CW01670277

Toy S

'A cool, urban tale of compelling antihero Gabriel's struggle for redemption from hard times, hard crimes and hard drugs in London's darker boroughs. Stephen Thompson's vital, gritty and gripping debut novel reads like a kind of *Trainspotting* in Hackney. Ali G could only wish for Staines to be this real'

19

'A frighteningly honest drugs and crime "seedy underbelly" tale that doesn't go for glamour, sentiment or shock value'

The Face

'This book offers an insight into an underworld which the films and documentaries barely hint at . . . Raw and unpretentious, it is largely written in the first person, as Gabby Power narrates his life story from a rehab in Notting Hill. The façade is familiar, all flash cars, lycra clad "dorises" and macho posturing, but what shines through Thompson's terse, unadorned prose is the sheer innocence of a lost boy searching for something that will "fill that hole" in his life'

The Hill Magazine

'Thompson's journalistic background is put to good use in this novel. The writing is crisp and assured . . . those who prate about "social exclusion" and who think that the solution is a war on drugs and the appointment, on fat salaries, of a coterie of "tsars" should read this book and think again'

Tribune

'Far more than the familiar story of drug addiction – it's a story about London and its barriers, about the crushing effects of poverty and racism that, uniquely, is as damning of black attitudes as white ones. Perhaps most impressive of all is the way Stephen tells the story'

Evening Standard

'*Toy Soldiers* is in no way a hackneyed glamorisation of the London underworld. Its autobiographical foundations give it a depth of motivation which most drugs and desperation novels fail to have . . . Stephen Thompson is someone you'll be hearing a lot more from'

Pil

'Well crafted and intelligently paced . . . the book finds a kind of hope in an otherwise bleak and threatening city'

Daily Telegraph

'*Toy Soldiers* differs from other "bad boy" books as it does not glorify nor glamorise crime . . . a promising debut and a damn good read'

Calabash

'For a first novel, journalist Stephen Thompson has produced something he should be very proud of . . . a beautifully constructed tale'

Dublin Evening Herald

'A Hackney lad who moves west to a Notting Hill rehab centre to get a new life, Gabriel's tough, crude, and full of attitude. It takes time to warm to him, but it's impossible not to in the end . . . one hell of a story'

Daily Mirror

Toy Soldiers

STEPHEN THOMPSON

SCEPTRE

Copyright © Stephen Thompson 2000

First published in 2000 by Hodder and Stoughton
A division of Hodder Headline
A Sceptre Paperback

The right of Stephen Thompson to be identified as the Author of the Work has been asserted by him in accordance with the Copyright, Designs and Patents Act 1988.

10 9 8 7 6 5 4 3 2 1

All rights reserved. No part of this publication may be reproduced, stored in a retrieval system or transmitted in any form or by any means without the prior written permission of the publisher, nor be otherwise circulated in any form of binding or cover other than that in which it is published and without a similar condition being imposed on the subsequent purchaser.

All characters in this publication are fictitious and any resemblance to real persons, living or dead, is purely coincidental.

A CIP catalogue record for this title is available from the British Library.

ISBN 0 340 75147 9

Typeset by Palimpsest Book Production Limited,
Polmont, Stirlingshire
Printed and bound in Great Britain by
Mackays of Chatham PLC, Chatham, Kent

Hodder and Stoughton
A division of Hodder Headline
338 Euston Road
London NW1 3BH

For Kate

'The aim is to live lucidly in a world where dispersion is the rule.'

Albert Camus

PROLOGUE

He needed a refuge, a sanctuary, a place to save himself from himself. Things had become desperate. For months he had been looking for a way to escape his hellish existence. He came across it purely by chance, on the tube one night, on his way back to Bethnal Green from Ealing Broadway, a journey he sometimes had to make in times of drought. He noticed the pamphlet on the vacant seat next to him. Bored, he picked it up. It had ten or so poorly printed pages, loosely stapled. He scan-read the first page. Its contents were so depressing he scrunched the pamphlet into a ball and dropped it on the floor. The tube pulled into Bethnal Green station. Before getting off, he picked up the ball of paper and stuffed it into the pocket of his grubby jeans.

Two days later, sitting on a bench in Downs Park, he fished the pamphlet from his pocket. He unfolded it very carefully, taking time to smooth out the creases as best he could. He had forgotten how poorly printed it was. Here was his way out, he thought, when he had finished reading it, here was his chance at salvation. He had been thrown a lifeline. He had to grab hold of it. Fuck what Jeff thought. Or Brick and

Gunhawk for that matter. Fuck what anyone else thought. He could not care less if he was seen as weak, as not being able to cope with the rigours of ghetto life. So what if he was seen as a victim, as a casualty, as someone needing, heaven forbid, help. He needed help, all right, and was no longer ashamed to admit it. Help that might have come from his family had they not washed their hands of him. In the eyes of his long-suffering mother and older brothers he may as well have been dead. This caused him no end of heartache – even junkies feel hurt when their own flesh and blood pretend not to notice them in the street.

Yet he was not dead. Somewhere beneath the rags and the grime and the stench, beneath the sack of brittle bones and the rotting skin, beneath the lies, the deceit and the self-loathing, somewhere beneath all of that his heart was still beating: faintly, erratically at times, but beating nonetheless. He was not quite in his grave yet. He wanted to live for some time to come, truth be told. All he needed to do was get away and fix himself, then come back as good as new, like a broken down TV returned from the menders.

The pamphlet listed various drug rehabilitation centres the length and breadth of the country. It gave addresses and telephone numbers. He ignored the ones outside London.

London it was, then. But which bit? He could not go south. He had ripped off too many dealers that side of the river. North London was out of the question for the same reason. So, since he lived in east London, he made the only decision he could: he upped sticks and headed west.

Part One

I

Notting Hill Gate. Spring 1989. Gabriel had just got off the tube. He was scared. This was unknown territory for him. Literally and figuratively. He chastised himself for his cowardice. He told himself to stop acting like a pussy. After all, he was only attending an interview. How difficult could it be? Being interrogated by Hackney police, now that was difficult. This little chat, by comparison, should be as easy as blinking. But he was scared. He could no more escape that fact than he could his own shadow.

He got lost. He was forced to seek directions from an English Rose. She eyed him warily, clutching her handbag. In a sloaney voice she pointed him on the right path, after which she gave him a plastic smile before hurrying off. He ogled her for a second or two while she strode purposefully away from him. Not a bad arse, he thought. For a white girl.

Walking along, he became convinced that everyone was watching him. Paranoia. He ended up in a very smart street. Huge Victorian mansions. Pastel paintwork. Window boxes. Not that he had a clear view of the houses. They were partially obscured by tall trees which lined both sides of the street, their canopies overlapping and casting a cool shadow from one end of the street to the other. As for the blossom, he had never seen so much of the stuff in his life. It covered everything. Road. Pavement. The parked Volvos and BMWs. Like freshly fallen snow.

Yes, he thought. This was a picture postcard of a street. The folk living there were not needy. What a world away from litter-strewn Hackney. But surely he was in the wrong street. Rehab? he thought. There? The toffs would not have it. Not on their doorstep. There would have been an outcry. Petitions drawn up. The local MP badgered to distraction. He mentally berated the English Rose for daring to give him wrong directions. Still, having come all that way, he thought he may as well be a hundred per cent sure he was in the wrong street.

He felt so self-conscious, he almost crept up to the front door of the five-storey house. He rang the doorbell tentatively. He had a longish wait. He half expected the police to arrive and cart him off as a would-be burglar. He imagined the phone call being made to the local police station by one of the residents. 'Could you send someone round right away? There's a rather scrawny-looking black youth loitering with intent.' 'OK, madam. Could you give us a more detailed description of him?' 'Why, yes. He's tall, over six feet, I'd say. You can't miss him. He's wearing one of those baseball caps turned back to front.' His heart raced at the thought. He was about to run off when a man answered the door. He had lank, grey, matted dreads, sported a goatee, and was wearing soiled dungarees and hand-painted DMs: yellow ones. He looked no older than twenty-one. Gabriel sized him up. Who was this person? he wondered. He seemed so incongruous amidst the splendour of the surroundings that Gabriel took him to be a painter-and-decorator in for the day. So he was surprised when the man beamed widely and said: 'You must be Gabriel.'

'That's right.'

'I'm John. Come in. We thought you weren't going to show.'

'Yeah. Sorry 'bout that, man. Got a bit lost.'

'Not to worry. Come on in.'

Gabriel followed him along a grey, linoed corridor, at the end of which was a cramped office whose walls were covered with anti-drugs posters. There were three other people in the office. John introduced them as Jo, Kevin and Marcia, his staff colleagues. The first two of this trio were, like John, rather shabby-looking: ill-fitting faded T-shirts, crumpled paint-stained jeans, grubby trainers. Marcia looked altogether more striking. There was a gothic quality about her that bordered on ostentation. She had extremely pale skin, almost translucent. This was offset by her jet-black hair, matt-black T-shirt and jeans, black-painted fingernails and toenails (her feet were bare). Her eyes, at odds with the rest of her appearance, were opaque blue. For the duration of the interview Gabriel kept stealing glances at them.

Jo offered to make tea. Everyone, including Gabriel, declined. Jo looked relieved. John lit a cigarette and chain-smoked throughout the interview.

'So,' he said. 'How did you hear about the house?'

'Read about it in a pamphlet.'

John nodded. 'Where did you get it?'

'Found it on the tube.'

'Oh.' Silence. Kevin scribbled some notes. John continued: 'When did you last use, Gabriel?'

'Over a week ago.'

This was not true. It had only been two days since he last used. He lied because he thought the truth might cost him a place in the house.

'So you haven't done a detox, then?'

'A what?'

'Doesn't matter. You've been clean a week. That qualifies.'

'Does it?' asked Gabriel. He was already confused. Too much jargon. The staff exchanged knowing looks. Then Jo said: 'Must have been tough for you.'

'What?'

'Staying clean for a week.'

'Can say that again.'

'How long have you been using?'

''Bout a year.'

'Not that long, then.'

'Long enough, believe me.'

'And what makes you want to give up?' asked John. He lit another cigarette.

'Had enough, innit?'

'For good or for now?' asked Jo.

'Can't say, really.'

Silence, save the sound of Kevin scribbling.

'Right, then,' said John. 'Let me tell you a little bit about the house, give you a bit of its history and what exactly it is we do here. OK?'

Gabriel shrugged indifferently and said: 'Go for it, man.'

John could have been reading from some kind of promotional literature, so wooden was his tone. Indeed, months later Gabriel came across the official house booklet and realised that John had almost quoted it verbatim.

The house was a registered charity. It was part of an organisation called, inexplicably, The Denton House Association. One of two houses owned by said association, it had opened in 1980 and catered for drug misusers between the ages of eighteen and twenty-five.

'Speaking of which,' said John. 'How old are you, Gabriel?'

'Twenty-two.'

'Oh, good.'

Policy was decided by a management committee which met once a month. The main objective of the house was to provide a 'supportive environment' for people looking to make the transition to a drug-free life. The residents, or addicts, were required to provide random urine samples. This, experience had shown, was the most effective way of ensuring a drug-free house. In addition, for the first month of their stay, residents were asked to confine themselves to the house. If they wished to go out they had to be escorted by a member of staff. After a month they were allowed out alone, but had to inform the staff of where they were going and when, approximately, they would be back. No resident was allowed out after midnight. As for the length of their overall stay, depending on individual needs, it could be anything from a few weeks to a couple of years. On a day-to-day level, there was no set programme as such. Instead, the residents had their progress monitored on a weekly basis. This took the form of an informal chat, one-to-one, either at the house, or, if the resident preferred, outside the house somewhere, 'perhaps at a café'.

Gabriel's eyes were glazing over. The information was coming at him too quickly. He did his best to concentrate.

By now John had moved on to detailing the residents' progress, which he said was divided into three clear stages. One, the residents were helped to gain 'emotional and physical strength'. Two, they were encouraged to pursue their own interests and to establish links with the outside community. Three, they were prepared for the time when they would have to leave the house. That about covered everything, except to say that the house had room for fourteen people: four staff, four 'Support Group' and six residents. Had Gabriel any questions?

'Yeah. Support Group. Who are they?'

The four members of the Support Group had a specific and important role to play, John explained. They brought to the house a certain 'normality'. They were not ex-users (neither were the staff). They had jobs outside the house. They were simply caring people who enjoyed communal living. Having them around meant – and this was crucial – that the house was not centred solely on the needs of the residents who, at all times, had to be discouraged from selfishness and self-obsession.

'If you all live in the gaff,' said Gabriel, 'how come only the addicts are called residents?'

'Good question,' said John. He fingered his goatee then said: 'All right. Let me ask you one. What would you prefer to be called, an addict or a resident?'

'Call me what you like, man. So long as it ain't nothing to do with the colour of my skin, na'am saying?'

John smiled, embarrassed. He felt the need to formally state the house's anti-racism policy. An awkward silence followed, broken only by the scribble of Kevin's pen. Marcia, more relaxed than her colleagues, winked covertly at Gabriel. The show of intimacy surprised him.

'So you don't mind being called an addict?' asked Jo.

'No. 'S what I am, innit?'

'That's interesting,' said Jo. 'We've never come across an addict who hadn't preferred to be called a resident. They find the word carries less of a stigma and we tend to agree with that.'

'Like I said. Call me what you like.' Then to John: 'I'd have to pay rent, right?'

'Yes,' said John. 'But not you personally. You'd qualify for housing benefit.'

'This samples bollocks. How you run it and shit?'

John was unsettled for a moment. Marcia sniggered. John gave her a frosty stare.

'In each loo,' said John eventually, 'there's a small cabinet with plastic bottles in it. When a sample's been taken we write the resident's name on it, plus the date and time it was taken, and by whom.'

'Come again. Did you say by who?'

'That's right. The name of the staff member who took the sample.'

Gabriel frowned and said: 'Shit! You mean you actually stand over them while they're having a slash?'

'Fraid so. It's not ideal but it's necessary.'

'They don't even do that down the dose clinic, man.'

John paused, thought about it, then said: 'That's probably because people who visit VD clinics have nothing to hide. Residents, on the other hand, quite often do. Usually it's the fact that they've been using in the house. They've been known to water down their urine.'

Marcia rolled her eyes at Gabriel who said:

'Well. S'pose you must know your shit.'

Silence. Kevin looked up from his notepad. John continued.

'How domesticated would you say you were, Gabriel?'

'Domesticated? Make me sound like a dog, bredren.'

He had used the word 'bredren' ironically, for he was talking to white people. Marcia had immediately grasped this, being a woman of the world. Her colleagues, however, looked at each other in brief confusion. Kevin, pausing from his note-taking, asked: 'Is that some breed of dog?'

'Can we get on, please?' said John irritably. 'Let me put it another way, Gabriel. If you were to move in, who do you think would do your cooking and cleaning?'

He knew what John was alluding to, so decided to play a game. He looked at Marcia and, smiling at her, said: 'Dunno. Someone.'

'Someone like who?'

'Cook and cleaner?'

'Not here, I'm afraid,' said John. 'The house is a commune in every sense of the word. Which means we all have to muck in. For instance, we take it in turns to cook and we each have a specific area of the house that we're responsible for keeping clean. It's all done on a rota basis. At the moment I'm on the downstairs loos. For my sins.' He looked at his colleagues with mock sadness. Marcia stroked his knee comfortingly.

'There, there, pet,' she teased.

'Right,' said Gabriel, trying not to look at Marcia, trying not to laugh. 'A commune. I'm with you now.'

'So,' said John. 'Think you could cope with that?'

Gabriel was not sure he could, but he still replied: 'Course. No probs, man.' He looked at Marcia. She shook her head at him, as if to say 'liar'.

'Good. Well, unless you have any more questions for us,' Gabriel shook his head, 'I think this would be a good point to end the interview. If you'd like to wait in the front room for a bit, we'll have a little chat amongst ourselves then let you know what we decide. OK?'

'Cool,' said Gabriel, rising and stretching. John also stood up. He opened the office door. As he did so the smoke that had been trapped in the office went rushing down the corridor like a demented genie. John pointed Gabriel towards the front room, which was back along the corridor near the front door.

'Shan't be long,' he said. 'The kitchen's downstairs if you fancy a cuppa.'

'I'm safe, man,' said Gabriel, before heading off down the corridor.

There was someone in the front room when he got there, a boy, aged eighteen or nineteen. He was lounging on one of two sofas in the room, reading a battered copy of *Viz*. His face was excessively pockmarked. A heroin addict, Gabriel assumed. He had seen enough of them in his life to know. The boy introduced himself as Jack. Gabriel had barely stated his own name before Jack had launched into his life story.

Originally from the Old Kent Road, Jack had already spent a good deal of his youth in one rehab after another. At twelve he had run away from home because his mother was unable to stay out of his room at night. He had ended up in care, then foster homes, before finally being adopted. More abuse had followed, this time of a violent nature and at the hands of his adoptive father who thought he was a 'fucking punching bag'. He had run away again, deciding to ignore the authorities and take his chances on the streets. The next couple of years were spent living rough, which made him vulnerable to every 'lizard' who sought to exploit young destitutes. Inevitably he had ended up on the game 'for money', on drugs 'for relief' and finally as a junkie 'for me troubles'.

While listening to this woeful tale, Gabriel felt as though his own upbringing, by comparison, had been positively cosseted. He was about to flee the house when John put his head round the door.

'OK, Gabriel. If you would like to come back in now.'

He was offered a place in the house and moved in the following day.

It was no coincidence that he was asked to move in the day after his interview. Tuesday was the day of the weekly house meeting, which had to be attended by every member of the household. Gabriel was paraded around like a prize pony. He became embarrassed, for two reasons. Firstly because he was welcomed with a round of applause; and secondly because, including himself, there were ten people in the front room that evening, and his was the only black face amongst them. In a desperate attempt to remove himself from the spotlight, he went and sat on a pouf by the huge bay window.

The air was thick with smoke, mostly John's. Tea and biscuits were on a small coffee table in the centre of the room. In one corner sparsely filled bookshelves had been built into the pastel-pink wall. Below these shelves were miscellaneous, nondescript items: coverless magazines, dusty old footwear, board-games. There was a large TV near the door, set on a four-wheeled trolley, beneath which, flat on the grey, industrial carpet, lay a video recorder. Framed black-and-white photographs, sea-scapes in the main, hung on all four walls, reminding Gabriel of a ticket agency, or a West End restaurant.

John presided over the meeting. He sat on the floor, crossed-legged, with a sheet of paper in one hand (the typed agenda) and a cigarette in the other. His staff colleagues were sitting to his left, bunched up on one of the two sofas. To his right, on the other sofa, sat a sombre-looking quartet who had been introduced to Gabriel as Marilene, Antony, Claire and Christopher. He had assumed their collective age to be roughly one hundred and twenty, and had divided the figure between them evenly. They were the Support Group he had been told about. Jack was sitting next to them, on a threadbare armchair, his face buried in the same copy of *Viz* he had been reading the previous day. For the second time in as many days, Gabriel felt like walking out.

John called the meeting to order. He had to shout to be heard above the din.

Item one on the agenda: crisis in the house. The lab had returned a positive urine sample which, they claimed, showed definite traces of opiate. Jack had been spoken to earlier that day and had been given another chance. His last. Silence. Everyone looked at Jack. He did not once look up from his comic. Gabriel felt for him.

Item two: divisions in the house. The staff felt that the house, over the last couple of months, had lost its 'communal feel'. Suggestions were invited as to the best way to recapture that 'essence of togetherness'. Mute response. John waded in with a list of recommendations he and his colleagues had compiled earlier that day. Namely, A: they should all make a greater effort to spend some time together after evening meals. B: not naming any names, one or two people should seriously look at their tendency to shut themselves in their rooms for hours on end. C: the cult of exclusive friendships had to stop. D: no more petty squabbling. E: some sort of democratic system was needed with regard to watching TV.

Item three: visitors to the house. The staff wished to propose that all visitors be subjected to random urine sampling. This, John said, was only fair on the residents. The proposal was instantly and universally rubbished by the Support Group. Gabriel was amazed at how quickly they and the staff were at each other's throats. The kernel of the Support Group's opposition was this: any sampling of their guests would, they argued, constitute a gross infringement of their civil liberties. Ten minutes of shouting produced nothing but deadlock. Eventually, frustrated, the staff decided on an interim measure – the matter would be discussed again the following week when 'people had had a chance to think about the implications of the proposal and could discuss it in a less emotive fashion'. Based on what he had just witnessed, Gabriel did not hold out much hope of that happening.

Item four: any other business. No one had anything to contribute so John hurriedly drew the meeting to a close. The Support Group fled as one, quickly followed by Jack. The staff repaired to the office. So much, thought Gabriel, for that 'essence of togetherness'.

He went up to his room on the top floor. Breathless, he sat on the edge of his bed and proceeded to unpack his meagre belongings. And they *were* meagre. Three dozen or so super-hero comics, half a dozen boxes of Subbuteo football teams, a letter his father had written to him ages ago, a few raggedy items of clothing. Once he had finished unpacking he let his eyes wander round the room. A bare light bulb dangling from the ceiling, a sink in a corner with a mirrored cabinet above it, a metal waste-paper bin on the floor next to these, and, near the window, a small rickety old table and a small rickety old chair. The room, he decided, resembled a prison cell. To make sure he was not actually locked up, he went over to the window and looked down onto the road. Nothing to see there either. Parked cars, the yellow glow of street lamps, trees. He wanted to cry but found he couldn't.

He went back over to the bed and lay on it. Staring at the

stained white ceiling, images of his recent past began forming inside his head and he suddenly felt an overwhelming desire to talk to someone, to unburden himself, to confess. Not that he was about to rush downstairs and bare his soul to the first person he happened across. He was far too secretive for that. And, to his mind, for good reason. He knew there were dark forces at work in the world, agents of the Beast who came in many guises; as friends, lovers, family, even. In short, no one but no one could be trusted. Besides, whatever positive changes he was about to make to his life, he and he alone wanted to take the credit for them. He had not come to the house seeking advice on how to live his life, was not looking to be taken by the hand and led in any particular direction. He had had enough of people trying to lead him. It was time he started thinking for himself, time he determined his own fate. All he needed was the right environment in which to start the process.

It was gone three in the afternoon when he finally woke up the next day. He had a perfunctory shower in the communal bathroom adjacent to his room, dressed in the bathroom, then went down to the kitchen in the basement.

It was a huge, light kitchen. The ceiling and walls were painted buttercup yellow. So, too, were the fitted Formica wall and floor cupboards. A very long table (pine-legs, chip-board top) dominated the centre of the cream-coloured, linoleum floor. It had about twenty chairs made from various materials positioned around it.

It would be a while before he developed an appetite for

breakfast more substantial than the tea and toast he ate seated at the long table, staring dreamily out of the burglar-barred window at the disembodied legs of passers-by. He finished his breakfast then washed up his mug and plate, in accordance with the note he saw stuck to one of the wall cupboards. Then he went upstairs to have a cigarette, once more in accordance with another note he saw stuck to yet another wall cupboard, this one outlawing smoking in the kitchen.

When he got to the front room, he was not surprised to see Jack sprawled out on one of the sofas, smoking and reading his copy of *Viz*.

'All right, mate?' said Jack. 'Didn't hear you come in.'

'Gathered that, hombre.'

Jack put the comic on the floor and sat up. Gabriel prepared to have his ears talked off.

'What's the coup?' asked Jack.

'Just slid out the pit, man.'

'You're lucky, mate. They got me outta bed at ten. Didn't bother you, though. First day and all that. Be different tomorrow. You watch.'

What new development was this? Gabriel wondered. Out of bed by ten? Surely not.

'Yeah, mate,' said Jack. 'Diabolical, innit? Every fucking morning without fail. Bang, bang, bang on my door. "Get up, Jack. It's ten o'clock."'

'Why, for fuck's sake?'

'Dunno, mate. Some bollocks about "structuring" your day. S'pose they want us to get up and do stuff. Fuck knows what, though.'

'So how d'you pass the time and shit?'

'It's 'ard. Mostly I'm in 'ere. Every now and again I go for a stroll down the Bella, but that's about it.'

'Sounds boring, man.'

'Boring ain't the word, mate. Honestly, don't think I've watched so much telly in me life. Must have read that thing' – he pointed to the comic on the floor – 'about fifty million times. I'm seriously thinking about checking into Phoenix House. At least there's people to talk to there.'

'Phoenix House?'

Jack explained. Phoenix House was legendary in the field of drug rehabilitation, renowned less for its record of achievement and more for its obstinate belief in, and aggressive adherence to, group therapy. There, the residents were encouraged to express themselves, which, roughly translated, meant they spent a lot of time running around screaming at each other supposedly in the hope of 'getting in touch with their feelings'. Jack had had two stints there, leaving on both occasions because of the sheer intensity of the place.

'Sound's fucking grim,' said Gabriel.

'It is. But at least it ain't dull. Not like 'ere. Wouldn't be so bad if there was people to talk to, but there's never anyone around.'

'That's a point. Where the fuck is everyone, man? Place was ram-jam last night.'

'Support Group are out working.'

'Oh yeah.'

'Jo's on holiday. Left this morning.' He mimicked a posh accent, said, 'Lake District, don't you know?' then resumed his cockney falsetto. 'John and Kevin went out around midday. Took the piss samples off to St Thomas's. Marcia's in the office. Probably having a wank.' He chuckled.

At that precise moment Marcia walked into the room. Jack's face straightened, like a child caught in some wrong-doing.

'Hiya,' said Marcia to Gabriel. 'Sleep well, did we?' Gabriel nodded. Jack picked up his comic and swung his feet up onto the sofa. 'So,' said Marcia. 'Have you had something to eat?'

'Yeah,' said Gabriel.

'Feel up to giving a sample?'

Gabriel did a double take.

'What, now?' he said. 'You mean like this minute?'

Jack cocked his ear.

'If you feel up to it,' said Marcia. 'Otherwise we can do it later.'

'No, no,' said Gabriel. 'I'll have a go. Might as well get it out the way, na'am saying?'

'That's the spirit,' said Marcia, condescendingly. 'Follow me.'

They walked along the corridor in silence, like two people about to do something heroic and death-defying and for which the only suitable preparation was a stoic, silent, focusing of the mind.

Next to the office was a small loo. They entered it and Marcia locked the door after them. It was very cramped inside. Both felt ill-at-ease being in such close proximity to one another. Marcia used a key from the many on a bunch she was carrying to open the small metal wall-cabinet. From this she took out a plastic bottle the shape if not quite the length of a tennis ball canister.

'Here we are,' she said, handing the bottle to Gabriel. She then took a step backwards to be nearer the door, so that Gabriel, with his back turned to her, could urinate into the bottle with at least a token privacy.

Gabriel unzipped his flies, pulled out his penis, poked it awkwardly into the bottle neck, then tried hard to relax his bladder. A few seconds later the first trickling of urine ran silently and unspectacularly down the inside of the bottle. He and Marcia then waited for the torrent, the one for the feel and sight, the other for the sound. It never came, and seconds later, with only a tiny fraction of the bottle filled, the trickling dried up. Gabriel shook his penis dry, put it back into his jeans, zipped up his flies, then turned and faced Marcia and handed her the bottle.

'Hmmm,' said Marcia. She held the bottle up and inspected the quantity of urine. 'Not a lot, is it?'

'Nah it ain't,' said Gabriel, disappointed. He felt like someone who had been told by his GP he had a low sperm count.

'Not to worry,' said Marcia, as if to cheer him up. 'It's enough. But I think next time we'll wait till you really feel like going. OK?'

Gabriel grimaced. Marcia labelled the bottle and put it back in the cabinet, which she locked. She waited for Gabriel to finish at the sink, washed her own hands, then the two of them went back to the front room.

As soon as they entered it Marcia picked up from the coffee

table that week's copy of *Time Out.* Standing in the centre of the room, she began paging through it absent-mindedly.

Gabriel studied her for a minute, noticing suddenly what a big woman she was: big bones, broad shoulders, five-feet-ten at least.

'Marcia,' he said.

'Yes, Gabriel,' Marcia replied instantly.

'Ain't disturbing you or nothing, am I?'

'No, no. What's up?'

Gabriel looked across at Jack (who was still on the sofa reading his comic) and was suddenly nervous.

'Well, don't take this the wrong way or nothing, it's just that I was sitting here wondering and I thought I might as well ask . . .'

'Yeeeees,' said Marcia warily.

'Well, what I wanna know is . . . you anaemic or something?'

Marcia smiled and said: 'What a funny question. Why do you ask?'

''Cause you're so pale you look like a corpse,' Jack suddenly interrupted. He looked at Gabriel for support, chuckling. Gabriel stuttered.

'You're not exactly flushed with colour yourself, you know, Jack?' said Marcia. She shook her head and looked across at Gabriel. To her surprise, he seemed embarrassed. After a few seconds silence she said: 'Come on, Gabriel, let's you and me go for a coffee. We need to have a chat.'

They went to a cafe on Westbourne Grove. Gabriel had

tea and lemon cheesecake. Marcia cappuccino and chocolate gateau. Apart from themselves and an old man in a linen suit who was sipping an espresso and reading a folded copy of the *Telegraph*, the place was empty. And quiet, except for the sound of the pretty Yugoslavian (the sole member of staff) busying herself behind the counter: dusting ashtrays, wiping down the coffee machine, rearranging the cakes in the display cabinet. Gabriel was sure she fancied him, for she kept looking at him and smiling. He smiled back at her over Marcia's shoulder.

Initially, conversation was difficult. Despite Marcia's probing questions, Gabriel was too vague and at times deliberately evasive. It soon became clear to him that Marcia's sole reason for taking him out was to get him to talk about his life. She was working.

Marcia was equally tight-lipped about herself, though this was due more to Gabriel's seeming lack of interest than any wilful circumspection on her part.

However, things improved dramatically when Gabriel, simply to puncture one of the many uneasy silences, said almost casually: 'So how'd you get into this game, then?' Marcia's response was fulsome to say the least. She told Gabriel a frank, rambling tale of the circuitous journey she had made to arrive at her present situation.

She had only been at the house a year. Contrary to what Gabriel might have assumed, she was not, like her three staff colleagues, your archetypal middle-class kid. In fact her background could not have been more ordinary and working class.

Originally from Dudley, she left school – 'a dull, totally

uninspiring comprehensive' – at sixteen, clutching a handful of CSEs of largely mediocre grades. 'Except for art,' she said. 'It's the one thing I showed aptitude for.' A year passed. During that time she signed on and began experimenting with sex and soft drugs. Her parents (he a postman, she a school dinner lady) became concerned about her lack of direction. They lectured her constantly. In the end she could take no more and moved out.

For a while she stayed with friends, sponging off them as well as the State, but her pride would not allow her to live that way indefinitely so she got a job waitressing. This enabled her to rent a 'box' of her own. Far from being happy at her new-found independence, which is what she had hoped for, she quickly became downhearted at the sheer drudgery of working away her nights and sleeping away her days. To lift her spirits she decided on a change of scene. She left her job, vacated her flat and moved to London. She was all of eighteen.

She found life in London harsh and the people unfriendly, yet she was determined to make a go of things. The alternative (moving back to Dudley with her tail between her legs) was simply out of the question.

Following a spell of living rough, she got work as a barmaid in a Soho pub. It was not long before she was sleeping with the customers. One of them, a middle-aged woman who lectured in American Studies at North London Polytechnic, encouraged her to further her education. Which she did, after a fashion, since it was her artistic education and not her academic one to which she returned.

In the absence of a portfolio of work, she talked her way into one of London's 'lesser' art colleges, enrolling for three years. Inside a year she dropped out to hitch-hike across Europe, on her own, to 'find herself', not because she felt especially lost, but because it was the in thing to do.

Eventually she returned to London, having been away the best part of a year. She found work hard to come by. Britain was in the depths of recession. For the second time in her life she was forced to sign on. She did this for six months, attending scores of job interviews in that time. Towards the end of this period, she thought seriously about going home. Then, out of the blue, courtesy of a contact she had made while sleeping rough, she got a job as a live-in residential care worker at a homeless hostel in Earls Court.

In terms of prestige, her job-title far outstripped her actual duties, which consisted of nothing more than turning keys, cooking and serving food, and lending a sympathetic ear to the down-and-outs. Having been herself a down-and-out, they were not duties she found difficult.

If there was one aspect of the job she hated, it was the location of the hostel. She found Earls Court seedy in the extreme and longed to move. Eventually, she found a similar post in a better area of London, hence her current job.

Most of what Gabriel heard went in one ear and out the other. The only piece of information that lodged was Marcia's off-hand reference to her lesbian fling. This had shocked him, which was precisely what Marcia had intended. When she had finished Gabriel could not help but ask: 'You a lesbian, then?'

'Would it bother you if I was?'

'No,' Gabriel lied.

'So why ask?'

He had never met a real live lesbian before. She had not claimed to be one. But did she not just say ... The fact that she slept with a woman once did not, per se, make her a lesbian. What was she saying, that she liked men as well? On the whole she preferred them. Then why had she slept with a woman? It was an itch she had to scratch – why, was he honestly trying to tell her that he had never felt sexual longing for another man? Never in his life – the very idea! So he was homophobic? What was that when it was at home? Did he not like homosexuals? He had nothing against them.

'Some of your best friends are gay, right?'

'No!'

'I was only joking.'

'Honestly, got nothing against them. So long as they keep their business outta my face, na'am saying?'

She asked him where his parents were from.

'Parent. Dunno my dad. My mum's from Jamaica. Why?'

When did his mother come to this country?

'Late fifties. Early sixties. Ain't too sure.'

Did his mother ever talk about that time?

'What you getting at?'

'I was just thinking that she probably experienced a lot of racism when she first got here. There was a lot of it about, apparently.'

'Yeah? And?'

'What's your mum's name?'

'Lucille.'

'Nice name. All right. Picture this. Lucille's just arrived here from Jamaica. She doesn't know a soul. She moves in next door to a white family. One day she decides to go and introduce herself, perfectly normal neighbourly behaviour, or at least it was then, so we're led to believe. Anyway, she knocks on her neighbours' door, perhaps even bearing a gift. One of the family opens the door, let's say the man of the house, for want of a more PC phrase. He opens the door and sees Lucille standing there with a smile on her face and friendliness in her heart. What do you imagine he says to her?'

'Dunno. Get lost?'

'Oh no. Nothing as direct as that. He gets all mealy mouthed. He stares Lucille in the eye, smiling the whole time, and says, "Listen. I've got nothing against your sort but . . . well . . . I'd appreciate it if you didn't come round here again. No offence, honestly." Sound familiar?'

Gabriel was having none of it.

'Gimme a break,' he said. 'Ain't the same thing, is it?'

'It's exactly the same thing. Bigotry is what it is. It might come in many guises but it's still bigotry.'

Gabriel shook his head and smiled sourly.

'Yeah, well,' he said. 'Say what you want, but some things are hard to accept, you get me?'

'Even harder when you don't try. Hitler killed six million Jews for that very reason.'

'Look. Mind if we blow this gaff?'

'Do what?'

'Can we go?'

'You all right?'

'Safe as houses. Can we make some tracks now?'

'OK. I'll just go and pay.'

She stood up and headed towards the counter. Gabriel went outside to wait for her.

They walked back towards the house in silence. It was clear to Marcia that Gabriel was sulking. Just as clear to her was why he was sulking. She had put him in his place and he had not liked it one bit. This had pleased her. For if, as she hoped, they were to get on, then he would need to be careful not to ride roughshod over her liberal sensibilities. She liked him, yes, but that did not mean she was going to close her eyes to his shortcomings, which, provided he stayed at the house long enough, she hoped to rid him of, as though she were a faith healer and he a disease-ridden unfortunate. He had potential. Of that there was no doubt in her mind. She would do her best to help him realise it.

For his part, Gabriel was not sure he could ever get on with Marcia. Discounting his mother, he was not used to having his opinions challenged by women. Least of all by white women. Still further, it was the way Marcia had challenged him which had upset him so much. She had dismantled his argument with a smile. Lacking a similar cunning, he had been forced into a moody, frustrated silence.

At the same time as being annoyed with her, Gabriel could not deny that he was attracted to Marcia, reasons for which he could not initially fathom. He wondered if he had suddenly developed a liking for white women, and concluded that this was unlikely, since to his mind they were the most un-sexy women on the planet, all flat bums and sickly complexions, two major physical defects which Marcia had most definitely been cursed with. Could it be that he harboured a purely egotistical desire to fuck her in order to shut her up? Yes. That was it. He wanted to bring her down a peg or two and the only way he could do that was to get into her knickers. And he would get into her knickers. He was certain of it.

These were their separate thoughts as they made their way towards the house. At one point Marcia began to suspect signs of improvement in Gabriel's mood. She noticed that his eyes had widened and that he had an almost imperceptible smile on his face. Her suspicions were soon confirmed, for just as they entered their blossom-covered street, he said: 'Newsagents round here, is there?'

'Round the corner. Need cigarettes, do you?'

She did not smoke, was disparaging of anyone who did.

'Yeah,' said Gabriel. 'Cancer sticks would be good. But there's something else I wanna get.'

'What?'

'A writing pad.'

Had some letters to write, did he? Not letters, no. What, then? Just stuff. What sort of stuff? About his life. If she had a penny for every resident who had ever said they were going to write their life story.

'Got a problem with that, have you?' he asked, defensively.

'Oh no! On the contrary. We encourage it.'

'But?'

'But saying you're going to do it, and doing it, are two different things. I can't remember a resident who actually managed to see it through to the end.'

'Yeah well, maybe I'll be the exception to the rule, na'am saying?'

'Hope so. I'm sure your life would make very interesting reading. Wish I could say the same for myself. Not that I've got literary pretensions, mind you.'

'Got what?'

'There's the newsagents,' said Marcia.

That night Gabriel found it almost impossible to do any writing. After a few aborted efforts he gave up and went and lay on his bed. His head was full of distractions. For one thing, he could not stop thinking about Marcia. What might she currently be up to in her room on the floor below his? He pictured her naked on her bed, with her legs spread apart, masturbating and thinking of him. The image aroused him and he proceeded to copy it; only, through sheer laziness, he kept his clothes on, simply unzipping his flies and taking his erect penis into his hand.

But even this pastime was abandoned after a while, for he was unable to maintain his erection as the thought of Marcia faded from his mind to be replaced by another, more worrying one: namely, that on a great deal of subjects he was completely ignorant. His chat with Marcia earlier that day had revealed this to be as clear as a newly polished window. His ignorance had been thrown into sharp relief and had been for him a humbling, humiliating experience. He was amazed at the gaps in his knowledge, and as he lay there on his bed he began to seriously think about them. Politics. Religion. Art. Science. History. On each and every subject he found his knowledge scant to the point of being non-existent. Profoundly alarmed, he decided to take action.

The following day he got John (who was on duty) to take him to the Ladbroke Grove branch of the Kensington and Chelsea library. He was delighted at the number of books he was allowed to borrow in one go. There were eight in total, each one well-thumbed, and, hardback and paperback alike, covered in cracked or peeling plastic. John was unable to mask his surprise at the eclectic mix of titles. As they left the library he commented: 'Man of many interests, eh?'

'Yeah. I am, as it happens,' Gabriel replied.

Back at the house Gabriel took his books straight up to his room. He placed them very carefully on the rickety old table, in two neat piles of four, next to his writing pad and chewed-up plastic biro. The table now resembled something of a study area. Gabriel stood back and admired the effect, fantasising about the scholarly hours he would spend hunched at the table reading. He wished he could have started right away, but John was waiting for him downstairs, having asked him to report to the office to complete some paperwork. He took a final loving look at his books before leaving the room, locking the door behind him for good measure.

John was now in an officious mood. This contrasted starkly with the chirpiness he had shown earlier when escorting Gabriel to and from the library. He got Gabriel to fill out a couple of forms: housing benefit and sickness benefit. Much to his annoyance, they took Gabriel the best part of an hour to complete. Afterwards John took him into the small loo adjacent to the office and made him urinate into one of the plastic bottles. Gabriel said nothing, but wondered if the staff, by sampling him twice in as many days, suspected him of using in the house. He dismissed the idea quickly, deciding it was probably standard practice with all new residents. Once he had given his sample he and John returned to the office. John immediately got on the phone and made a couple of calls, registering him with a local GP and a local dentist. The two then left the office again, in order for John to point out the various emergency assembly points in the house. Gabriel received a quick, unenthusiastic rundown of the emergency procedure while he and John climbed the stairs to the very top of the house, literally passing through a skylight (using a step ladder) and up onto the roof. Before he had had time to appreciate the bird's-eye view, Gabriel found himself clambering back through the skylight behind a rapidly disappearing John. Back inside the house, John then showed him the other assembly points plus all the fire escapes and all the fire extinguishers.

The tour completed, they returned to the office. John slumped onto a chair, sighed and said: 'And that, as they say, Gabby, is that.' He lit a cigarette, his first since Gabriel came down to see him. He took a long drag on it then said: 'That's the one part of the job I can't stand. All that administrative malarkey.' He shook his head at the thought of it then took another long drag on his already half-smoked cigarette. Gabriel sat on one of the three director's chairs in the room and stared at him. There was, he thought, no escaping the fact: John cut a very sorry figure indeed. His goatee was pretentious to the point of parody. His matted dreads were screaming to be shorn. His clothes were nothing but rags. Had they met outside the house, Gabriel would have openly mocked him. He wanted to, even now. But there was something about John, something in his watery brown eyes that spoke of a fundamental compassion, which, in spite of his bufoonish appearance, intrigued Gabriel and checked his scorn.

'Done with me, then?' he asked.

'Yes,' John replied. 'You can go off and read now. I know you're dying to.' Gabriel smiled. 'Or perhaps it's your writing you can't wait to get back to.' Gabriel's face tightened. John, suddenly unsure of his facts, added: 'Your life story? You're writing it, aren't you?'

'Who you hear that from?'

'Marcia. Hope you don't mind. So. Is it true?'

'Not really. Just jotting down a few things, that's all. Getting stuff off my chest and shit.'

'I hear you. Hope you keep it up. Something to do, isn't it? Still, you must try not to spend too much time in your room. That would be counter-productive, so to speak. You know what I mean, don't you? Remember what we discussed at the house meeting?'

Gabriel nodded and said: 'No probs.'

'Great,' said John, smiling. 'Well, don't let me keep you.'

Gabriel left the office and went up to his room.

How naïve he had been, how careless. Marcia had betrayed him. How foolish of him to think he had her confidence. Who was he to her? He had only known her a day. His secret was out.

The staff would now be sitting around the office discussing him, comparing him to ex-residents, making fun of his plans, seeking ways to undermine him, to disassemble the jigsaw of his confidence which he was so painstakingly trying to piece together, plotting against him. Agents of the Beast, the lot of them.

Berating himself and the staff thus, he had been pacing the room, muttering under his breath, working himself into a state. Matters worsened when he began to experience the most violent of crack cravings. He had been thinking about crack off and on all day. Now it was all he could think about. As he had been doing all day, he tried, to no avail, to will away the craving. Consequently, with his senses now heightened to an almost preternatural level, he fled first his room, then the house.

He reached as far as Bethnal Green where he got off the tube, crossed to the opposite platform, waited five minutes, then caught the tube going back to Notting Hill Gate.

On the way back, standing in a compartment packed tight with the rush-hour crowd, he reflected on how close he had come to undoing all his good work of the last few days. Two things had brought him to his senses. First, having thought it through (the tube journey to Bethnal Green had been sufficiently long for him to do so), he realised the ridiculousness of what he had contemplated. He had almost fallen at the first real hurdle en route to his recovery. This had made him feel weak and inadequate. Moreover, the logistics of the thing had been fraught with danger. What if he had run into any of the various people to whom he owed money? And on the subject of money, since he had none, how would he have bought the crack? Would he have dashed into the nearest shop and grabbed money from the till? If so, what if he had been caught? Would he have made police bail? Or would he have had to spend the night in the station, then on to court the following morning?

The second thing which made him see sense was an unconscious by-product of the first, in that, by thinking about all of the above, he had not been able to concentrate on his craving, which, he discovered to his relief, had completely subsided long before the tube had pulled into Bethnal Green station.

When he got back to the house Marcia, who had earlier relieved John, took him into the office and persuaded him to tell her the whole story. When he had finished, she made it clear that whilst she empathised with his reasons for leaving the house unescorted without permission, that kind of behaviour was unacceptable. If, in the future, he was experiencing any sort of 'crisis' then he must, she stressed, come and talk to a member of staff. That was their role, to help him through such times. And if for some reason they happened to be unavailable, he should seek out a member of the Support Group.

Gabriel, in a penitent tone, countered by saying that it was very difficult for him to confide in people. This had always been the case with him, especially with regard to strangers. Marcia understood. In this, she said, Gabriel was hardly unique. Nevertheless, she maintained that his inclination to 'go in' on himself would, if unchecked, only hinder his progress at the house. More besides, these so-called strangers would remain strangers if he did not take the time to get to know them.

Gabriel recognised this as a thinly-veiled charge of selfishness. He did not pursue it, since he knew the charge to be well founded. However, he emphasised to Marcia that for him to confide in someone, he would first need to know that he could trust that person, that whatever he mentioned to them in confidence would remain in confidence. Speaking on behalf of the staff, Marcia said she could not foresee any problems on that front, provided he spelt out to his confidante what should and should not to be aired abroad. Gabriel privately regretted not having been so explicit with her about his writing. Then, as though she had read his thoughts, Marcia, qualifying her last statement, told him that purely on a professional basis the staff did not keep secrets from each other. It would be unethical, she said, and the residents were strongly discouraged from trying to manoeuvre members of staff into such potentially compromising positions. That was not to say, however, that if a resident revealed something private to one member of staff it would go any further than the others. They practised, if Gabriel liked, a sort of collective confidence. All of which sounded like double-speak to Gabriel. He asked Marcia to define what the staff deemed to be professional matters, since it would influence what he may or may not tell them in the future. He found her answer maddening in its vagueness. More or less anything, she said, which took place inside the house was subjected to the staff's professional scrutiny.

The incident passed. For Gabriel it proved to be a turning point of sorts. Never mind the staff, he himself wanted no repetition of what had happened. The trouble, he realised, d been caused by his thinking about crack. What began s a passing thought had gradually turned into a physical craving similar to that felt by heroin addicts in the first agonising throes of cold turkey. He knew he could not stop thinking about crack, not completely, and certainly not while the stuff still polluted his blood. What he could do was lessen the amount of time he spent thinking about it, meaning he would have to occupy his every waking hour. He already had his books. Then there was his writing. So his mind was taken care of. But what of his body?

He became a member of the Kensington New Pools, a misnomer for what was actually a proper leisure centre. He went swimming there every day for two months. It became something of an obsession with him. For the first month, because he was still on restrictions, he was escorted there by a member of staff. John and Marcia liked to join him in the pool, unlike Kevin and Jo, who preferred to sit waiting for him either in the public gallery directly above the pool, or in the canteen, where they would drink copious amounts of weak machine tea while constantly looking at their watches.

Once off restrictions, he went swimming on his own. He was a man on a mission. Length after length he would swim, increasing his total by at least five lengths each day. Soon his physique was transformed.

Naturally vain, he developed the habit of staring at himself in the body-length mirror in the changing room, turning this way and that in front of it, admiring himself, even caressing himself on occasions, like a body-builder.

But he did not visit the leisure centre solely to swim. He

did not see himself as the type to get into the pool, get out, get showered, then get lost. For him, a bit of socialising before, during and after swimming was all part and parcel of the afternoons he spent down at the New Pools. He met a lot of people this way, became friends with one or two.

One such person was Marcus. He was a popular, ebullient dread to whom Gabriel took an instant shine and who quickly became his confessor in chief. They spent a lot of time together in the canteen. Marcus would lecture him on anything from Haile Selassie's underrated impact on the world to the suspect ethics of journalists. 'Them have no scruples, man,' he would say of journalists. 'Every year them come to carnival looking for trouble, even starting it, just so them can go away and write about how "blacks riot" and so on.' Gabriel told him all about his life in Hackney, about his addiction, and about life in a drug rehab. He found Marcus surprisingly relaxed about the whole thing. 'Crack,' he would say. 'Invented by the white man to kill we off. Glad you never let them get you out, bredren. Glad you survive to tell the tale. So many others won't.'

Marcus worked at the leisure centre, but Gabriel hardly ever saw him do any work in his capacity as pool attendant. What he did see, often, was Marcus breast-stroking and front-crawling with the best of the centre's patrons. 'Perks,' according to the dread.

Marcus knew a lot of people. This became especially evident whenever he and Gabriel went for leisurely lunch-time strolls down Portobello Market. Every few yards he would be approached by some person or other and either have his fist punched, his palm slapped, his back patted, or his ear whispered into. Black, white and green girls would lock him in luvvy-style embraces, releasing him only to stand back and flutter their eyelashes at him, or praise his tumult of impressive dreads, or gawp at his fantastically toned physique. He would introduce Gabriel to these fans. 'This is me bredren Gabby from Hackney.' Judging by the looks he got, Gabriel may as well have been from Warsaw.

At the outset of the friendship, and being the younger of the two by ten years, Gabriel saw Marcus as something of a father figure. This was an illusion which Marcus unwittingly shattered. He needed very little effort to achieve this: explicit chats about sexual positions, plus philosophical discussions about the havoc wreaked on one's sex life by venereal diseases. The result was that Gabriel came to see that no self-respecting father would ever dream of being so candid with his son. That fact duly accepted, their friendship scaled new heights.

A favourite pastime of theirs was visiting the many parks in the neighbourhood, where they would bait foreign girls and play with King, Marcus's white Staffordshire bull terrier. They also liked to lounge about Marcus's basement flat on Ladbroke Grove. Spacious and clutter-free, it was, in Gabriel's opinion, the very epitome of the bachelor pad. He imagined all the girls Marcus must have brought back there and put through their paces. They did little at the flat except listen to 'roots' reggae and watch banned videos featuring black American political activists like Al Sharpton and Louis Farrakhan. Sucking on his spliffs (which Gabriel steadfastly refused to share, in fact he had given up smoking altogether) Marcus would shout at the TV screen whenever he was touched by a certain part of what was being preached. 'Tell them, Farrakhan, for them need to hear it! Tell them, me say! Warn them!' Watching him watch those videos, it was easy for Gabriel to see where Marcus drew inspiration from for his own outspokenness. He was one of those types who are not afraid to speak their minds, no matter the subject or in whose company. His confidence, which stopped just short of arrogance, was gargantuan. 'The white man say we black people have no culture, that we not civilised. What rubbish them talking, Gabby. Don't make them fool you, bredren. We was civilised when them was still running around on all fours clubbing each other to death in caves and shit.' He made statements like this constantly, and with such vim, it was comical, which, when added to his flair for smutty innuendo, meant he often had Gabriel in stitches. 'I like to keep a *breast,*' he would say, cupping his hands over his chest, smiling, 'of what going on in the world.' Or: 'Stick by me, darling. I will keep you *cunt*-tented.' Clutching his sides and wondering when he had ever laughed so much, Gabriel often had to beg him to stop.

2

Slowly but surely, Gabriel gave shape to his days, or 'structure', to quote the staff. Typically, he would be up by ten each morning. The staff were pleased they no longer had to knock on his door. By eleven he would be down for a hearty breakfast, his appetite now befitting a man of his size – six-feet-three and fourteen stones. Once he had eaten, he would complete whatever chore he had been assigned that week. Then it was off for a swim. Or to Holland Park, where, the distraction of beautiful girls notwithstanding, he would find a secluded spot and do some reading. Sometimes, if he had a day off or an extended lunch break, Marcus would join him in the park. By early evening he would be back indoors. He would have dinner at eight, squeezed up with the others at the long table, conscious of his colour, his nose invariably turned up at the fare before him, longing for an end to what, for him at any rate, was a particularly dismal part of the day. After dinner he would go and watch TV with the others in the front room. This pastime held very little attraction for him or anyone else, except Jack, who would hog the remote control and become positively tyrannical in his desire to watch whatever he chose.

The others, including Gabriel, merely humoured him. For them, watching TV was a purely functional activity in the larger scheme of things. They were each aware of the need to be seen to be sociable. With the passing hours, they would drift off one by one to their rooms, leaving the TV to Jack. Up in his room, Gabriel would read for a couple of hours, then write for perhaps another couple, before turning in, usually around two or three in the morning.

Before he knew it, three months had flown by. On the whole he felt good about himself and the progress he had made. Spring gave way to summer and the improved weather further enhanced his sense of well-being. Even his paranoia had waned a little. Which is not to say there had not been off days, days when he could have killed for just a sniff of crack. In fact, on two occasions (three when added to his initial near-relapse) he almost certainly would have given in to his craving were it not for Marcia's patient counselling. The first time she had actually caught him sneaking from the house at one in the morning. She had been out and arrived back just in time to catch him leaving the front door on the latch. Though she knew perfectly well what he was intending to do (the look in his eyes spoke volumes), she demanded an explanation from him, her tone nothing short of matronly. He came clean and begged her not to betray him. Against her better judgement, she promised not to, provided he gave her his solemn oath never to repeat his actions. 'Cross my heart and hope to die,' he swore. For the next two hours they sat in her room (for privacy's sake) and talked and talked.

She would have sat up with him all night if necessary, but

eventually, his crisis now behind him, Gabriel thanked her and went upstairs to bed. It took him a while to get to sleep. He was worried that Marcia, having slept on it, would go back on her promise and reveal all to John and the others. When he came down for breakfast the next morning he fully expected to be called into the office and lectured, possibly evicted. When this failed to happen, his relief was akin to that of a condemned man reprieved at the eleventh hour. On top of that, Marcia, by keeping her promise, had given him the clearest indication to date that there was something between them. And it was for this reason that he purposely sought her out the second time he was tempted to go down to the All Saints Road and blow his sickness benefit on crack. He felt he owed her that much. In a repeat of the first episode, Marcia brought him to her room and took pains in talking him round. Pleased that he had acted so responsibly, her faith in him was now immeasurably increased. And such was his faith in her, he now looked for any excuse to be alone with her.

They went for walks. They pottered around in the back garden, where Marcia, believing herself to be green-fingered, was attempting to get a flower-bed going. He posed for one of her paintings which she framed and gave to him. It now occupied pride of place on the wall at the foot of his bed. They visited the New Pools together, though Gabriel became more interested in frolicking than swimming. During their water wrestles, he often allowed his hand to brush against her in a seemingly innocent, yet suggestive manner. She did not mind, provided he never felt emboldened or lewd enough to actually maul her, a temptation he was finding increasingly difficult to resist. The sight of her body (large full breasts, shapely hips, long strong legs) never failed to arouse him.

They spent a good number of evenings together down the pub. They drank moderately, at her insistence, lest he developed a dependency on alcohol which, according to her, would have been a straight substitute for his previous dependency on crack. Ordinarily, he would have taken offence at the suggestion he could not hold his drink. He did not take offence because he wanted to believe her advice was born more out of a desire to henpeck him than any real fear for his sobriety. It was, he hoped, her way of saying she cared for him not as a member of staff, but as Marcia. He hoped her feelings for him ran deeper than professional concern. His feelings for her were certainly deep. And getting deeper by the day. Much to his confusion. He wanted her in a way he had not wanted a woman before. This worried him. Perhaps he was succumbing to that fabled emoton, love. And for a white woman at that! Whatever next?

He was also getting on better with the other staff members, spending an increasing amount of time in their company. He enjoyed going to the cinema with John whose taste in films (Hollywood blockbusters) mirrored his own. He no longer found it an ordeal to help Jo do the weekly shopping, especially as he was able to persuade her to buy foodstuffs he liked: biscuits, Jamaican Ginger Cakes, full-fat milk. And he felt downright responsible whenever he accompanied Kevin to St Thomas's Hospital with the urine samples. He felt as though Kevin were a wimpy cashier bringing his firm's takings to the bank and he a burly bodyguard sent along to protect him from robbers.

He had also established something of a rapport with the Support Group. Whenever he could, on those rare occasions when they were actually around the house, he would make an effort to talk to them.

Contrary to what Jack had led him to believe, he did not think they were at all stuck up. In fact he always found them warm and attentive. However, he knew he would never be thick with any of them. He and they had nothing in common whatsoever. To begin with, there was the age difference. He was in his early twenties, they were all in their mid-to-late thirties. Then there was the little matter of their lifestyles, which tended towards middle class. They liked jazz, they drank wine, they went to the theatre. Yet in spite of the differences between himself and them, Gabriel privately looked up to the Support Group, envied them, even, though nothing or no one could ever make him admit as much. He envied their privileged backgrounds, their education, the way they spoke, their money and the freedom it gave them, their confidence. All of which made him feel a little intimidated in their presence. When talking to them, for example, he put on airs, becoming hopelessly tongue-tied as he struggled in vain to match them linguistically. Conversations with them, far from making him feel their equal, served only to highlight his poor command of English. This was a handicap he would have to overcome if he wanted, according to his mother, 'to get on in this country'. Improving the way he spoke, she had always said, would open doors for him. Previously he had dismissed her advice as being the ramblings of an immigrant with an inferiority complex. He had now come to view it as a pearl of wisdom. Especially now that he had decided to go to college. He certainly was not intending to show up for his classes to be stereotyped by lecturers and students alike as black, dunce and inarticulate.

Still, while in many ways they were his role models, there were also a good number of things about the Support Group that stuck in Gabriel's craw. For one thing, he loathed their untidiness. He was constantly stumbling over their shoes and socks which they left lying around the front room, as well as magazines, newspapers, items of clothing, half-eaten snacks, dirty plates, dirty cutlery and dirty mugs. When assigned to cleaning the front room he found it galling to have to clear away their mess. And they were deaf to his subtle and not so subtle pleas for a bit of consideration. But this chore paled in comparison to washing up after one of them had cooked.

Each member of the Support Group was renowned for extravagance when it came to cooking. They made no concessions whatever to preparing simple meals. Christopher, a chef by profession and inclination, was especially guilty of this crime. He bought weighty, hardback cook books and attempted to exhaust their hundreds of complicated recipes. He followed these recipes assiduously, sometimes travelling as far as Spitalfields Market in pursuit of some rare ingredient. Whenever he cooked the kitchen was out of bounds for up to three, four hours at a time, while he, like a mad scientist shutting intruders from his laboratory, went about concocting his exotic dishes. Which were invariably lavished with praise even before they had been tasted, though not by Jack or Gabriel. Especially not Jack. If he did not like the look, never mind the taste, of a particular dish, then his reaction could be blunt in the extreme. 'What the fuck is this?' he might say, or, 'I ain't eating this rubbish.'

The full extent of the damage done to the kitchen by Christopher was only ever truly revealed once the meal had ended and everyone repaired to the front room. The mess was spectacular time and again, requiring at least two hours hard slog to clear it away. The first time this job fell to Gabriel he absolutely refused to do it without help. In the end Marcia took pity on him and donned a pair of rubber gloves. On subsequent occasions he was obliged to do the washing up alone, seething with resentment, swearing under his breath throughout and making one hell of a (deliberate) noise with the pots and pans.

And there was one other thing he could not stand about the Support Group. They were tight with money. He came to this conclusion after giving some thought to what lay behind their decision to live, of all places, at a drug rehab. OK, so he had been told they were people who simply enjoyed communal living. Perhaps they were. But if so, why not pool their finances and rent, no, buy a place of their own? They would not have to observe so many petty rules and could avoid having to expose their friends, families and lovers to recovering drug addicts. No. Their decision to live at the house, Gabriel was forced to believe, had to be fiscally based. In other words, the rent they were paying was cheap and inclusive. Quite simply, as Gabriel saw it, they had stumbled upon a cushy little number and were exploiting it to the full. For this, he resented them. To his mind, they were able to and should have done better. Apart from anything else, the house was part of a charitable organisation which surely could ill-afford to bank-roll their excesses. And if, by living at the house, they were not solely interested in making financial savings, then they must have had another ulterior motive. Middle-class guilt, perhaps. Or a desire to be trendy, to be seen to be living close to the edge. This was certainly what Jack thought, and he accused them of it repeatedly, both behind their backs and to their faces. Gabriel remembered one particular exchange Jack had with Antony. Antony had been waxing eloquent on the virtues of living in the area, highlighting some of its chief attractions: the hustle-and-bustle of Portobello Road, the pageantry of the annual carnival, the seediness of All Saints Road. At the mention of All Saints Road Jack jumped in with: 'That's why you live in this house, innit, mate? You think it's cool, don't ya, living with junkies and all that? Something to talk about at your poncey dinner parties.' Antony, taken aback, initially hummed and hawed before going on to protest, a little too vehemently, his innocence. Gabriel, sitting nearby and pretending to read one of his books, thought he had gained an invaluable insight into what the Support Group were really all about.

But if he was getting on better with the staff and Support Group, after three months Gabriel was still no closer to Jack. And he was not helped by the polarity in their attitude to drugs. Jack had moved into the house merely to take a break from heroin. He fully expected to return to 'jacking-up' at some point. Gabriel, on the other hand, hoped never to see another crack pipe for as long as he lived. Jack talked fondly of his time on heroin. Gabriel could see nothing positive to take from his time on crack. In short, Jack saw himself as a junkie on a sabbatical. Gabriel saw himself as someone who had escaped a pernicious vice by the skin of his teeth, as someone who had cheated death. For him to return to crack would have been no different than a lung cancer patient taking up smoking again after being cured by extensive chemotherapy. At his initial interview, the staff had pointedly asked him if he intended to give up crack 'for good, or for now'. He had not been sure at the time. Three months later he had become unequivocal on the matter. There was no going back to his old ways. He had made those feelings plain to Jack. As a result, they had not been able to establish the solidarity that, by rights, should have existed between them. At best they could be described as being on speaking terms. Which made the staff happy enough. At least they were not constantly bickering, or fighting, so often the case with residents.

Gabriel was eventually asked to prepare his first house meal. He was awed by the sheer size of the task facing him. He had never taken the time to observe any of the others in the process of preparing a meal and now wished he had. For he would surely have picked up a few handy tips on how to minimalise the amount of work that went into cooking for twelve people. Still, at least it would only be twelve. He had stated quite firmly that there could be no guests for his first culinary effort. The others had agreed to this stipulation. Not because they wished to spare him any extra labour. Rather they feared for the palates of their guests.

The eve of the big day arrived.

'So who wants what tomorrow, then?' Gabriel asked after the house meeting had just broken up.

The others were wise to him.

'I'll eat whatever you cook,' said Christopher. 'So long as there's no meat in it.'

'Me, too,' said Marcia.

'Me three,' said Jo.

'Ditto,' said Kevin.

'Right,' said Gabriel. 'That's the veggies done and dusted. And the rest of you lot? John?'

'Don't really mind,' said John. 'So long as it's got meat in it.' He smiled and looked round the room at the others, stroking his goatee smugly, as if expecting applause for his witticism. Gabriel sighed wearily. He was getting no help whatsoever. And he noticed that the others seemed to be enjoying his discomfort.

'And I s'pose the rest of you'll eat whatever I cook, right?' They were all in giggling agreement. 'Hmm,' Gabriel added. 'How did I know you were gonna say that?' The others laughed.

He woke the next morning in a state of panic, in two minds whether to stay in bed and feign illness for the rest of the day. Steeling himself, he rose, showered, got dressed, then went down to the kitchen and had his breakfast. Afterwards, still without a clue as to what he was going to cook that evening, he went up to the office to get the shopping money and to seek advice from whichever member of staff happened to be on duty. It was Marcia.

'Help,' he said, as he walked into the office.

'What's up?' asked Marcia, concerned about the look of terror on his face.

'Dunno jack about cooking, Marce. Or even what to cook.'

Marcia smiled, relieved. 'Oh that,' she said. 'Just keep it simple. You'll be fine. Let me give you some money.' She opened the safe and took out a black metal cashbox. From this she took out and gave to him exactly thirty-six pounds, three pounds for each person in the house. 'Remember to get receipts. And bring back any change. Good luck.' She raised her brows a couple of times, mischievously.

'Very funny,' said Gabriel. He turned to leave but Marcia halted him mid-stride.

'Want me to come shopping with you?'

'Suit yourself.'

'Do you want me to or not?'

'Why, you wanna come?'

'I asked you first.'

Gabriel rolled his eyes and said: 'This is a joke.'

'All you have to say is whether you want me to come shopping with you. It's simple.'

'All right. All right. Don't go on, woman. Yeah. OK? Yeah. I do. Satisfied?'

Marcia smiled and said: 'There. You see? Simple. Can't.'

'What?'

'Can't.'

'You serious or what?'

'Deadly. Waiting for an important phone call. Sorry.'

'But . . .'

'I know, I know. And believe me, I'd love to hold your hand. But . . . well . . . what can I say? I can't.'

'I'm outta here.'

He stormed out to the sound of Marcia's raucous laughter.

Somehow the shopping took care of itself. Occupied with thoughts of Marcia, he wandered along the market in an almost trance-like state, as though he had been hypnotised and sent on an errand. Ploddingly, he went in and out of various shops, emerging from most empty-handed after leisurely viewing the goods on display. Soon he happened upon a shop under the Westway, a veritable Aladdin's cave of vegetarian cuisine. Nut roasts. He then popped into a nearby halal butchers and bought a chicken, chopped into eight pieces. Finally, on his way back to the house, he stopped at a vegetable stall and picked up the necessary for a salad.

Marcia answered the door to him.

'Oh. That didn't take you very long, did it?'

'No thanks to you.'

'You sure about that?'

The penny dropped. He pushed past her into the house and went down to the kitchen. Within minutes she had joined him. He ignored her and busied himself putting the shopping away. Marcia sat at the long table and watched him. She said, after a time: 'What we having, then?' He did not answer, just carried on putting the things away. 'You're very childish in a lot of ways, aren't you?' He swallowed the bait.

'You can bloody talk,' he said.

'I'm sure I don't know what you mean.'

'No?'

'No. Tell me what you mean by that.'

'Yo, listen up, Marce. If you've come down here trying to wind me up, you can forget it. I ain't playing your game, you get me?'

'What game?' asked Marcia, smiling.

'That game,' said Gabriel. He had finished putting the shopping away, so, just for something to do, he poured himself a glass of orange juice.

'Yes please,' said Marcia.

'Yes please what?'

'Could I have a glass of that?' He poured the drink and brought it over and plonked it down in front of her.

'Cheers.' She took a sip from the tall glass. He tried not to look at her. 'Sit down a sec.'

'Why?' asked Gabriel. He looked out the window, just as a pair of legs (female, tights and heels) walked by.

'"Why", he says. Because I want to talk to you, that's why. Go on. Sit.'

'Talk to me about what?' He ran his forefinger round the edge of his glass.

'Nothing in particular. Just thought we could have a talk. Don't you want to talk to me?'

'Nah, not really.'

'Why not? Go on. Sit down. You're making me uncomfortable.'

'I don't wanna siddown, thank you very much.' He compromised by resting his bottom against the edge of the table, his back turned slightly on Marcia who was sitting about three inches to his right. He sipped his drink.

'Why not?' Marcia repeated.

'Why not what?'

'Why don't you want to talk to me?'

'Because you're always trying to make a fool of me and shit.'

'How so?'

'Who are you, old bill?' Silence. They sipped their drinks simultaneously. Then Gabriel added: 'Can't work you out, Marce, na'am saying?'

'No I don't. Tell me exactly what you're saying. Fun and jokes aside now. Go on. Tell me. I'm all ears.' She put on her most serious, attentive face.

'Oh you know what I mean. You're always teasing me and shit, always trying to wind me up.'

Marcia smiled, shook her head and said: 'You must try not to take everything so seriously, Gabby. I'll catch you later.' She rose and went out the door. Seconds later she was back. She walked over to him, stroked him softly on the back of the neck and said: 'Be patient, OK?' She went out again. Gabriel sat down at the table and stared out the window. He heaved a sigh of relief. For a brief moment there, he thought he had lost her. He would have to be careful from now on. No. He would have to be 'patient'.

His meal proved a qualified success. The veggies only mildly appreciated their nut roast, whereas the meaties loved their stewed chicken. Especially John. Between sucking the spicy juice from a wing bone, he said:

'So what do you call this type of chicken, Gabby?'

'What?' asked Gabriel, confused. 'Just chicken, innit?'

'But it's West Indian, isn't it?' asked John.

The others ate on in silence. They knew John was digging himself into a pit.

'Yeah, John,' said Gabriel. 'The thing flew here from the West Indies.'

Laughter. John flushed from his neck upwards and said: 'You know what I mean. It's a West Indian dish, is what I'm saying.'

'Actually, it's a Jamaican dish,' said Marcia. 'Isn't that right, Gabby?'

They exchanged smiles, healing, at a stroke, their earlier rift. Then Antony said: 'Never mind where it's from. What I'd like to know is how you cooked it. What's in it?'

'Why you wanna know that for?' asked Gabriel. He was, for the first time since moving into the house, actually enjoying being the focus of attention.

'Well,' said Antony. 'I might like to have a go at it myself.'

'Why?' asked Gabriel.

'Well I . . .' he sputtered. 'Well, for one thing, it means I could eat your kind of food more often.' There was immediate silence around the table. It was now Antony's turn to flush red.

'My kinda food?' asked Gabriel. 'What's that, then, bredren?'

'You know,' said Antony. He glanced round the table looking for support. He got none. He looked back at Gabriel, expecting to be finished off.

Gabriel spared him by saying: 'What's that nut roast like, Chris? Ain't too dry is it?'

'No, no,' said Christopher, quickly swallowing a mouthful of the excessively dry nut roast. Silence, broken by the sound of cutlery against crockery.

For a few weeks nothing of any significance happened in the house. The emphasis was very much on routine and each member of the household was happy to take the others' presence for granted. In fact, most of the time the house was empty, the weather being so good. Even Jack had taken to going out more, where to no one knew. The staff were reasonably pleased with the progress he and Gabriel were making and for the most part left them to their own devices.

Then Lou-Anne moved in and shattered the calm.

She made waves right from the off. She shouted at the staff to 'fuck off' when they knocked on her door in the mornings. She employed numerous evasive tactics when asked to provide urine samples. She was openly hostile to the Support Group, describing them variously as retentive, snobbish, boring and chinless. She neglected her chores. She was disruptive at the house meetings. Referring to Gabriel's infatuation with Marcia, she called him (not to his face) an 'arse-licker', a 'traitor', a 'groveller'. The one person to escape her bile was Jack. In him she recognised a kindred spirit.

The staff were lenient with her. They genuinely believed it would only be a matter of time before she settled down. A fortnight sped by. No change. Pressured by the Support Group to do something, they finally brought her to book.

They summoned her to the office one afternoon and asked her to leave immediately. She refused. They were stunned. Residents simply did not behave this way. They were politely asked to vacate the premises and were expected to do exactly that. Not Lou-Anne. She had called the staff's bluff. What would they do now? They were completely bereft of a contingency. They could not physically remove her from the house, for they would lay themselves open to charges of assault. They could have called the police and had her removed but shrank from that option because of its potential for melodrama. The image of Lou-Anne being dragged kicking and screaming from the house by a couple of muscly wooden-tops, in broad daylight, in full view of the neighbours, was not one they wished to see played out.

They decided to seek advice from their shadowy superiors, the management committee. That afternoon a delegation comprising John and Marcia (the seniors in the quartet of staff) took off to meet with this mysterious group. They came back hours later looking drawn and dejected. The management committee, seeking to up the number of residents in the house (which had a direct bearing on their funding), advised them to give Lou-Anne a second chance. So long as she atoned for her sins and promised to be a model resident in the future. They put these stipulations to Lou-Anne and told her to take a few days to think them over. The following day, much to everyone's surprise, Lou-Anne capitulated. Her anger at the staff in particular and the world in general had burned itself out. In any case, it was in her interests to calm down, for she simply could not afford to be evicted.

Lou-Anne's story was a classic one. Broken home, arrested development, crime, drug-addiction. She was only twenty but had already lost faith. She certainly did not believe in the usefulness of drug rehabs. Like Jack, she had been in and out of them more times than she cared to remember. Recently out of prison (she had served two years of a five-year sentence for GBH), she was only at the house as a condition of her parole agreement. Eviction would have meant going back to prison and finishing her sentence. It was not a difficult choice for her to make.

The repercussions of the whole business were felt by everyone in the house, for weeks afterwards. The Support Group had fully expected to see Lou-Anne evicted. They were shocked to discover she had been reprieved. As far as they were concerned the staff had been cowed by a resident. This to them was a significant event, the like of which they had not witnessed before. Lou-Anne obviously possessed a tenacity to be reckoned with. The Support Group stayed out of her way as much as possible.

The staff viewed things differently. Lou-Anne's antics had confirmed to them something they had always believed about the psychology of residents; namely, that when a resident first moved into the house, he or she needed to be mollycoddled, pampered, fussed over. This need was a direct consequence of the years they had spent abusing themselves with drugs.

It was a need similar to that of a runaway child who craves the love and attention of its parents when first it returns to the family nest. If this need went unsatisfied then the resident (again analogous to a child) was likely to throw tantrums, which usually took one of three forms. Some residents became moody and withdrawn (Gabriel). Others complained that they were being deliberately ignored (Jack). While still others took it upon themselves to be at every turn confrontational (Lou-Anne). For the staff, recognising these behaviour patterns was easy. Dealing with them was something else altogether.

Shortly after the incident, the staff assembled everyone in the front room for a clear-the-air discussion. Marcia presided.

'First of all,' she said, 'we'd like to thank you all for making the effort to be here. I know one or two of you had other commitments you've had to break. We appreciate that.' She glanced in the direction of the Support Group who, as ever, were bunched up together on one of the sofas. She cleared her throat before continuing. 'It's been a difficult last few weeks, to say the least. A lot's happened and there are grievances that need airing. Whatever they might be, now's the time to speak up, basically. We know it's not easy. But it's got to be done. So . . .' She looked round the room. Silence. Then Christopher began to stir. He spoke very quietly.

'Well, I can't speak for anyone else, but I have to admit it, I've seriously considered moving out. You were right, Marce. The last few weeks have been a real strain. I mean, I've been here nearly two years now and I can honestly say it's the first time I've ever felt this way. It's reached the point where I'm now dreading coming home.'

'Why's that, exactly?' asked Marcia, prompting him to go further.

'Why?' replied Christopher, incredulous. 'I would have thought that was obvious.'

'Maybe,' said Marcia. 'But please, feel free to be as frank as you want.'

'That wouldn't get us very far, would it?' said Claire. 'We don't want a slanging match.'

'That's true enough,' said Marilene, timorously, nodding her head in agreement.

'For God's sake!' cried Marcia, exasperated. 'Why are people so afraid to speak their minds in this bloody place?' She shook her head wearily before continuing in a calmer tone: 'I just wish we could have a bit more openness, that's all.'

'It's all right,' said Lou-Anne to no one in particular. 'You can all say what you want. Call me names. Punch me in the face. Do whatever you want. I don't care. That's what this is about, innit? Well go on. Lay into me. See if I give a toss.'

Lou-Anne's outburst was not exactly what Marcia had wanted, but at least, she hoped, it would get the discussion going. She waited for someone to respond. There was much biting of nails and fidgeting and staring into space.

'Antony?' said Marcia, her voice growing wearier by the minute.

'Hey, Marce,' said Antony, holding his hands up resignedly. 'Pick on someone else, please.'

Marcia shook her head and smiled sardonically. It was

beginning to dawn on her, and everyone else, that the meeting was a fruitless exercise. There was a marked lack of honesty and bravery on show. Marcia spoke words to this effect and, in a deliberate show of disinterest, closed the meeting.

The following week, however, at the official house meeting, an outing to Margate was suggested as a means of re-establishing the group identity. The staff stressed what a good idea they thought this was, adding that any objections to it would be seen by them as clear evidence of an unwillingness to bury the recent past. There were no objections. In fact, a universally convenient date was immediately decided upon.

The outing took place one fine Sunday afternoon. Tablecloth, hamper, picnic. To the casual onlooker they seemed like a group of close friends enjoying a day out at the seaside. They were all making the effort.

'God!' said Christopher. 'Did I make these sandwiches? They're disgusting.'

They were gathered around a patch of tall grass well away from the bustle of the sea-front.

'Look at those shorts, Lou-Anne,' said Claire. 'Honestly, I don't know how you can wear them.'

'They're not shorts, actually,' said Lou-Anne. 'They're hot pants. But then you wouldn't know nothing about that, would you?' She stroked her legs lovingly and added: 'Showing off me pins, innit? If you got 'em, might as well flaunt 'em.' She gave Claire a half-smile.

'You saying I haven't got nice legs, Lou-Anne?'

'Dunno, Claire,' Lou-Anne replied. 'We never see 'em.'

Tense tittering.

'I'll have you know,' said Claire, pompously. 'I've got great legs. But they're for my boyfriend's eyes only.' She raised her eyebrows superiorly. Jack, always on the lookout for an opportunity to side with Lou-Anne, hummed the theme tune to the Bond movie with the similar-sounding title. Nervous laughter.

'Art thou art a feminist, Claire?' asked Kevin, his mouth full of crisps.

'Every woman's a feminist,' Claire replied. 'But they're not all exhibitionist.'

'Oooh, I don't know about that,' said Marilene. 'I would say it's the other way around.' She laughed. Gabriel was getting bored.

He said: 'Off down the beach. Anyone up for that?'

Quite a few of them were. But when Marcia stood up and said 'I am' they all remained silent and seated.

The beach was crowded. Gabriel felt extremely self-conscious being the only black person on it. They walked and talked, Gabriel with his hands stuffed into the pockets of his cut-off jeans, Marcia with her battered espadrilles in one hand, intermittently stooping to pick up pebbles with the other. Her black batik wrap flapped in the wind.

'Boy it's windy,' said Gabriel, clutching his bare arms.

'It's lovely,' said Marcia, bending her neck backwards, allowing the sea-breeze to kiss it.

Gabriel admired the pose for a few seconds then said: 'Wonder why none of them lot came with us.'

'Wouldn't worry about it. I'm glad they didn't.'

'Are you?'

'Course. Aren't you?'

'Yeah,' he said. He paused then added: 'Don't really like that lot, do you?'

'Who?'

'Put it this way. I'm not on about Jack and Lou-Anne.'

She shrugged and said: 'They're all right. Their hearts are in the right place and all that.'

'But?'

'They're just a bit silly.'

That did it. She had left him in no doubt. He was special to her. He felt like bursting into song.

They continued walking along the beach. After a while Marcia stopped and said: 'I've got to get home, Gabby.'

'Home?' asked Gabriel, surprised. 'We've only just got here.'

'To Dudley, fool.'

'Oh.'

'Haven't seen my parents since I moved to London.'

'Miss 'em, do you?'

'Dreadfully.'

'Ain't seen 'em not once?'

'That's bad, right?'

'Not necessarily.'

'I speak to them on the phone all the time, of course. But it's not the same, is it?'

She swooped on a pebble, smoothed it between her fingers, then flung it into the choppy sea.

'At least you talk to 'em on the phone,' said Gabriel, ruefully.

Silence. Marcia eventually broke it.

'Still haven't called your mum, eh?'

'Nope.'

'You must, Gabby.'

'Yeah, yeah, I know.'

'Tonight. As soon as you get back. Poor woman must be beside herself.' Gabriel shuffled his bare feet in the sand, a worried look on his face.

'Oh come on,' said Marcia. 'It can't be all that bad.'

'S'pose not,' said Gabriel, thoughtfully. He paused before adding: 'Wouldn't mind going to Dudley with you one day.'

'That'd be nice.'

'One day, eh?'

'Then again,' said Marcia, playfully, 'my parents would have a fit if I brought a black man home.'

'Only a fit? Shit! That ain't jack. My mum would keel over and die if I brought a white woman home.'

They laughed. A flock of seagulls flew by overhead, making a racket.

'Ever been out with a white woman?' asked Marcia.

'What?'

'You heard me.'

'No. Never. You?'

'Just the one.'

Gabriel rolled his eyes and said sarcastically: 'Man, you're funny. I meant . . .'

'I know what you meant,' said Marcia, nipping in. 'Yes I have.' Gabriel raised his brows. 'You look surprised.'

'I am.'

'Why?'

'Dunno. Just am.'

'I hate to shatter your illusions, but you're not the first black man I've known. Told you, my life hasn't been as sheltered as you might think. There were plenty of black people where I grew up. Lenny Henry's from Dudley, you know?'

They sidestepped a few toddlers playing in the sand. A gust of wind whipped up Marcia's hair and her batik wrap. Gabriel caught a brief glimpse of her black knickers.

'So what about you?' she asked. 'Never even fancied a white woman?'

'Not till now.'

She smiled and said: 'I'm flattered.'

'So you should be. I'm a catch, me.'

Marcia laughed and said: 'You're a catch, all right. The original big prize fish.' They smiled at each other. Then Marcia added: 'We should get back, really.'

'You're the boss,' said Gabriel. They turned and headed back.

The rest of the day dragged for Gabriel. Even the fairground failed to amuse him as much as he had hoped. He could not wait to get back to the house. There were a couple of things he needed to do. First, he would call his mother. It was true, he had left it long enough. Then, once everyone had gone to bed that night, he would creep down to Marcia's room and 'light her fire'.

He rang her from the residents' payphone. As soon as he heard her voice his eyes welled up. As soon as she heard his voice she choked up. For the first time ever, Gabriel heard the heart-rending sound of his mother crying. Speaking through trembling lips, he tried to get her to stop. The fact that it took Lucille a good few minutes to do so, tipped him over the edge and he, too, began to sob. A desperate ten-minute conversation followed, during which Lucille, by turns angry, incredulous and relieved, got the salient points of his story. The conversation ended with her demanding that he 'haul his arse' to see her the very next day. He promised he would and hung up.

A few hours later, lying in bed, staring at the portrait of himself painted by Marcia, he had a crisis of conscience. He knew he should have been reflecting on his mother's suffering. He was the author of it, after all. But the fact was he was dreading going to see Lucille, and did not want to lie awake all night brooding on it. So instead he tried to think of something else, of someone else. Marcia.

He arrived at six the following evening. His brother, Malcolm, answered the door.

'Shit! What you doing here?'

'Nice to see you, too, bro,' said Malcolm.

'I s'pose Devon's here as well, is he?'

'Well, well,' said Malcolm. 'Look at you.'

'Get out my way,' said Gabriel, and he pushed past Malcolm into the flat and began to mount the stairs. Malcolm sighed resignedly and said: 'Still got your manners, then?' He followed Gabriel up the stairs.

Devon was there all right, sitting on the sofa in the front

room next to an austere-looking Lucille. When Gabriel and Malcolm walked in he said: 'Here he is. The prodigal son.' He whooped and cheered.

'Oh shut it, Devon,' said Gabriel. He went over and kissed Lucille on the cheek. She regarded him coldly. 'All right, Mum?' he asked.

'Don't you allright me,' said Lucille. 'You have a damn cheek disappearing like that without tell nobody. Who you think you is, Gabriel Power? Eh?' She kissed her teeth, folded her arms about her bosom, snorted and looked away from him.

'Said I was sorry, didn't I?'

'Sorry, sorry, can't buy soldier lorry,' said Lucille, obstinately.

'I knew it,' said Gabriel. 'I'm gonna get nothing but grief.'

'Grief!' Lucille shrieked. 'What the blasted hell you know 'bout grief? Little pissin' tail bwoy like you. What you know 'bout grief? Eh?' Her eyes moistened.

'All right, Mum,' said Devon, putting his arm around Lucille's shoulders. 'Don't go upsetting yourself. He's here now.' Then to Gabriel: 'You ain't got a clue what you've put her through, have you? Idiot. Don't know why she bothers with you.'

'Same reason she bothers with you, innit?' said Gabriel. 'Burgled any drums lately?'

Malcolm, who was standing beside him, boxed his ears.

'What you doing, you damn arse?' asked Gabriel, rubbing his ears, furious.

'Shut you raas and siddown and be quiet,' said Lucille, suddenly.

Gabriel stood there bemused. He had not bargained on such a hostile reception. The rehab, faults and all, suddenly seemed like paradise. He longed to be back there pouring his heart out to Marcia. Reluctantly, pouting, he went and sat on the straight-back chair next to the cluttered mantelpiece, directly opposite Lucille. Malcolm then squeezed up next to her and Devon on the brown, threadbare sofa. The three of them stared at Gabriel. Gabriel, trying to avoid their eyes, started looking round the room, at the second-hand furniture, the old paisley-patterned carpet, the once-white-now-grey peeling wallpaper, the moth-eaten, tobacco-stained net curtains. All of it drab and depressing. What a difference to how the room had looked when he had returned home from the Detention Centre all those years ago. Something about its appearance made him suddenly sure that he would never return to live in Hackney.

Lucille finally broke the silence.

'Go and put the fire under the food,' she said to Devon. 'And don't eat none of it while you out there. And don't turn up the fire too high.'

Devon went out.

'So,' said Malcolm. 'Drug rehab, eh, bro?'

'Don't start, Malcolm,' said Gabriel, wearily.

'Who's starting?'

'Yeah well, I'm just telling you, you get me?'

'Can't believe it took you so long to phone the old dear. We honestly thought you were dead.'

'Maybe that's what I wanted you to think.'

'Because,' said Lucille, 'you don't care 'bout nobody but

youself. You was always like that. Imagine, you never once think to youself, "... Oh, I wonder how me poor mother getting on ..." Imagine that.'

'Oh come on, Mum. That's a bit strong, innit? Thought about you all the time. What you take me for?'

'Me and Dev looked for you all over the place,' said Malcolm. 'We even went to the old bill and reported you missing and shit.'

'Why?' asked Gabriel, unimpressed.

'Cause we were worried, you idiot. Can you believe this guy?' He threw his arms up in despair.

'You two,' said Gabriel. 'Worried 'bout me? Gimme a break. You practically disowned me when I was strung out.'

'What were we supposed to do, smartass?' asked Malcolm. 'We warned you 'bout that crack business.'

'Warned me? Warned me? More like beat me up.'

'Warned you,' Malcolm maintained, for Lucille's benefit. She pretended not to be listening.

Over dinner Gabriel was pressed for details of his stay at the rehab. His brothers did the interrogating. Lucille, though she listened keenly, remained silent, aloof and indignant. Gabriel had injured her and she was making him aware of it, would go on doing so for weeks to come. As for Devon and Malcolm, for all their teasing, they were pleased to see that Gabriel had managed to clean himself up. After all, when push came to shove, he was their kid brother and they loved him. Teasing him was their way of expressing that love. And beneath his martyr's veneer, Gabriel knew this. As did Lucille. Which is why she gave the three of them such leeway to bicker. Eventually, though, she grew tired of their noise and went to bed.

Gabriel rang her every day for the next week and visited her three times during that period. After that, once he sensed she had softened, his calls and visits all but ceased. Lucille was unconcerned. She was content just to know where he was, that he was doing all right. She saw no need for him to ring her every day. Yes, in an ideal world, he would still be living at home where she could fuss over him and keep an eye on him. It was just that she could not bear the thought of him roaming the streets of Hackney. The further he was away from the area the easier she slept at night.

3

It was a balmy midweek evening when Gabriel finally summoned the courage to invite Marcia to the cinema. Much to his surprise, she readily accepted.

They decided to walk to Notting Hill Gate rather than take the bus. Marcia was wearing a smart (black) chiffon shirt, a smart pair of (black) cotton trousers and a smart pair of (black) Mary Poppins boots. Gabriel was conceited enough to believe she had made the effort for him. He had certainly made an effort for her. He was wearing a recently purchased, bottle-green tracksuit and a gleaming pair of white Nike trainers. As a final seductive flourish, he had dabbed on some inexpensive aftershave.

'You look nice,' he said as they strolled along. 'Black really suits you, you know?'

'That's because I'm so pale. Pale and interesting,' she joked.

'Wanna hear a joke?' Gabriel asked. Marcia groaned. 'You'll like it. Trust me. What d'you call an Irishman dangling from a ceiling?'

Marcia waited for the punchline. It was clearly not going

to be delivered so she said monotonously: 'What *do* you call an Irishman dangling from a ceiling, Gabby?'

'Sean de Lear,' said Gabriel, and he fell about. Marcia smiled. Then Gabriel said: 'All right, all right. Got a next one. Got a next one.' Marcia rolled her eyes. 'Heard about the Irishman who decided to swim the channel?' Marcia quickly shook her head, eager for him to get on with it. 'He got halfway across, said he felt tired, then swam back.'

They got back to the house on the stroke of midnight. Jack and Lou-Anne were in the front room watching TV. Gabriel and Marcia went downstairs to the kitchen. There was some left-over dinner waiting for them on the stove. They ate, washed the food down with some tea, then sat side-by-side at the long table openly flirting with each other. He ruffled her hair. She poked his nose. They played 'footsie' under the table. She 'read' his palm, forceasting fame and fortune. Afterwards, still holding his hands in hers, she said: 'You've got beatiful hands, you know that?'

'They're only hands.'

'To you, maybe. To me they're strong yet graceful, destructive yet creative.' She cupped them around her cheeks. 'And they're smooth.' The warmth of her face shot right through his body. 'You obviously haven't done a hard day's work in your life, boy.' She lowered his hands from her cheeks and placed them ever so lovingly on her lap. Gabriel looked at them. He tried to see in them what she had seen. He then looked into her eyes and said: 'You got mad eyes, d'you know that?'

'Really? Just as well I'm sane, then, isn't it?'

'I don't mean mad like that, you idiot.'

'I know what you mean.'

'Do you?'

'Yes. You like my eyes, right?'

'Love 'em.'

They smiled at each other. Then he leaned forward and put his face right in front of hers. He was surprised when she did not back away. He could feel her warm breath on his face. They began to kiss. A few seconds later Marcia pulled away and said: 'We shouldn't, Gabby.'

'Why not?'

'We just shouldn't. It's not right. I should know better.'

He sighed.

'Listen,' she said. 'I should be getting to bed.'

'Tired, yeah?'

'A bit. You?'

'Not really.'

'What are you going to do now?'

'Dunno.'

'Well, I'm going up, OK?'

She rose and left the room.

Two hours later Gabriel was fast asleep when there was a knock on his bedroom door. Groggy with sleep, he went and answered it. For a brief moment they stood in the doorway looking at each other, not speaking. Then he noticed she was wearing her blue towelling bathrobe. He thought it was the most beautiful piece of clothing he had ever set eyes on.

They saw each other every night for the next week. Their

appetite for each other was insatiable. Then it ended abruptly. One night Marcia announced that they would have to stop.

'I've been spoken to,' she explained.

'Who by?'

'The others.'

'They know?'

'They suspect.'

The following afternoon they went to 'their' café on Westbourne Grove to discuss the matter further. They had been going there at least once a week since Gabriel moved into the house. Marcia had been assigned to him as his key-worker and the café was where they supposedly went to talk about any problems he might be having. Put officially, it was where he went to have his progress 'monitored'.

The pretty waitress brought them their coffees, smiled at Gabriel, then went back to busy herself at the counter. Marcia sipped her cappuccino, Gabriel his latte. He had developed a liking for coffee, in all its many forms: Marcia's influence.

'So,' she said.

'So what?'

'Don't look so sad,' said Marcia. 'Believe me, it's for the best.'

'Is it?'

'Of course. You didn't think it could go on for ever, did you?'

He shrugged. Over Marcia's shoulder he saw the waitress smile at him. He did not smile back. That afternoon he was in no mood to flirt with her. Marcia said:

'It was good while it lasted, wasn't it?'

'Brilliant,' said Gabriel, sourly.

'Oh come on, Gabby. Do you want to see me lose my job? More importantly, do you want to be kicked out the house? Pull yourself together.'

Later that evening he decided to go and see Marcus. He needed to be away from the house.

He found Marcus in a slightly downcast mood.

'Come in, bredren. Don't see you for the longest time. Where you been, man? You don't go swimming no more. You don't call round. What's happened to you, lately, star?'

'Been a bit busy, Marcus.'

'Doing what?'

'This and that, blood. You know the coup.'

They went through to the front room. King was snoozing on the rug in the centre of the floor. He looked up briefly, wagged his tail half-heartedly when he recognised Gabriel, then settled down again and closed his eyes, his big head resting on his small front paws.

'You want anything?' asked Marcus. 'Food, drink, a spliff?'

'You know I don't smoke that stuff, Marcus.'

'Yeah. And me still can't believe it. Whoever hear of a black man who don't smoke weed?' He chuckled and sat next to Gabriel on the sofa then proceeded to roll himself a spliff.

'So how you been, bredren?' asked Gabriel.

'Tell you the truth, Gabby, boy, not too good.'

'Why, what's up?'

'Me fed up, man. Fed up with this flat, fed up with work, fed up with this blasted country as a whole. There must be something better for me some place else. The West Indies maybe. Some place where a black man can be himself. You follow?' Gabriel nodded. Marcus lit his spliff and took a deep drag on it. 'I mean,' he continued, squinting through the smoke he had exhaled, 'London's fucked up, man. Getting more so by the day. Especially round here. Place is full of toffs now. Not like the old days.'

'Where exactly in the West Indies would you go?'

'Jamaica, of course.'

'Born there, were you?'

'Yeah. But me left when me was ten. Don't go back since. Been meaning to for years now. Going to be sooner rather than later, the way things are.' He sucked on his spliff.

Gabriel was relieved. He had always suspected Marcus of being English-born. This would have explained why his accent was about as authentic as a Rolex bought from a man down Petticoat Lane. As it had now been revealed, it was simply a case of his accent being diluted. He was not, as Gabriel had always imagined, a fraud.

'So you think London's fucked, do you?'

'Fucked right up, Gabby.'

'And you feel you could function better somewhere else?'

'Me don't feel it, me know it.' His spliff had gone out and he rested it in the ashtray on the arm of the sofa. 'In this country black people can only go so far. And we don't help weself by trying to be accepted by the white man. What we need in this country is more radicals. Damn place full of coconut black man.'

Gabriel thought about his own desire to assimilate and wondered, briefly, if he was in danger of turning into a 'coconut black man'. He said: 'You hate gringos, don't you?'

'Got nothing against them. Just don't want them in me face the whole time.'

Gabriel decided to try something. He said, paraphrasing Marcia: 'Some people might say that was reverse racism.'

'Maybe it is,' said Marcus. 'Tell you one thing, me could never fuck a white woman. If that is racism then so be it.'

'But you know tons of white women, Marcus.'

'True. But that don't mean nothing. Me might play with them, but nothing more.'

'I've fucked a white woman.' It just popped out. He had surprised himself.

Marcus raised his brows, taken aback. He said, after a few seconds: 'Really?' He then sniffed and added: 'Each to they own, I s'pose.' He relit his spliff and sucked on it. 'So,' he said, exhaling a copious quantity of milky smoke, 'you with a white woman at the moment?'

'Sort of,' said Gabriel.

'What you mean? Either you is or you ain't, man.'

Gabriel explained, in some detail, with as much candour as was decent. For all his fire-and-brimstone black radicalism, Marcus's response revealed him to be something of a closet liberal. He said, without a trace of rancour: 'Admit it to youself, Gabby. You love the woman. And from what you say, it sound like she feel the same 'bout you. But she right. It won't work while the both of you still living at that place. Maybe if one of you was to leave. But never mind all that – tell me – she can fuck?'

Gabriel smiled and they punched fists. King snoozed on, oblivious.

Two days after his chat with Marcus he cornered Marcia in the office and apologised for being so surly with her recently. He then hurried down to the kitchen, praying she would join him. She followed within a minute, finding him standing at the window staring through the burglar bars. She came up behind him, kissed him softly on the back of the neck and said: 'Friends?' He did not say anything immediately. Nor did he turn round. He saw a couple of fat pigeons walk by, followed by a mangy mongrel sniffing the ground. He watched the dog disappear from his view then said without looking round: 'Friends.'

The whole business affected Gabriel in ways he had not foreseen and was reluctant to accept even when the evidence was staring him in the face.

For a time he found sleep elusive. His appetite shrank. He became somewhat reclusive, spending half his days holed up in his room. When alone, he found it difficult to pass the time. He wrote in short bursts. He could not concentrate when reading. Actually, it was around this time that he decided to take a break from his books. Truth be known, they had ceased to engage him long ago. Yes, he found them informative, educative, but he no longer wished to read simply to acquire knowledge, knowledge of things which he had quickly discovered bore little or no relevance to his everyday life. Dull, scholarly works on, say, Ethnology, or Palaeontology, written by egg-head professors preaching to the converted and talking in an exclusive language, were hardly likely to rid him of the melancholy that had recently settled over him like a dust-sheet. Thus one afternoon, having returned the last eight books he had borrowed, he came back from the library, for the first time since joining it, empty-handed. John, who answered the door to him, was more than a little surprised. Stating the obvious, he said: 'Not get any out today, then?' 'No,' Gabriel replied, brusquely, and without further ado stepped past John into the house. He went straight into the front room where he switched on the TV and settled down to watch an old episode of *Quincy*. Seconds later John came into the room, followed shortly afterwards by Jack and Lou-Anne who, as usual, were giggling at some private joke. Gabriel shushed them and they went and sat on their favourite sofa. John went and sat in the old threadbare armchair. Before long they were all three captivated by the activities of the impassioned old Medical Examiner.

Quincy triumphed, the titles rolled and Lou-Anne and Jack immediately left the room. Gabriel switched off the TV by the remote. He rose to leave but John, who had been eyeing him intermittently for the last hour, stayed him by saying: 'Not so fast, mate. I need a sample.'

His tone was playful, but it had little effect on Gabriel who recoiled as though affronted.

'You what? You need a sample? Off me?'

He had not been sampled in months. He had thought, naïvely he now realised, that the staff had given up on him in that respect. He had come to believe that they trusted him. He should have known better. Why would they trust him? He did not even trust himself.

'Let's get it over with,' he said.

When they came out of the loo, he was about to start climbing the stairs to his room when again John held him up.

'You all right, Gabby?'

'Why?'

'You seem upset by something.'

'I'm safe, man. Don't worry 'bout me.'

'You sure?'

'Positive.'

'Well, if you're sure,' said John.

'Laters,' said Gabriel.

He went up to his room and lay on his bed and began to think about nothing in particular. He soon drifted off to sleep, a habit he had developed recently owing to his insomniac nights. About an hour later there was a knock on his door. He woke with a start and asked grumpily: 'Who's that?'

'It's me,' a voice replied.

'Oh. Hold on a sec.'

He got up, straightened his clothes, wiped his eyes, then went and answered the door.

'Were you sleeping?' she asked.

'No,' he lied. The staff frowned on residents sleeping in the afternoon. 'Coming in?'

'I won't. Just came to see if you were all right.'

'Why wouldn't I be?'

'Well, I was talking to John and . . .' she let it hang.

'What did the white rasta say?'

'Nothing much, that you didn't seem yourself and that

maybe I should come and have a word with you. So everything's all right is it?'

'Yep.'

'I brought you something.'

She brought her hand from behind her back and held out a book, a paperback novel. Gabriel took it from her, turned it over a few times in his hand, then said: 'News certainly travels fast in this gaff.'

'Thought you might like a change.'

'Me? Like a novel? You kidding me or what?'

'Give it a go. You never know. I'll see you later.'

Love In The Time Of Cholera. A pithy title it was not. The book itself was bound to be as boring as rye bread. How he disliked novels. Not that he had read many. Two in his entire life to be precise. *Kes* when he was at school and something by William Trevor he found lying around the house when he first moved in.

It took him three sittings in as many days to finish the Marquez book. There were things about it he did not like, not least the subject matter. The kind of love depicted in the book was not one he recognised. It was far too sentimental. Nor could he relate to the characters and their world. On the other hand, he found himself mesmerised by the language.

When he delivered his verdict on the book, Marcia invited him to accept it as a present.

'Nice one,' he said.

'Well?'

'Well what?'

'Don't I get a kiss?'

His heart skipped a beat. He quickly moved forward and tried to kiss her on the mouth, but at the crucial moment she turned her head and proffered her cheek. He hesitated momentarily, pecked her cheek, then backed away to a respectable distance, a crooked, embarrassed smile on his face.

'So. What else you reckon I should read?' he finally asked.

She offered to lend him any number from the dozens of books she had on shelves in her room, but he politely declined the offer. It was high time he started a library of his own. Could she write him a list?

'It's going to be a long list,' she said.

'I got time to read 'em.'

'Yes, but how are you going to afford them?'

'Never heard of second-hand bookshops, woman?'

'Still going to cost you a bit.'

'Aint gonna buy them all in one go, am I? Rome wasn't built in a day, you know?'

'I suppose not.'

The list *was* long. It contained some thirty-odd titles, the first seven of which Gabriel bought the following day from a second-hand bookshop on Portobello Road for the princely sum of ten pounds. The bookseller, a florid pensioner with a cut-glass accent, put the books into a crumpled old plastic bag and said to him: 'You drive a hard bargain, young man.' She had wanted two pounds per book, but Gabriel, with only twelve pounds on him and not wanting to leave himself broke, had haggled. 'Still,' said the old woman as Gabriel was all set to leave, 'I hope they bring you hours of pleasure. You've certainly got some good ones there. And don't be a stranger. Come and see me again.' Gabriel said she could count on it, thanked her, bid her goodbye and left.

Of the seven novels, five were written by women. Initially this escaped his notice. In days gone by he would have seethed with resentment and plotted revenge on Marcia for her treachery. He would have seen it as yet another example of her trying to emasculate him. Now he merely shook his head and smiled at the folly of his male chauvinism.

The list presented him with one small problem: which of the books should he read first? In the end he took the safe option. He would read Shiva Naipaul's *Fireflies* because it was set in a part of the world (the West Indies) he could relate to, being the son of a Jamaican.

The story of a family of Trinidadian Indians torn apart by in-fighting, *Fireflies* proved to be a revelation, a little gem of a book. It was difficult for Gabriel to imagine a time when he would read anything as wholesome, anything as moving, anything as beautiful. He found himself thinking about it weeks after finishing it. On the actual night he finished it, he felt so inspired, so envious, he went to his desk and wrote and wrote. And he carried on writing every day without fail until he had finished his story.

Part Two

SCHOOL DAYS

Primary school was shit. Won't even bother with it. Can't remember a lot of it anyway. Can remember my first day at secondary school, though. Seems like yesterday. I'd been looking forward to it. Going to secondary school meant I was now a man. Me and my mate, Laughie, had on our crisp new uniforms. His didn't fit him properly. They were so new and shiny you could have combed your hair in them.

I remember us being shown round the school. Couldn't believe how big the place was. It had two playgrounds. And it had some massive classrooms. And a gym. Even a swimming pool. Hackney Downs Secondary had real glamour.

The teacher who was showing us around took us into a few classrooms to see some lessons in action. As soon as we walked in heads turned. Especially the third and fourth years. They stared us out like they couldn't wait to start beating us up. I'm no fool. I never looked any of them in the eye. Not Laughie, though. The damn arse pulled faces at them. Couple of times I had to say to him: 'You got no sense or what?' 'They don't frighten me,' he said. 'I'll fight any of them any time.'

He meant it, too. Laughie was always fighting. And always

getting his arse kicked. He had all the verbal in the world but fuck-all to back it up with. He was all skin and bones. One good slap and he'd be out. He thought he was so bad, but he was just stupid.

I liked Hackney Downs. I settled in quickly. Did OK in my lessons. Especially English. Made a few friends. Was OK at most sports. Football especially. And I liked to think I got on well with the teachers without actually being their pet. I hadn't gone there to fart around. It was uni next for me.

Laughie on the other hand was forever in hot water. Not a day went by when he wasn't in detention for something or other. Every second the Head wanted to see him in his office. Most mornings after assembly Barraclough (the Head) would read out a list of names of the pupils he wanted to wait for him outside his office. Laughie's name was always on that list. Sometimes we'd be in the playground and all of a sudden his name would come over the Tannoy. WOULD LEROY SMITH PLEASE REPORT TO THE HEADMASTER'S OFFICE AT ONCE. REPEAT ... WOULD LEROY SMITH ...

Laughie broke every rule in the book. He gambled. He smoked. He pinched stuff. He bunked off. You name it he did it. It was like he went to school for a joke. He certainly didn't go to learn how to read and write because he could do neither very well. He was always the last person into class and the first to leave when the pips went. And how he carried on in class. Of course he sat at the back in every lesson, the better to pull silly faces at the teachers and crack jokes and whack the other kids over their heads with his ruler and stick gum on their chairs and fly paper planes and pass notes and generally act the clown. God he loved attention. Then one day he went too far and got expelled.

One afternoon we'd just gone for science. As usual Laughie came in late. He was vexed because he'd lost all his money playing penny-up-the-wall. 'Late again Smith,' said Mr Jawal the Paki science teacher. Laughie just ignored him and went and sat down. Mr Jawal wasn't one for confrontations so he went back to his demonstration involving test tubes and Bunsen burners and shit. Laughie sat there with his jaw in his hand, staring out the window, his face as long as the Blackwall Tunnel.

Mr Jawal then left the room, to get something from his office. Suddenly I heard this argument going on behind me. It was Laughie and Joe. Joe was the class bully. Fuck knows how the argument started but all I could see was Joe slapping Laughie and telling him on each slap: 'Don't . . . fuck . . . with . . . me . . .'

Joe was a big lad. He had muscles. And a beard. Even in the third year for fuck's sake. Laughie was no match for him physically. So he picked up a beaker of acid and drenched Joe's face with it. The whole class was shocked into silence. Joe was screaming and holding his face. One or two boys rushed over to him and got him to put his face under the tap. It helped. Joe's face was burnt all right. But not hideously. There was just a few pink patches here and there. Laughie marched out the classroom without saying a word (not even to me) and was never seen on the school grounds again. He got expelled in his absence and there was talk that he'd been prosecuted and sent to some sin-bin school. As for me, well I liked Laughie and everything. But what he did to Joe chilled me to the bone. I was glad to see the back of him.

I found a new sidekick. Carlton Cook. We became inseparable. Always, after school, I'd either be round his drum or him round mine, playing Subbuteo and shit. We loved Subbuteo.

Mum definitely preferred Carlton to Laughie. She would feed him up and fuss over him like he was her own son. She liked him because he was the complete opposite to Laughie. He wasn't aggressive or rude. He took his education seriously. He was bright. And most definitely going places. That's how I liked to think of myself and I felt privileged to be his friend.

But he wasn't perfect. Not by a long chalk. In fact he had one serious flaw. He was pathetic at sport. For instance, on the football pitch he was so awkward and clumsy all he did was get in the way of the other more gifted players who would slag him off and make him leave the field. He was no better at cricket, either. If he was batting he'd be lucky to make a single run before he was either clean bowled or caught or had run himself out. In the field he lacked all co-ordination. Even if the ball was coming straight at him he'd find some way to let the thing slip through his fingers. But if he was rubbish at football and cricket then he was completely and utterly clueless when it came to athletics. He wasn't the quickest in the world so he concentrated on distance running. But to see him going round the track with his arms flailing like a fucking lunatic then you'd realise that no matter how much he practised he'd never be good at any sport ever. It wasn't long before he was dubbed Queen Carlton and Lady Cook. His appearance didn't help him, either. He was tall and gangly. His hair was always so fucking neat. His tie was always done up. He wore National Health specs. And there was just a general girliness about him that he couldn't hide. This made the other boys feel uneasy around him. No one but myself sat near him in class. The others said I only did it to copy his work. Either that or we were sweethearts. Of course it was all bollocks. Yet the more I denied it the more they accused me of it.

When we queued up in our house room for lunch the other boys would fight each other so they didn't have to stand behind Carlton. It was like he had some kind of disease they were afraid to catch. He became the butt of every poofter joke under the sun. He never once stooped to their level though. He didn't get involved in slanging matches and name calling. If you threatened him he would just go and tell the nearest teacher. He was a grass and proud of it. He'd say to me: 'Honestly, Gabby, if those idiots think I'm gonna dirty my uniform fighting them, they best think again.'

He was a ladies' man. Or should I say girls liked him because he posed no kind of threat to them. At lunch-time we'd usually go up to Dalston Mount girls' school, a few minutes' walk up the road from our own school. We'd get there and the most delicious Dorisses would flock to Carlton. He was like the Fonz. Of course all the attention embarrassed the shit out of him. He only went up to Dalston Mount because it was something to do at lunch-time. It was the only time the other boys spoke to him. They realised his worth to them and couldn't afford to upset him. It was at these times that he could really make them grovel.

I loved going up to Dalston Mount. We all did. Even Carlton in his way. But then something happened which got us banned from going anywhere near the place.

It happened one autumn afternoon. The sky was grey and the leaves were being whipped up by a wicked wind. I'll never forget that day.

As usual, we'd gone up to Dalston Mount at lunch-time. The girls were hanging around outside their school gate waiting for us. Posing and shit. On the way up there we'd decided to try and get them away from their school for a change. A boy called Jeff was the sort of unoffical leader of out little firm, and he put the idea to the girls. They grumbled a lot at first and pretended they weren't interested but in the end he managed to persuade them.

With the girls up front (so we boys could ogle their fit backsides) we walked towards Downs Park. The wind was so strong we had to lean into it as we walked. One or two of the girls' skirts blew up. What a sight! Putting one foot in front of the other was a major effort. Carlton immediately started to whinge. He wanted to go back to school. I told him to do as he damn well pleased but I wasn't going anywhere. Just then Jeff and some other boys started chasing a few of the girls, trying to grope their tits and shit. The girls scattered every which way, laughing and shrieking. I abandoned Carlton and joined in the chase. I remember a few of us (Jeff included) chased these three girls right the way across to the far side of the park, the bit directly in front of our own school. Two of the girls had had quite a head start on us and, deftly, athletically, they scaled the railings to the safety of Downs Park Road then dashed back in the direction of their school. The third girl wasn't so lucky. Because we were hot on her heels she tried to scale the railings too quickly and got stuck on one. I mean it actually impaled her. The sight of her froze us in our tracks. I'd never seen so much blood in all my life. The girl didn't make a sound. She just flopped sideways and passed out.

Like I said, it happened right in front of our school. Which turned out to be a good thing for the girl, if not for us. A few first years saw what happened and ran into school to get some teachers. They came back with Miss Cummings, Mr Pervis and Mr Campbell. A fat crowd had gathered by now, gawping at the girl and shit. A few of the boys who'd been chasing her (not me, I was too terrified) were doing their best to hold her upright so she wouldn't do any more damage to her insides. The teachers eventually got her down and laid her out on the pavement. The whole of her skirt and legs were drenched in blood. Miss Cummings checked her breathing and pulse. She was still alive. Miss Cummings then turned to us and ordered us to get into school. None of us moved. Then, like a lollipop man, Mr Campbell stepped into the road and stopped an oncoming car. It was a tired-looking Cortina Mark I. I remember the driver was a grumpy-looking old black man with a mini fro. He was wearing a Hackney Council donkey jacket, probably on his way back to work from lunch, either that or he was skiving. The teachers explained to him what had happened. He looked more irritated at being inconvenienced than concerned about the girl's well-being. The teachers put the girl into his car (he complained about blood on his car seat) then got in themselves. The old bloke then drove them to Hackney Hospital.

We saw the girl a few days later. She was fully recovered. We found out that she hadn't been injured as badly as all that. The blood had made everything seem worse than it really was. Did I feel relieved or what?

Needless to say, all of us involved got a right roasting from Barraclough. He suspended all of us for a month then followed up by banning all Hackney Downs pupils from going up to Dalston Mount. The ban was still in place when I left school.

After we got banned from Dalston Mount Jeff told us not to worry because there were other girls' schools. Skinners in Stamford Hill for one. He said that the girls up there were far superior in fitness to the drab Dalston Mount lot. He needed to say no more. I was sold. But he couldn't convince the others. Their excuses were various. 'It's too far, Jeff.' 'We can't afford the bus fare, Jeff.' 'We'll never make it back to school in time, Jeff.' And three bags full, Jeff. He told them they were all faggots. I agreed with him. Something I'd been doing a lot of lately.

So it was just the two us who'd catch the 106 up to Stamford Hill. We went up there every lunch-time come rain snow or shine. We loved it up there. And Jeff was right. The girls were fitter than the ones at Dalston Mount. We'd stand across the road from their school gate and wolf whistle them and shit. But because there was just the two of us and about thirty of them at any one time they'd just giggle amongst themselves and shout insults at us from the safety of their school gate. Me and Jeff would dare each other to cross the road and talk to them. But we'd usually chicken out at the last minute. To the girls we must have looked like a right couple of plebs standing across the road eating our chips and pointing out who we fancied from who we didn't fancy.

We were usually late back for school. When we walked into lessons the teachers would lecture us about punctuality and shit. We'd just kiss our teeth and go and sit down. If the teachers carried on then Jeff would slag them off and order them to leave us alone or else ...

Some days we didn't bother going back to school at all. Instead we'd go and play space invaders or roam the streets getting into all sorts. I remember we went on this mad shop-lifting spree. Mostly newsagents. There was one in particular we used to fleece regular as clockwork. It was owned by a decrepit old Jew called Kosinsky.

Now in those days newsagents didn't have the bell over the door. So we'd creep into Kosinsky's when the old bugger was round the back somewhere. We'd come out of his shop with fags, chocolate, crisps, sweets, you name it. We'd end up with so much stuff we'd have to flog most of it at school the next day. And it was like Kosinsky didn't even miss the stuff because believe me we raided his shop every day for about a month. But he turned out to be a smart fucker.

We'd been casing the joint all afternoon. We walked back and forth past it a million times, waiting for Kosinsky to go round the back. It didn't even occur to us how suspicious we must have looked. Anyway, finally we saw the old Jew disappear round the back. We crept in. We didn't have to worry about anyone walking in on us because the shop was always deserted. We used to wonder how the fuck Kosinsky made a living.

Once we got inside we immediately started to stuff our pockets with whatever we could lay our thieving hands on. I must have grabbed about twenty Twixes. Jeff dashed behind the counter and swiped about four hundred Embassy Filters. I was now looking round for the next thing to nick. It never entered my mind to open the till. Eventually I sank my hand in a box of Mojo chews (the strawberry ones) and came up with about a hundred of the damn things, spilling them all over the floor in my haste. I stuffed as many as I could into my pockets. By now we were causing such a commotion we couldn't believe Kosinsky hadn't heard us. Jeff came from behind the counter and the two of us were headed for the crisps when Kosinsky stepped from behind a stack of Golden Wonder boxes. We froze. Stunned. Before we knew what the fuck was happening Kosinsky had locked the door with a key and bolted it for good measure.

'You two devils are going nowhere,' he said, grinning like a madman. Then he marched past us and went round the back claiming he was going to phone the old bill. I don't mind saying it, I was frightened. The old bill. This was some serious adult shit. We'd been caught bang to rights. I thought about the beating I would get from Mum. Me and Jeff stared at each other, the swag bulging in our uniform pockets. Then Jeff put his finger to his lip. His face told me he'd figured out some plan of escape. He whispered it to me. Kosinsky came back.

'You two devils,' he said. 'You think you are smarter than old Kosinsky, eh? Well you are wrong!' He had some kind of accent, Polish maybe. He leaned against the counter watching us, smiling like someone who'd laid a mousetrap the night before and had woken up to find not one but two dead mice in it. 'That's it,' he said. 'Just stand right there. Just like that. Then you can tell the police what you were doing in my shop. I am . . .' Before he could say another word Jeff pounced on him. He tried to struggle but he was too old and weak and in no time Jeff had his arms pinned behind his back.

'Get the key,' Jeff shouted. 'Get the fucking key.'

'The key?' I asked, all foolish-like, as if I didn't know where it was.

'In his pocket!' Jeff screamed. 'Quick arsehole.'

As I approached him Kosinsky rammed his withered old knee into my stomach, winding me. I had to ignore the pain. Jeff was shouting at me. Kosinsky was getting hysterical, shouting for help from imaginary passersby. I was confused and scared. In my panic I clubbed Kosinsky over his head with a bottle of red-top milk. He groaned and collapsed to the floor. I thought he was a goner. Jeff said he was just knocked out. He fished the key from Kosinsky's pocket. Seconds later we sprinted out the shop.

We decided to lay low for the next few days. In that time we were model pupils. We went to every lesson every day on time. We paid attention in class. We even stopped going up to Skinners.

Carlton noticed the change in me and wanted to be my spar again. Even though I'd been ignoring him for months. I didn't mind. If I was hanging out with him instead of Jeff I knew I wouldn't get into any scrapes. Then one morning, just when I thought I'd heard the last of the Kosinsky business, I looked out my form room window and my heart nearly stopped beating. Kosinsky and two uniformed old bill were coming through the school gate.

My whole body was soon drenched in sweat, even though it was the middle of winter and as usual our radiators were knackered. I started to fidget. Carlton was sitting next to me. I didn't dare look at him in case I gave myself away. I looked across the room at Jeff. He looked back at me, puzzled. I made a gesture with my eyes as it to say 'we're done for'. He didn't understand me. I gave up. Seconds later Kosinsky walked in with the two old bill.

Our form tutor Miss Lavender asked us all to be quiet because the old bill wanted to speak to us. I looked over at Jeff. He looked like he'd seen a ghost.

'Now then boys,' said one of the old bill. 'There's no need for alarm. The reason for our visit today is quite simple. On Monday of last week at approximately 12.30 p.m. Mr Kosinsky here was attacked in his shop by two youths he has reason to believe attend this school. Right then. We'll be going round the whole school today visiting all the classes and yours just happens to be the first one on our little tour.' The innocent pupils all looked at each other, searching for the culprits. I turned my face away from Carlton. My heart felt like it was mad to jump out my chest. The copper went on. 'Now this was a particularly nasty attack. As you can see Mr Kosinsky has suffered a very serious injury. Now I feel confident, and your teacher here has assured me, that you would all wish to co-operate with us in trying to clear up this matter.' I looked at Kosinsky. I felt a sudden pang of remorse for what I'd done. He had a whopper of a bandage on his head. It looked like a skull-cap. 'So,' said the copper. 'What we'll do now is get Mr Kosinsky to go round the class and see if he can identify his assailants. OK?' The pupils whispered amongst themselves. This was a nice, unexpected, exciting start to the day, and they were loving every minute of it. Unlike me and Jeff. Carlton asked all excited-like: 'Who you think it was, Gabby?'

The copper ushered Kosinsky forward. He started to walk slowly down the central aisle, scrutinising all the faces on his left. He looked frail and half dead. He could barely drag himself down the aisle. When he came to me he looked me dead in the eye, just like the old bill must have told him to. I was nervous like hell but I didn't flinch from his gaze. He'd recognised me. But I could see he wasn't a hundred per cent sure. He looked at me long and hard. I could feel the whole class watching me. Kosinsky gave me one last penetrating stare then walked on. Just as well he did, because I was about to break down and confess, and I would have grassed up Jeff in the process.

Kosinsky started scrutinising the faces on his right, walking leisurely back along the aisle, taking his time with each row of pupils. Eventually he came to Jeff. Jeff gave him the evil eye and he quickly moved on. I sighed to myself. Close call. But we'd escaped. Kosinsky finished and went back and stood near the two old bill. They thanked us for our co-operation and started to usher Kosinsky out the door. Just before he stepped through it we heard him say to the old bill: 'This is useless. They all look the same.'

Instead of learning my lesson I hooked up with Jeff again. It was the end of my friendship with Carlton. We'd simply outgrown each other, just weren't into the same things any more. I certainly didn't want to sit around in the evenings playing Subbuteo. That was kids stuff.

Me and Jeff started going back up to Skinners. We bunked off even more than before, like we were making up for lost time. We started shop-lifting again, though we never again went near Kosinsky's place.

The few times we were actually in school we were unruly and disruptive. And abusive to the teachers. They didn't know what the fuck to do with us. They tried everything. The old divide and rule tactic. Detentions. Suspensions. Lectures (I got a lot of those, much more than Jeff did, the belief being that I had, academically speaking, more to offer than Jeff). Bad reports. Even violence (more than once Mr Pervis literally knocked our heads together). None of it worked. In the end they gave up on us. To them we were lost causes. Maybe they were right, because we certainly had no interest in school. We only showed up when we got bored with wandering the streets. And when we did all we wanted to do was play cards and smoke in the classrooms and generally take the Michael. We figured if the teachers didn't care about what we got up to then why the fuck should we?

There was another tactic they used to try and straighten

us out. They sent lots of letters to our drums. We'd wait for the postman and intercept them. And if any did get through then we just accepted that we were going to get some serious beatings. I remember the beating I got from Mum after she found out I'd bunked off school for a month straight. She ripped into me with the thickest leather belt. She beat me long and hard, as if she was trying to give me a month's worth of punishment in one session. She sweated like a pig while she beat me, that's how much effort she put into it. When she'd finished, about two hours later, she was completely shattered. I can laugh about it now. But at the time I thought about doing one of two things, killing her or running away. Of course I did neither. In fact by the next day I'd forgiven her. Forgiven, mind. I'll never forget.

SCHOOL'S OUT

Midway through the next year, we gave up the pretence and quit school for good. Jeff's dad beat him and eventually kicked him out. Mum beat me but couldn't quite bring herself to show me the door. But she did say I would have to find work. She wanted rent. She said if I wanted to play at being a man then she'd show me what it was to live as a man. I got a job in McDonald's. My wages were sixty quid a week. Mum took half. I stayed at Micky Dee's two months then chucked the job. For that Mum gave me the most grief. We argued constantly. Then she just started to ignore me. We were living under the same roof yet we hardly spoke two words to each other a day. My brothers, Devon and Malcolm, urged me not to throw my life away. I was deaf to them. They gave up on me. Their pleadings had only been lip service, anyway, more to keep in with Mum than anything else. I didn't see why I should listen to them. It wasn't as if they were good role models. Devon, at nineteen, was already a convicted burglar. And Malcolm, at twenty-one, was a compulsive gambler.

Jeff had no intentions of working. Nor did he intend to be skint all the time. He couldn't sing or play an instrument.

It was too late for a career in sports (for a time he'd held the school record for the two hundred metres). So the only option left open to him was crime. Either that or starve. No. He had plans, Jeff. Big plans. And as usual I allowed myself to get roped into them.

By now Jeff was living in a squat round the corner from my drum and I was round there every day. We'd sit and smoke weed and plan our next caper. We did everything. The squat was our Aladdin's cave. It was full of stuff we couldn't flog, like betamax videos and black and white tellies. At times it got so cramped in there we had to give stuff away or chuck it.

At the end of every mission we'd go back to the squat and chill till the heat wore off. Then we'd go and see our man up at Samson's caff, our fence. What a bastard he was. We were only kids to him so he gave us whatever he felt like for our gear. But we had no choice. Some money was better than no money at all. At least we could rely on him to always have ready cash. We spent most of our wonga on clothes. We thought it was important not to look like oily lamps. We shopped in all the pukka stores. Scotch House was my favourite. Jeff preferred Aquascutum.

At night, if we weren't out on the thieve, we'd spend the time at some shebeen or other, where old black men and tired old white women got legless to the sound of ancient reggae tunes. Actually, these shebeens weren't all that bad, especially if they had a half-decent pool table, which most of them did.

We only went to shebeens in the week, when fuck-all else was happening in the manor. The weekends were a different kettle of fish. Then we'd get dressed to the nines and either go to Cubies in Dalston Junction where Sir George's sound system held sway, or we'd go down to Kingsmead Estate's community centre and listen to Sir Biggs. To tell the truth, neither of us really liked Sir George. His crowd was a lot of poofy black guys, or 'sweet boys', as we called them. And he played far too much lover's rock. No. We definitely preferred Sir Biggs. Being at Kingsmead suited us to the max. It was a more rough and ready dance. You could wear whatever you liked. There weren't as many girls there as there was at Cubies, but the few that did go weren't as stuck up either. But the best thing about Kingsmead was the music, rebel music, and Sir Biggs had the weight in his speaker boxes to send it straight to your soul. Yep. Kingsmead was a bad boy's dance, full of gangs and posses and shit. We loved the place.

Jeff's squat was useful for other things as well. We'd bring girls back there and fuck 'em and dump 'em. The place used to reek of sex. We didn't give a shit. If anything it was a turn-on. We'd finally discovered pussy and we just couldn't get enough of it. We called ourselves the Martini Boys because we tried to pick up girls any time any place anywhere. Whether it be on a bus or in a kebab shop. If we saw a fit girl everything had to be dropped till we'd had a go at chatting her up. We'd attack them without warning, firing questions and compliments so rapidly they wouldn't have time to think. Like a comedy duo we'd take the piss out of each other, forcing them to laugh. Make a girl laugh and you're halfway there. Then before she knows it you're tucking away her digits and watching her backside jump as she walks off down the road.

Me and Jeff had our share of problems with girls, though. For a start he got more numbers than me. I used to sulk about this and we'd end up arguing. I just couldn't work it out. He wasn't particularly better-looking than me. In fact he had an egg-head and a big fuck-off nose. It definitely wasn't because he had the gift of the gab over me. He was crude and offensive mostly. His spiel was full of talk about titties and pussies and what he liked to do them and how. He was forever feeling up his crotch and inviting girls to admire the size of his bulge. Yet all this slackness seemed to work for him.

I went for the opposite approach. I tried to keep the conversation away from sex, as if it was the last thing on my mind. I tried to make the girl feel good about herself, tried to get her to relax, to trust me. It was a reasonable approach, but in no way as successful as Jeff's bullying tactics. Because at the end of the day that's what it was, bullying. To this day I'm convinced that Jeff only fucked so many girls because he terrorised them into having sex with him. 'Boy, Gabby,' he'd say to me, shaking his head. 'You got time sweet-talking them. Just beg them a fuck and be done with it. They can only say no.' He really used to piss me off with that shit.

But no matter what our different approaches were, we both had the same problem when it came to getting rid of girls. Once we'd had our ends away that was it for us. We weren't into all that boyfriend and girlfriend shit. Bucks, garms, raving and dope. Those were our top priorities. Girlfriends came way down the list.

They used to come round the squat at all hours, ringing down the doorbell and shit. Of course we wouldn't answer it. They'd get really mad and start shouting our names from the street, effing and blinding and carrying on. We'd just sit indoors giggling, knowing that sooner or later they'd get the message and fuck off out of it. If they had any pride that is. Sure we felt guilty. But cruelty was the only language some of them understood. They'd get their revenge on us, though. Normally we'd see them a few weeks later on the arm of some new bod, when we'd immediately regret dumping them. From then on, mad with jealousy, we'd do all we could to win them back. Sometimes we succeeded. Sometimes not. But whether we did or not, they wouldn't half make us grovel and beg in the process of trying.

At this point in our lives we didn't have a care in the world. At sixteen we thought we'd arrived. Our lifestyle was the lifestyle. We laughed at people stuck in boring nine-to-fives. And we weren't frightened of the old bill, either. In fact we took the piss out of them. We went thieving for fun. Our bank-books were fat (for kids our age), yet we still hit the streets every day. We had to. Crime was a drug and were we hooked.

By now we'd learned to drive. Not because we paid for lessons or anything nerdy like that. No. We went TDA crazy. The first car we nicked was an old Austin 1100. We smashed it up round Pembury flats trying to master the basics. When we'd wrecked it good and proper we went out and nicked another one and did the same thing all over again.

Once we were competent behind the wheel we went halves and bought something of our own, something with a bit of bite, a Triumph PI. We didn't so much drive the thing as fight with it. It was all screeching tyres and Formula One gear changes.

From the word go we decided to take no police checks in it. Neither of us had a licence so we couldn't afford to. We had the most police chases. Luckily we were never caught once. I was never behind the wheel for any of these chases. Good thing too, because I certainly wouldn't have pulled the same death-defying stunts as Jeff did. I remember this one chase we had which kind of sums up his daring.

We'd just left Samson's caff. We were on our way to see a man in Well Street about some stolen giros we were trying to flog. Jeff was driving. I was in the passenger seat munching on a saltfish dumpling. By the time we'd reached the junction of Sandringham Road and St Mark's Rise a police Rover was flashing us from behind.

As usual I panicked. Quite apart from not having a licence we had no tax and no insurance. Plus we had all the stolen giros on us and about half an ounce of weed. As soon as Jeff saw the Rover he put his foot down.

'Shit!' he said, eyeing the old bill in the rear-view mirror. 'They must have been waiting for us.'

'Step on it,' I said. 'They're on your heels.'

'Relax, Gabby. You worry too much. This is a PI, remember?'

We belted it down to the junction of Cecilia Road and Sandringham Road. The old bill were still flashing us. They were really quite close now. Jeff wheelspun right into Cecilia Road then mashed his foot down. He must have clocked forty going up to Dalston Lane. He was giving himself room because when we got to Dalston Lane there was the usual amount of heavy traffic going by. Jeff nosed the car into it, the traffic slowed and let him in, then he screeched left round the corner and raced down towards Amhurst Road. By now I had the weed and the giros in my hand, the window open, ready to fling the lot if necessary.

The old bill were still close behind, their siren wailing now. I looked over my shoulder and I could see one of them on his radio. When Jeff got to the zebra crossing outside Amhurst Primary school I thought he was going to hang a right into Spurstowe Terrace, fly past the dole office, then disappear into the flats behind it. There was no oncoming traffic so he could have done. But no. He surprised me and the old bill by shooting round the left corner into Sigdon Road, a tiny little side street. He must have taken that corner doing at least thirty because he had real problems straightening up once he'd gone round it. Good thing for us there was nothing coming the other way, else we'd have both been goners.

Jeff burned down towards Wayland Avenue. When he got there he hung a right into it, a sharp left back into Sandringham Road, another sharp right into Ferncliff Road, and finally a quick left into the dead-end driveway behind Cromer Terrace flats. He parked up and killed the engine. He looked at me, smiled, said 'Triumph PI. Don't ramp with it', then held out his palm for me to give him five. I did and we both cracked up laughing.

After that the old bill really took a liking to us. Every second they were looking to pull us over. We always managed to give them the slip. In the end, though, we were forced to flog the PI. It was just too well known by the old bill. We bought a Triumph Dolomite Sprint instead. Now *there* was a fucking motor.

Greed is a fucked-up thing. It's the reason I first got nicked. I can't remember where Jeff was that day. Probably banging some Doris back at the squat. But I'm sure if he'd been with me then I wouldn't have done the stupid thing which got me three months in a Detention Centre. Like a father having to restrain his foolish son, he wouldn't have let me.

It happened on a particularly roasting summer's day. I'd just come out the Abbey National on Kingsland High Road where I'd gone to put some funds into my account. So it's not as if I was boracic. Anyway, as soon as I came out the Abbey I saw it, the fattest ducket I'd ever seen in my life. It was round the neck of this old biddy. She walked by me just as I stepped out onto the pavement. The sun bounced off the ducket and almost blinded me, even though I was wearing shades. I realised when it was too late that I should have just turned and walked away. I already had the most tom, including duckets. But no. I started following the old biddy who was heading towards Ridley Market. There were loads of people on the High Road at that time of the day and I had real trouble keeping her in view. But I managed to see that she'd gone into the newsagents a few yards shy of the market entrance. I stood outside Ravel's shoe shop and waited for her to come out.

She did eventually. She carried on walking towards Ridley. I remember she was lugging a shopping trolley, so I thought she must be going to the market. If I was going to snatch her ducket then I knew I'd have to do it well before she reached the market entrance. I picked up the pace, but because there were so many people between me and her I couldn't get to her before she reached Ridley. I slowed down, prepared to accept that she'd got away. That's when the old biddy surprised me. She walked straight past the market entrance and stopped outside Mothercare. This gave me fresh hope. I broke into a trot. I was careful not to run too fast. The last thing I wanted was to draw too much attention to myself. I trotted past the old biddy then stopped and turned and faced her. Our eyes met. In an instant she knew what the coup was. Instinctively she went to protect her ducket. She was a fraction late. I'd already swiped it from her neck. Actually, the ducket itself fell on the ground, leaving me with the flimsy chain in my hand. The old biddy bent down to pick it up. Again she was late. I swooped on it, scooped it up in one movement, then dashed off towards Dalston Junction. Only then did the old biddy start to scream. 'Oi! Stop him! Thief! Help! Thief! Stop him!' She was causing a right racket. When she realised I was escaping she resorted to racial abuse. 'You fucking black bastard!'

I knew I had to get off the High Road. I was heading rapidly for the next left turning, Ashwin Street. I thought I'd never reach it. When I eventually turned into it I suddenly felt sick. My stomach was churning like mad. I'd been running way too fast. I was knackered and out of breath and sweating like a road digger. Then, in the distance, I saw a figure walking slowly towards me. I refused to believe he was old bill, even though he had on the uniform. I had to believe it when I heard behind me: 'Stop him officer! He's got my pendant. Stop him!' I couldn't understand it. The old biddy with the varicose veins who I'd left some two hundred yards up the road had miraculously caught up with me.

I had to think quickly. My thoughts were all over the shop. Should I turn and run back in the direction of the old biddy? Or should I carry on in the direction of the copper who was now on his radio talking police language? I went for the second option. There was no way I was going back on the High Road. Too many have-a-go heroes to contend with. If I could get past the copper, I thought, then I knew I'd be away. It turned out to be a big if. As I tried to sprint past him the copper gave me the mother of all rugby tackles. He literally flung himself at my legs, without so much as a care for his own safety. My knees buckled under me. In a flash the copper had my arms pinned behind my back . . . cuffed. We scuffled on the ground for a while but it was pointless. I was nicked. While we were still on the ground the old biddy came up alongside us and clubbed me over my head with her ridiculously heavy handbag. The thing felt like it had rocks in it. She was about to club me again when the copper saved me from certain brain damage. 'It's all right now, love,' he said, hauling me to my feet. 'Leave him to us now.'

Four weeks later at Highbury Corner Magistrates Court I was sentenced to three months' DC, what Maggie Thatcher called at the time the Short Sharp Shock.

SHORT SHARP SHOCK

I'd seen a few prisons in my time, from the outside, driving past in the car and shit. The Ville, Scrubs, Wandsworth. Thank fuck Hollesley Bay was nothing like any of those grim-looking places. It didn't have any high surrounding walls or fences. No cell blocks. Just a lot of little wooden buildings all over the place.

Hollesley Bay was a self-supporting colony. To get to it you had to cross this narrow little bridge. It was the only way in or out. That's why there was no need for high walls and shit. Any 'absconders' were normally caught trying to cross the bridge.

The minibus crawled along towards Reception. One of the kangaroos on board, a right bumpkin, gave us a guided tour of the colony. In a thick ee-by-gum accent he pointed out the farm, boasting about how it produced the grub for all the other DCs and YCs in England. 'We be growing everything 'ere,' he said. 'Apples, plums, all sorts.' Then he spotted something in a distant field and suddenly pointed and said: 'Take a good look, boys. I bet yees aint never seen that much hay in all of your lives.' He laughed, but as we looked at the massive haystacks on the quivering horizon we couldn't see anything funny about them. 'Get used to them,' Bumpkin said. 'For yees'll be having to stack those soon.' Again he laughed. He was getting less funny by the second.

The farm was surrounded by sorting, packing and storing sheds. I could see boys in overalls carrying crates, escorted by fag-smoking kangas. The boys seemed happy enough. One or two were even smiling. I couldn't believe there was anything on earth they could have to smile about.

Bumpkin took particular delight in pointing out the jam factory. As the minibus crawled past it he told us to 'smell that aroma', pushing up his bulbous nose and breathing in deeply. The geezer was a right fucking idiot. Then he drew our attention to the dairy farm. Again I noticed boys milling about in overalls. I presumed their jobs must have been to milk the dozens of mud-splattered cows I could see lolling around, all of them stinking to high heaven. Honestly, we could smell them even from the minibus. Later it would be my job to shovel their shit.

I noticed other things on the way down to Reception that Bumpkin hadn't bothered to point out. I saw a footie pitch, and a massive dome-shaped building that I found out later was the gym, and everywhere I looked I could see small, evenly spaced trees dotted about perfectly kept lawns. There were little tarmac roads everywhere, snaking off the main one and disappearing among the oblong-shaped, unpainted, wooden dormitories. Then I saw a sprawling, red-brick building with a free-standing sign outside it. The sign read: HOSPITAL. In fact there were sign posts on every road bend. Some pointed the way to Warren Hill (the closed section of the colony), while others pointed the way to the 'units' in the open section. The whole place was like Toy Town. Only I didn't feel like Noddy.

Finally we got to Reception. I didn't know what to expect, so naturally I was nervous as hell. Sixteen of us (all Londoners) bundled out the minibus, handcuffed in twos, with a couple of kangas up front, and Bumpkin bringing up the rear. Directly in front of us stood a low, flat-roof, concrete building. On the front wall a sign read: RECEPTION.

The first person we came across inside was a grumpy-looking orderly, busy mopping the floor. He looked pissed off at having to attend to a bunch of new arrivals. It was his job (which we found out a couple of hours later) to see that we were showered before taking our civvy clothes and issuing us with regulation DC ones. What a job, I thought, having to handle skid-marked underpants and sweaty socks.

Then we saw a kanga whose BO was stinking out the place. He was standing at this long counter with great big sweat patches under his arms and a fag dangling from his mouth. He looked serious as fuck. Bumpkin handed him our papers, took off our cuffs, then went and sat down with his two mates on a bench by this big old window. Without looking up from the papers Bumpkin had given him, Serious Kanga ordered us to line up facing him. Once we'd done this a white boy at one end of the line, a spotty punk, sparked up a fag. Serious Kanga bared his teeth.

'Put that fucking fag out, you! There's no smoking in 'ere.'

He puffed on his own fag. Punk, terrified, quickly mashed the fag between his fingers.

'Sorry,' he said, all meek-like.

'Sorry!' Serious Kanga bellowed. 'Sorry what?'

'Sorry I sparked up, innit,' said Punk, confused, looking along the line at the rest of us for help.

'Sorry, *sir,* you prat. You address officers as *sir.* Prat.'

The rest of us giggled. Serious Kanga silenced us.

'And what the fuck are you lot laughing at? Shut the fuck up. There's no laughing in 'ere.'

We all stared at our feet, cowed.

'Don't worry,' laughed Serious Kanga. 'You'll learn soon enough the way we do things 'ere.' He looked down at the papers Bumpkin had given him. Seconds later he looked up again and barked: 'Right! Jones?'

A lad stepped sheepishly from the line and walked up to the counter.

Once we'd showered and changed we were put into a room to await dinner. By now I was so hungry I felt like I hadn't eaten for years. I stared out the window, my back turned on the others, not really wanting to be drawn into no kind of banter. At one point I felt a gust of self-pity blow right through me. I started to shake and my eyes filled up. But then I thought . . . *fuck this feeling sorry for yourself shit Gabby, get a grip, you're here now, doing bird, like everyone else, paying for your cowardly crime, just grit your teeth and get on with it.*

I looked around me, mostly white boys bragging about their crimes. I noticed this black guy whose face looked familiar. I'd seen him on the minibus and had been waiting for the right time to talk to him. I walked over to where he was sitting and sat on the bench next to him. He eyed me warily.

'Where you from, star?' I asked.

'Why?'

I was surprised by his answer. Not to mention his tone.

'You look familiar. Where you from, Hackney?'

He shook his head and looked away from me. I thought I wasn't going to get anything out of him, so I was surprised when he said out of the blue: 'Tottenham.'

'Oh yeah? Whereabouts? The Farm?'

'Nah. But I'm up there a lot.'

'That must be it then. Up there myself sometimes.'

'Isn't everyone?' he said, all matter-of-fact-like.

Yep. He was a sarcastic mother-fucker. I didn't like him one bit. He had that typical, tough-headed, the world's against me attitude. I was tempted to ask him what he got sent down for but the look on his screwed-up face told me it could only have been for one thing, violence. Everything about him said 'fuck with me at your peril'. He reminded me of Joe. Joe who'd had that spat with Laughie at school.

We eventually had our dinner, if you could call it dinner. Soggy cabbage and cold spuds and dog-food meat stew. A kanga then came and told us to pick up our bedclothes and stuff from the pile near the counter then make ready to go over to our designated units. A few minutes later Bumpkin took me, Punk, Screw Face and one or two others over to Hartsmere, our particular unit.

When we got there Bumpkin marched us straight to our dorm. He showed us how to make our beds, then marched us back along the narrowest of corridors to see the SO, Mr Mainwaring, a bald, bespectacled, middle-aged coot. Bumpkin stood behind us while Mainwaring gave us a quick rundown of the rules on Hartsmere, what kind of behaviour was expected of us, and a whole load of other stuff too boring to mention. He then gave us our EDRs (earliest date of release) and asked us if we had any questions. We didn't, so he told Bumpkin to escort us to the TV room where we met the other detainees on the unit who'd all just come back from work.

The first week dragged. By the second I was into my stride, if that's the right phrase.

We had to be up by seven in the morning. Seven! Our dorms had to be ready for inspection by eight. Breakfast was at eight thirty. By nine thirty we'd be lined up on the old parade ground ready to go off to work, dressed in boots and overalls.

On the parade ground we'd be grouped into four work parties. Party one, the farm. Party two, the dairy farm. Party three, the unit cleaners. Party four, the cow-shit shovellers. For the first two weeks I had to fall in with party four. Privilege of being a newcomer. I was gutted.

Before we went off to work, Mainwaring, an ex-soldier, loved giving us ten minutes of marching drill. The old codger was sad in the extreme. He'd march us up and down the parade ground, shouting instructions the whole time.

'Atteeeeeention! By the 'eft, quiiiiick . . . march! 'Eft, 'eft, 'eft, right, 'eft. 'Eft, 'eft, 'eft, right, 'eft.'

For some reason he never pronounced the L at the beginning of the word left. We'd get to the end of the parade ground and he'd suddenly shout: 'Halt! Mark time.' Which meant marching on the spot. Then he'd shout: 'Abouuuut turn. By the ’eft, quiiiiick . . . march! ’Eft, ’eft, ’eft, right, ’eft.’ We’d deliberately march out of step, treading on one another’s heels, shoving one another in the back, talking, giggling. We used to get the old boy so mad he’d threaten us with all sorts.

But what really got his goat was if one of us shouted ‘Birdseye!’ He was a ringer for Captain Birdseye from the fish finger adverts. He’d immediately start pacing up and down, his face red with rage, his hands behind his back, demanding to know who the culprit was. ‘Who said that? Who said that? Come on now. Own up.’ At first no one would. But once he started to threaten us with no TV or Canteen the guilty person, goaded by the murderous looks he got from the rest of us, would eventually come clean. The punishment for shouting ‘Birdseye!’ was severe indeed. If you were found guilty of this particularly vile crime then you’d have to spend a couple of lonely days (and nights) down the block, scrubbing the floor with a toothbrush.

The worst part of the day was early morning. It was for me anyway. I just wasn’t used to getting up that early, wasn’t used to the mad rush of having to do everything by a certain time. I preferred the evenings. After ‘tea’ we’d go to the TV room and smoke ourselves silly with Old Holborn while watching kids programmes, though we were strictly forbidden to do either till the kanga on duty had to told us to ‘spark up’ or ‘turn the telly on, lads’.

They treated us like infants, and didn’t miss a chance to show us who was in charge. For instance, we weren’t allowed to turn the TV on until we were absolutely dead quiet. It might not sound like a lot to ask, but it is when you’re dealing with forty-odd rowdy teenagers. If a boy farted the kanga would send him to bed. If another coughed: bed. And if after fifteen minutes of unbroken silence yet another boy cracked and screamed at the top of his voice (this happened a lot) everyone had to go to bed.

On the Wednesday of the second week I had my first circuit training session. I can't say I'd been looking forward to it. In fact I'd been shitting myself over it for days, because one evening in the TV room, a couple of days before the actual circuit, these white boys told me some real horror stories about Mr Farquhart the PI.

According to them, if Farquhart asked me to jump, my only response should be 'how high, sir?' They said he drove you to the point of death. He was a real 'cunt', they said, and told me that if I had any sense at all I wouldn't fuck with him. They said in the gym he watched you like a hawk. If he caught you cheating at the exercises he'd make you and everyone else come back and do the circuit all over again the next day. Then they went on to talk about the actual circuit, which they said was extremely gruelling and designed to stretch you to your very limit. They must have seen the terror on my face because this one boy, Chris, said: 'Don't worry mate, you're new, you'll only have to do the green circuit.'

'Green circuit?' I asked.

'Yeah,' said Chris. 'You got three colours on the circuit. Red, black and green. Red means you gotta do each exercise twenty times. Black's fifteen. Green's ten. Plus, you gotta go round the circuit three times in all. So for you that'll be thirty goes on each exercise.'

By now I was thinking up some excuse that would get me out of having to do this circuit bollocks. Epilepsy, asthma, angina! But I knew this Farquhart bod must have heard them all a hundred times before.

'Boy,' I said to Chris. 'What's he trying to do, murder us?'

'Green circuit's a piece of piss,' Chris continued all braggy-like. 'Do it on me head, mate. What you gotta worry about is the red circuit. Ask anyone 'ere, it fucking kills ya. Every time. I ain't joking. No matter how many times you do it, it leaves you dead for days afterwards.'

He almost made the green circuit sound easy. But I knew it was going to kill me, especially since I'd done no serious exercise since leaving school. My legs and arms looked like twigs. And as for stamina, what little I might have been born with had been completely blown away by ganga abuse. I suddenly remembered when I'd tried to have it away with the old biddy's ducket. I'd only reached a couple of hundred yards before I was ready to chuck up. No. There was no getting round it. The circuit, be it pink, yellow or mauve, was going to kill me stone dead.

Farquhart came for us at ten. He looked arrogant and fitter than a horse. Even his face had muscles. We'd been waiting for him on the parade ground with our gym kits tucked under our arms, having a quick after-breakfast smoke. Although he was wearing trainers, shorts and vest, Farqhuart still had a walkie-talkie strapped to his waist. It said to us that he was a kanga first and a PI second. A few of his colleagues were standing by the back door of the kitchen, smoking and swapping home-life tales. He went over and chatted with them for a while, completely ignoring us. Finally he moved away from the other kangas, approached us, then said in a bored voice: 'Let's be 'aving you then. In twos. Come on, line up. Be quick about it. That's it. Now let's have some jogging on the spot. Get you 'orrible lot warmed up.'

He glanced over his shoulder at his mates. They smiled back at him, enjoying our humiliation. We did as he commanded without a murmur between us. He had a real air of menace about him and not even the most unruly among us dared upset him.

'Now,' he said. 'We're going to jog to the changing room and I want no talking on the way. Got that?'

'Yes, sir!' we replied sharply and as one.

'Good. Follow me. And keep up.'

When we got to the changing room (an outbuilding near the gym) Farquhart told us we had exactly five minutes to get changed. He said if any of us took longer then it was circuit again the next day. For all of us. I'd never seen people shed their clothes so fast in my life. Luckily we managed to change in time, just. Again we had to line up in twos and jog on the spot. I was already whacked and the circuit hadn't even begun yet.

'Now,' said Farquhart. 'We're going to sprint to the gym. And I mean sprint.'

I groaned to myself. OK, so we could see the gym only fifty yards or so up the paved footpath. But nonetheless . . . Once again Farqhuart led from the front. We made a mad dash for the gym.

When we got inside, us first-timers started leaning against the wall trying to catch our breath. We noticed that the veterans had carried on jogging on the spot. We soon found out why.

'What the fuck are you lot doing?' Farquhart growled at us. 'You never stop moving in the gym. Never. Now get the fuck off that wall and let's 'ave you jogging on the spot.'

We eased forward as quickly as our aching limbs would allow us and joined the others in the centre of the parqueted gym floor, more walking on the spot than jogging. The others looked at us as if to say 'Don't fuck up you lot. We don't fancy this shit again tomorrow.' I looked to my left and saw Screw Face with a murderous look in his eyes, a look he'd trained on Farquhart, as if he was planning to knife him later. I knew how he felt.

Spread out round the gym were all the various exercises. Farquhart spoke. We jogged on the spot and pinned back our lug holes.

'For the benefit of you newcomers, I'll go round the circuit and demonstrate the correct way to do the exercises. Pay attention, 'cause I really will only do it once.'

Punk was jogging next to me. He made me look fit in comparison to him. His face was twisted with pain as Farquhart started his demonstration. Farquhart moved round the gym with a soldier-like agility, running between the exercises and talking to us at the same time. The geezer was fit bad. And it wasn't as if he was doing some puny exercises. Step-ups. Press-ups. Chin-ups. Sit-ups. Leg-raises. Star-jumps. Squat-thrusts. Burpees. Bench-presses. When he finished his demonstration, he didn't even break sweat. He looked at the stopwatch dangling from his muscly neck then told us how much time we had to complete the circuit. We got into position, like impatient steeple chasers waiting for the gun. Farquhart checked his stopwatch one last time, clicked it on, then shouted 'go!' Seconds later he had to click it off when Chris said: 'Which colour we doing, sir?'

'Oh. Yes. The newcomers do the green. The rest of you can do the black.'

He looked at his stopwatch again then clicked it.

At the first exercise we all bunched up and got in each other's way. Before long, though, some of the veterans had moved on and gradually we thinned out around the gym. Farquhart was standing in the middle of the floor. He kept swivelling left to right so he could keep tabs on us.

'Now remember,' he shouted, his voice echoing round the gym. 'Run between the exercises. I'm watching you.'

I tried to pace myself. Yet I couldn't go too slowly in case I didn't finish in time. Some of the exercises, at least the first time round, weren't so bad. But others, like the burpees and the bench-presses, were slaughtering me.

I was slowing down almost to a crawl by the time I'd finished the first lap. At one point I was doing bench-presses, the weight bar across my shoulders, when I noticed Screw Face doing some leg-raises. He could barely get his legs off the floor. Another time I was doing star-jumps when I noticed Punk on the chin-up bar. He was under some serious pressure. His face was all red and shit and his eyes looked glassy as hell. The rest of the newcomers were all similarly struggling. I was glad. At least I wasn't the only one dying on his feet.

By the end of the second lap I was ready to give up. I felt sick. It was torture. I was dragging myself between the exercises. I couldn't have run if you'd paid me. Screw Face had a grim, determined look on his face, as if he'd decided he must finish the circuit or die trying. Punk looked dead already. Foam had gathered at the corners of his mouth and he was sweating so much he looked like he'd just come in out of the rain. His gym kit was literally clinging to his bony body. His face, arms and legs were redder than a redcurrant. Farquhart must have seen us wilting because now he was shouting:

'Come on. Keep going. No slacking. Keep going I say.'

Forty-five minutes or so had passed and us newcomers were still going round. The others had all finished and were jogging on the spot near the door. We only had about three more exercises to do when Punk collapsed. I was on my umpteenth squat-thrust when I saw him fall flat on his face on the press-up mat. Farquhart rushed over to him.

'Get up!' he shouted at Punk. 'Get up! You want to be responsible for circuit two days in a row? Get up I tell you.'

I couldn't believe the man's attitude. He was a monster. We all could see that Punk was in a bad way. Still, I didn't say a word. All I wanted to do was make sure I finished. Pride and all that. Besides, it was a black thing. I couldn't make all those white boys see me as a quitter. The veterans started shouting at Punk.

'Fucking get up you woman.' 'There ain't nothing wrong with you.' 'If we do circuit again tomorrow you're dead.'

And so on. Farquhart eventually held up his hand and silenced them. He said to Punk: 'Now maybe you'll get up.'

By now the rest of us first-timers had finished. We went and sat on the floor by the back wall, shattered. To our surprise, Farquhart didn't insist on us jogging on the spot like the others. The state Punk was in, maybe he was worried he might actually kill one of us. He was still standing over Punk, though, threatening him. Eventually Punk got to his feet and completed the circuit with a few minutes to spare. But Farquhart wasn't quite done with us yet. He ordered us all to line up in twos then told us to sprint back to the changing room, shower and dress in five minutes, then sprint back to the unit.

The dining hall doubled as the visiting room. When I walked in I couldn't see them at first. I stood in the doorway peering through the fog of smoke and over the mass of heads. Finally I spotted them in a far corner, looking really self-conscious.

At the table was Mum, Devon, Malcolm, Jeff (I'd put his name on the visiting order so he could give Mum a lift – neither Devon nor Malcolm drove, the tossers), and Lana, this girl I'd been knocking off before I got sent down. In my letter to him I'd deliberately told Jeff not to bring her. I didn't want her seeing me inside. I didn't need her pity. Besides, she was too clingy, always coming round the squat and cramping my style and shit. Silly bitch really thought she was my woman. I took a deep breath then weaved my way between the tables towards them.

Mum looked drawn. She'd obviously been fretting. I suddenly felt deeply ashamed and sorry for what I'd put her through. I smiled at her awkwardly. She smiled back, slightly embarrassed. I leaned over and kissed her on the cheek and sat down. Only then did I acknowledge the rest of them. I looked at Devon and Malcolm. They shook their heads at me, as though they pitied me. Then I glanced at Jeff and Lana. 'What's happening, bro?' said the one. 'All right?' said the other. I nodded at them then looked round the dining hall, just to avoid having to speak. I didn't have a lot to say. Mum broke the silence.

'You look so skinny.'

'You think? I don't. If anything I've put on weight. Been eating well and exercising. Food's all right in here. And as a green-tie I can go up for second helpings.' I explained that detainees who'd been at the centre over two weeks were given green ties, allowing them extra privileges. Jeff and Lana laughed. It must have been the thought of me eating prison grub and enjoying it so much I actually went back for more. I didn't think there was anything funny in it.

'What's so funny?' I asked.

They shook their heads and wiped the smirk from their smug faces. Mum pulled out a plastic Tupperware container from her handbag.

'What's that you got there?' I said.

'Just a little something me cook last night. You want it?'

She shoved it across the table at me. It was four dried-up fried dumplings and two shrivelled-up chicken drum sticks. God bless her, I thought. Even after all I'd put her through, she was still worried about me eating properly, as if I was going off on some school outing and she'd prepared me a packed lunch full of nutrients so I didn't have to stuff my face with unhealthy crisps and fizzy drinks.

I tore into the chicken. It tasted like rubber. Jeff laughed. So did Mum. I must have looked like a savage because Lana said: 'You hungry, Gabby?'

'Starving,' I lied, for Mum's benefit.

I looked at Jeff sitting so familiar-like next to Lana, and wondered, just for a second, if he was fucking her.

'So what kind of food them feed you in here?' asked Mum.

'White man food, of course,' I said. 'But it's safe. Especially the puddings.'

'Just like school,' said Jeff to Mum. 'He always used to love the puddings at school.'

Mum laughed. It was a heart-warming sight.

The kitchen orderly came over to our table. He asked us if we'd like tea. I knew him. Singh his name was. Paki, I think. Could have been Indian. Same difference. We all took tea from his plastic tray, tea in plastic cups.

'I'll be back for the cups later, Power,' he said, then moved off to another table.

'Well,' said Devon. 'I hope you learn your lesson from this.'

It had started.

'Please bro,' I said. 'Spare me the lecture.'

'You should listen to your older brother,' said Mum.

'Why?' I asked.

Silence. Devon and Malcolm shook their heads at me again, suggesting this time it was pointless trying to talk sense to me.

Then Mum started laying into me. I bowed my head in shame and let her get it off her chest. Like Devon, she hoped I was going to learn my lesson. Maybe now I would see the error of my ways. With time now on my hands maybe I would get to thinking about how I was throwing my life down the drain. She was at the end of her tether. She certainly wasn't going to spend her life traipsing all over the country to come and visit me in prison. She'd done all she could for me, said all she could. It was up to me now. If I didn't . . .

'All right Mum. I get the message for fu . . .' I just about held it in. 'Just don't go on. This ain't the time or place.'

I was embarrassed now, mostly because Jeff and Lana had seen Mum coating me off. I stared into my plastic tea cup. A few seconds later Jeff passed me a lump of hash he'd been holding in his hand the whole time. It was wrapped in cling-film, sweat from Jeff's palm all over it. Singh came back for the empty cups. We made eye-contact and I dropped the blow into one of the cups. He winked at me, picked up the empty cups, then walked off.

'What you going to do with that now?' asked Mum.

'Smoke it. What d'you think?'

Laughter all round.

We sat there for another half hour or so, mostly in silence. Every now and again Mum would ask me a question – when exactly was I being let out? – was I doing as I was told? – that kind of thing. Eventually a kanga called time. I got to my feet immediately, desperate to see the back of my visitors. I slapped Jeff's palm, nodded at Lana, kissed Mum, and hissed at Devon and Malcolm. Then I turned and walked out the dining hall without looking back.

I got to my dorm and slumped onto my bed. For the next five minutes or so I replayed the visit in my head. Then suddenly I had a thought. A depressing one. Four weeks. Four whole weeks before I could go home. It might as well have been four years. My eyes filled up.

I started counting the days to my release. I decided not to send out any more VOs. I just wanted to do my last four weeks and get the hell out. I made a calendar and every night before lights out I'd put a cross on it. It felt good to see all those crosses mount up as the big day got nearer and nearer.

For the next couple of weeks I got my head down. I was in a world of my own, making plans for when I hit the streets. I didn't feel close to any of the other boys. There wasn't one of them I could have called a friend. Their plans for when they got out didn't coincide with mine. They were all aiming to continue with, not give up, crime. They didn't seem to care about doing bird, didn't seem to give a monkey's about being banged up. They treated the whole thing like one big holiday. In fact, a lot of them called Hollesley Bay, Holiday Bay. The white boys were especially flippant about the whole thing. For most of them, doing bird was like a feather in their caps. The majority of them were on their second and third stints inside. They boasted about it, for fuck's sake. Their mentality was wack in the extreme. I didn't want it rubbing off on me. I'd be going straight when I got out, so I had to keep them at arm's length. Mentally.

We were always kept occupied so the days went by fairly quickly. During the week – except Wednesday, which was gym day – we worked all day long. After the first two weeks I'd managed to wrangle a cushy cleaner's job, which meant I didn't even have to leave the unit. The other boys said I must have arse-licked some kanga to get it. Of course I did. I didn't give a shit what they thought. All I knew was that I didn't have to leave the unit and that my wages were upped by a quid a week, which made a massive difference to the amount of stuff I could buy at the canteen on a Friday.

In the evenings there were classes for anyone dunce enough to need them. I went along a few times. Not because I wanted to do Maths or English or anything. No. I went because the teacher, Miss Hornby (Horny Hornby we dubbed her) was seriously fit. For a white woman. And by all accounts, she was game, too. Rumour had it that she gave blow jobs after class and was particularly into black boys. Of course the rumours were all bollocks, but that didn't stop most of the black boys on my unit from going to her class every evening without fail. She must have wondered why she had no white kids in her class. Maybe she concluded that they weren't so in need of educating as us black boys.

On a Saturday, if you didn't have a visit, you could either play footie, or, in season, cricket. On Sundays we went to church for the first half of the day (falling asleep during the chaplain's long-winded sermon) and for the other half of the day we watched TV or played table tennis.

Nothing major occurred on the unit for a while. There was the odd drugs spin. One or two boys were sent to the block for fighting or baroning or, whenever the block was empty and needed filling, for simple 'insubordination'. Detainees left. Others replaced them. But apart from that, nada.

On the whole, the kangas were really friendly to us. So long as we did as we were told, toed the line and shit, they wouldn't pay us any mind. It was just a job to them. Some of them even told us how much money they earned (a pittance by any standard) and about the size of their mortgages and families. In this way we were able to get a picture of the kanga away from work. I remember a chat I had with this one kanga, Mr Davies. Not only did he drone on about his home life, he seemed genuinely interested in hearing about mine. Then he started banging on about the generation gap between me and him, saying how lucky I was to have youth on my side and my whole future ahead of me. He had a really wise, caring way about him that was in no way patronising. We all liked him for the same reason: he looked for the person behind the stereotype and encouraged us boys to do the same. A man of his talents, I remember thinking, should have been a mechanic and not an oily rag. I put this to him one day.

'Sir,' I said. 'Don't take this the wrong way or nothing, but you're getting on a bit now, right?'

'You saying I'm past it, Power? I've only just turned fifty, you know.'

'No, sir. You're getting me all wrong. What I mean is, how come you never made SO or PO?'

'Ain't me, son,' he said, shaking his head. 'Been offered, but it ain't me. This is where the real fun of the job is, Power. Sitting here in the TV room with you lot. Not stuck in some office. Know what I mean?'

I did. It's funny, but even after all these years I can still remember the old boy vividly. He spoke to me that day as if I was his son.

Before I knew it I only had two weeks left. I was over the moon. The end was in sight. It got so I became unbearable on the unit. The newcomers hated me. I wound them up something rotten. They called me Gate-Happy-Gabby. I just couldn't resist going round the unit reminding them of the little time I had left. 'Only thirteen and a breakfast now, mateys.'

Then something happened which made me shut my gob for the last week of my stay.

One afternoon we were having lunch in the dining-hall. As usual I was winding up the newcomers. 'Only six and breakfast. Only six and a breakfast.' This giant white boy called Jamie, who thought, stupidly, that he was the daddy of our unit, said to me: 'Give it a rest, Power. Like a stuck record, you are.'

'Come again,' I said, shocked. Surely this white boy couldn't be talking to me.

'You heard,' he said.

I kissed my teeth and said: 'Just do your bird, arsehole, and be quiet.'

'Never mind my bird,' he said. 'Someone's shagging yours on the out.'

Everyone at the table cracked up laughing. Even Screw Face managed a snigger. It was too much for me, my own kind laughing at me like that. I had a quick glance round the hall to make sure no Kangas were watching, then chopped Jamie in his forehead with my metal dinner tray. He immediately brought his hand to his forehead, checking for blood and shit, but he hadn't been cut, there was just a massive lump on his forehead that was growing before my eyes. He sprang at me, lunging at my throat, knocking me over in my chair. Four kangas swarmed us and hauled us before Mainwaring.

I claimed Jamie had attacked me. Jamie said he'd only retaliated. Owing to his rep, Mainwaring didn't believe him. He got sent to the block to 'cool off'.

Then Mainwaring said to me: 'You're skating on thin ice, Power. Be careful. You do want to go home on time, I presume?'

'Yes, sir. I do, sir.'

For the next six days I was almost invisible.

HOME-COMING

I had mixed feelings about being home. On the one hand I was glad to see the back of that poxy DC. Yet on the other I felt like a stranger in my own manor.

A lot of stuff had happened in the eight weeks I'd been away. To start with, Mum had a new job. She'd left her cleaning job at Hackney Hospital and was now working as an overlocker in some sweat shop on Brick Lane. She'd also spruced up the house. There was new carpet and wallpaper in every room, new curtains as well. She was dead pleased with the new look but I couldn't share her feelings since I felt guilty at not having been around to give her a hand. I felt as if I'd missed out on something major and was really quite cut up about it. Still, when Mum asked me what I thought of the new look I forced a plastic smile and told her it looked great. Which it did.

The first week back I didn't go anywhere. I didn't want to go out or speak to anyone or do anything. I certainly didn't want to see Jeff. I felt ashamed that I'd done bird and the last thing I wanted to do was talk about it. I wanted to put the whole sorry episode behind me and start afresh.

During that first week back me and Mum got closer than

we'd ever been. She must have sensed the mood I was in because she gave me a lot of time and space to think. Before she went off to work in the mornings she'd stick her head round my bedroom door to tell me she was off and that she'd left some breakfast for me on the stove. When she came home in the evenings she'd cook us dinner and we'd sit and watch telly till we felt tired and went to bed.

That was the first week. By the second she was on my case again. Now, on her way out in the mornings she'd shout from outside my bedroom: 'Gabby, get yourself down that job centre today.'

'I will. I will. Don't worry.'

'Yes, well see that you do.'

It wasn't long before I was locking my bedroom door. I had every intention of looking for work, or at the very least enrolling at college, but I wanted to do it in my own time, at my own pace. Plus there was still the little matter of explaining it all to Jeff. I'd avoided him for almost two weeks, but one morning I got out of bed and went round to his squat. What I had to say to him could wait no longer.

I found his squat boarded up. They'd finally kicked him out, I thought. Two guys from the Cromer Posse (a right bunch of terrorists), who were hanging out at the entrance to Cromer Terrace flats, spotted me and one of them shouted:

'Yow! Who you looking for, Jeff?'

I walked over to them. They were roughly my age but because they'd gone to different schools I didn't know them as such. They were just faces in the hood to me, both smoking spliffs and trying to look mean as hell.

'You two know Jeff?' I asked.

'You're Gabby, right?' said the one who'd shouted earlier.

'How you know that?'

'Jeff. Just finished a stretch, yeah?'

'Eight weeks,' I said.

They laughed and the one who hadn't spoken yet said: 'That ain't no stretch. More like a shit and a shave.'

'Jeff's living in Nightingale now,' said the one who'd spoken first. He kept dabbing his spliff because it wouldn't burn straight.

'Whereabouts exactly?' I asked him.

He told me the address and said that if I saw Jeff's ride in the flats then he would most probably be in.

I couldn't see the ride in the flats. I took the lift up to the fourth floor anyway, thinking that Jeff could have parked some place else. I knocked on the door and waited. Not a dickie bird. I knocked again. A minute later I was about to walk off when I heard footsteps behind the door. The door didn't open immediately. The person was spying on me through the peephole. Eventually I heard the lock rattle then saw the door open slightly. This girl with the living jerry curl put her greasy face round it.

'Yeah,' she said. 'What d'ya want?'

Cheeky bitch, I thought. 'Who are you?' I said. 'Don't Jeff live here?' She must have got frightened because she put the safety chain on.

'Wait here,' she said.

She shut the door. Seconds later it was opened again, this time by Jeff. His face relaxed when he saw me.

'Yow, Gabby, my man. Come in, come in. When'd you get out?'

'Last week.'

He opened the door wider and I stepped inside. We went through to the front room. I couldn't see the girl anywhere and I thought she must be in the bedroom since Jeff only had his Y-fronts on.

'Last week,' he said. 'And you're only coming to see me now?'

'Yeah, well, you know how it is. Had to spend some time with the old dear.'

'Course. Course. So. How'd you find me?'

'Saw a couple from that Cromer mob.'

'Oh them. I told them to look out for you. What you waiting for, man? Bill a spliff.' He threw me some Rizzlas. 'Back in a sec. Let me get some garms on. Siddown for fuck's sake. You're making the place look untidy.' He went out.

I sat on his leather three-seater sofa and looked round the room. It was a decent pad, I had to admit: well furnished, framed Bob Marley and Marcus Garvey posters on the walls. There was also a poster of John Lennon, the only white singer to ever be truly accepted by the black community. In the centre of the room was a smoke-glass coffee table with a bag of weed and some fags on it. I helped myself to some of the weed, eased back into the sofa and started to roll my spliff. Jeff came back in dressed in tracksuit and trainers.

'Put on some sounds, Gabby, man,' he said. 'Place is like a morgue.' I looked at him and shook my head. He was always telling me what to do. But that was all about to change.

'You put something on,' I said. 'I dunno what's there.'

'Seen Lana yet?' he asked suddenly.

'Fuck Lana.'

'Oh stop pretending. You know she's your woman.'

'Got no woman, bredren. Unlike you.'

He smiled, leaned forward and said all quiet-like: 'She's breeding, you know?'

'Who, Lana?'

'No, arsehole,' he whispered. 'Gloria.' I frowned, confused. He nodded in the direction of the hallway.

'Oh,' I said. 'Really?'

'Yep. Just found out.'

'Well, well. Can't believe it. You a dad.'

'Believe it, bredren. And believe this as well: my yoot ain't gonna want for jack.'

He finished building his spliff. He sparked it, took two deep drags on it, let the smoke out slowly through his tunnel-like nostrils, then started filling me in on what had gone down while I was away. For starters, the reason I hadn't seen our Dolomite Sprint in the flats was because he'd flogged it and bought a gas-guzzling Rover 3500.

I asked him what the score was with him and the Cromer Posse. He told me he'd been hanging out with them for weeks. This surprised me. He'd always dismissed them as hot bods and sworn he'd have nothing to do with any of them. When I challenged him on this he just shrugged and said: 'They're all right, really. Once you get to know 'em. Besides, in this day and age you need a firm behind you, otherwise you ain't saying nish.'

If I was surprised by that, then what he told me next completely blew me away. He said he'd stopped going on the thieve and had started selling weed on Sandringham Road, which everyone was now calling the Frontline. At first I thought he was winding me up. As far as I was concerned, selling weed was big people business. But then he pulled out half a weight of Malawi from under his sofa and showed it to me. I'd never seen so much weed in my life. I was flabbergasted. He told me there was easy money to be made selling weed and that I shouldn't waste time getting involved.

'I ain't exactly skint, you know, Jeff?'

'So you got a few quid in the bank,' he said. 'Big deal. How long you think that's gonna last? Wake up, Gabby, man.'

'Yeah, well, we'll see.'

We both dragged on our spliffs.

'Fair enough,' he said, suddenly all jovial again. 'But when you make up your mind, let me know. I'll sort everything. It'll be just like before. You and me. Partners. Safe?'

I nodded. I'd finished my spliff and my throat was dry bad.

'Got anything to drink?' I asked. 'Soft, preferably.'

He got up and went out the room. I started to think. There were so many things I'd planned to say to him. When it came to the crunch I hadn't bothered because I realised it would have all sounded like self-pitying bullshit. He came back with a glass of Vimto.

'Nice one,' I said, taking the glass from him. 'What time is it, by the way?'

He looked at his watch.

'One.'

'I gotta blow, Jeff.'

'Where you going?'

'Got a couple of moves to make.'

'Where?'

'Here and there.'

I wondered if he knew I was fobbing him off.

'That's cool. So when you checking me again?'

I finished my drink, stood up, stretched, yawned, then said: 'Dunno. Later this week, maybe.' We headed for the front door. When we got there I turned and said: 'Tell Gloria I've gone.'

'No probs,' he said. He opened the door for me. I stepped outside. Before I walked off, as if reading my mind, he said: 'Just remember, Gabby, anything us black people want from life we gotta take by any means necessary. No stupid nine-to-five's gonna give us the things we need. The cards are stacked against us, bredren. Remember that.'

I nodded and told him I'd see him later.

On the way down in the lift his words echoed in my brain. I hated him. I hated him for the way he thought he knew me. I hated him for the way he thought he was always so fucking right about everything. But most of all I hated him for the way he had faced his reality a long time ago, whereas I was still struggling to even recognise mine.

I had no intention of going to see Lana that day, but from the moment I clapped eyes on Gloria's figure, I knew I would. Twenty minutes after leaving Jeff's I was standing outside her drum in Lower Clapton. She lived with her parents in this crumbly, two-storey, terraced gaff, and for a moment I hesitated before ringing the doorbell. I was worried that her parents might be in. Then I remembered they both worked. I rang the bell. Lana was at the door in a matter of seconds.

'Gabby! God! When did you get out?'

'What's happening, babes? Got out a week ago.'

'Yeah? And it's only now you're coming to see me?'

I smiled. She shook her head, as if she pitied me. I couldn't believe it. She was genuinely hurt. Girls. She stepped aside, her arms folded all indifferent-like. I went in and she slammed the door shut behind me. Girls.

We went into the front room. I suddenly remembered how much I hated being in her drum. Her parents. Their presence was all over the gaff. You could feel it. You could feel it in their cosy furniture, their potted plants, their wedding photos on the mantelpiece, both of them staring at you, their eyes following you everywhere, all accusing-like. I always felt like I was burgling the place, for fuck's sake. I could never relax.

As usual I was standing about awkwardly. Lana told me to sit down because I was making her uncomfortable. *Me* making *her* uncomfortable. I sat on the arm of one of the two cosy armchairs. She sat across the room from me, with her legs curled up, on the other. She switched the stereo on and the pirate station's familiar jingle came sing-songing out the tinny-sounding speakers: LWR, YOU ARE IN TUNE TO THE BEST IN LONDON TOWWWWWN . . . Dub Bug, or one of their other joke DJs was spinning the tracks, talking over the records in that fucking annoying way pirate DJs do, totally in love with themselves and the sound of their fake American accents.

I took a good look at Lana. I knew I'd have no problems getting the pussy that afternoon. It was the way she was sitting, with her legs curled up underneath her but wide apart, all inviting-like. We looked at each other for a long time, smiling at each other, neither of us saying a word yet communicating our thoughts all telepathic and shit. Eventually she broke and said: 'What?'

'What?'

'This is crazy,' she said.

'What is?'

'This.'

'What?'

'Listen,' she said. 'You want a drink or something?'

'Something soft, please.'

She sprang to her feet and skipped out the room. Her arse looked fit as hell in her tight jeans. My cock stiffened on me. I had to think of Arsenal to get it to settle down again. Lana came back with two glasses of fizzy lemonade. She handed me one then went and sat where she had been before, across the room from me. I got up and went and sat on the arm of her chair.

'What you doing?' she asked, smiling. I didn't respond. She knew damn well what I was doing. I sipped my drink and looked down at her. 'Don't start, Gabby,' she said. 'Just don't start.'

'Shut up,' I said, and I lunged forward, grabbed her arm and pulled her to me. 'Give us a kiss.'

'No.'

I let go of her arm, sipped my lemonade and waited. Predictably enough, after a few seconds she tilted her head upwards, grabbed my face with both hands, pulled it towards her aggressively, looked into my eyes all intense-like, then stuck her tongue into my mouth. She rolled it around inside for a minute then pulled it out abruptly.

'That's all you're getting,' she said.

'Hold on,' I said, desperately, my cock stiff again. 'One more time.'

'Don't beg,' she said.

'Oh go on. Please. Please.'

'Don't beg, I said.'

'Please, please, pretty please.'

'Shut up will you,' she said, smiling. She then grabbed my face again. This time she snogged me long and hard. I tried to come up for air but she kept her lips pressed firmly against mine, her eyes shut, working her tongue like a demon inside my mouth. My cock was aching.

Finally I tore my lips from hers and said breathlessly: 'Let me just put down this drink.' I put the glass on the carpet. 'Now, then. Where were we?'

We started snogging again, both of us breathing hard while trying to tear each other's clothes off. Lana managed to unbuckle my belt. She slipped her hand inside my jeans and wrapped it quite tightly around my cock, as if she wanted to rip it off. I almost came in my boxer shorts. By now I had my hand inside her blouse, squeezing her tits through her bra. Then suddenly she jumped up from the armchair and stood looking at me, a wild look in her eyes, as if I'd tried to rape her or something. I didn't know what to think. I just sat there on the arm of the chair with my cock hanging out. Finally I said: 'What's up?'

She shook her head quickly and stuck out her hand for me to take. I took hold of it and she pulled me up from the chair. She led me out into the corridor. For a second I thought she was going to kick me out. But no, she started to climb the stairs, still holding my hand.

'Go into my bedroom,' she said, when we reached the landing, 'and take your clothes off. I'll be there in a sec. Got a surprise for you.'

She walked off down the landing and went into the bathroom. I stood there for a while, alone on the landing, my cock still hanging out, now drooping slightly, going over Lana's instruction in my head. Then I said out loud, to myself: 'Whatever you say, babes.'

When I got to the bedroom I stripped off my clothes in seconds, like I'd learned to do at DC before circuit training. Once I'd taken my clothes off I didn't know what the fuck to do next. I wanted to strike some kind of pose for when Lana came back but I got all confused trying to decide on which one. In the end I lay down on the bed, spread-eagled, and started to wank my cock leisurely, trying to revive it before Lana came back.

When she did a few minutes later she gave me the shock of my life. She stood in the doorway buck naked with a giant dildo in her hand. She looked me straight in the eye and said: 'I want you to fuck me. Then when you've come I want you to use this on me.'

After I left Lana's I went straight down the job centre. I browsed for a bit looking at one or two vacancies on the display boards. Eventually I took a card from one of the boards and sat down to wait for a free interviewer. While I was sitting there I started scrutinising the faces of the people around me, my fellow job seekers. What a totally beaten, depressed-looking, motley bunch they were. Sitting opposite me was this bedraggled white woman of about forty, smoking a fag and biting her nails and looking nervous, like she was about to go in front of a judge. Next to her was a ridiculously skinny old black man in a grandad's cap. He was scanning the racing pages of the *Sun*. He looked too withered to be even thinking about work. Sitting on one side of me was this African, dressed in a white suit matched by white shoes. He reeked of cheap aftershave and kept mumbling to himself in his language, pissed off at being kept waiting. I knew how he felt. On my other side was this young half-caste girl, sixteen at the most. She was clutching this dirty-looking baby to her chest. In fact, when I looked closely, I noticed that the baby was sucking on one of her stretch-marked tits. I winced at the sight and looked away.

I finally got to see one of the interviewers, this Asian bod in a crisp white shirt and black tie, the very picture of the minor civil servant. I handed him my card. He took it without looking at me. Then he started reading the card out loud, so that even Martians could hear my business. I was boiling inside.

'Salesperson in a local chemist. Must be bright and presentable . . .' He looked at me for the first time, down his nose, as if I was anything but 'bright and presentable'. He looked at the card again and went on. '. . . Must be bright and presentable and capable of working in a team. Approximately forty to forty-five hours per week, including some Saturdays. Eighty pounds per week to start. No formal qualifications needed. Experience necessary. References required.' He looked up at me again and asked: 'Got experience of this kind of work have you Mr . . . sorry, what did you say your name was?' I told him my name. 'Got experience of this kind of work, Mr Power?'

'No.'

'But the card specifically states . . .'

I kissed my teeth and slumped into my chair and said: 'Never mind what it states, Ranjit, just ring 'em.'

'My name's not Ranjit, actually.'

'Well Gupta, then, or whatever your bloody name is. Ring 'em. Ain't got all day.'

He sighed all superior-like, shook his head and said: 'Have you worked since leaving school?'

That did it. I lost the plot. This bod was clearly trying to wind me up. I stood up, looked him in the eye, pointed my finger at him and said:

'You know what you can do with your fucking job, don't you? You can ram it up your arsehole.'

I stormed out. When I got outside, I was so mad, I felt I had to go back inside and sort out Ranjit. So I turned on my heels and went back through the door. I walked straight up to Ranjit's desk and started ranting and raving.

'You think you're fucking hard, don't you? Well, if you're so hard, step outside. Come on. I dare you. I'll show you not to fuck with black people. Step outside you fucking Paki cunt.

Come on. I'll fuck you up, I swear!' Everyone in the place was looking at me. 'Don't worry,' I shouted at Ranjit. 'You gotta leave here some time today, and when you do I'll be waiting. Fucking Paki bastard!'

And with that I was out.

When I got home from the job centre that afternoon I didn't leave the house for another two days. I slept most of the time.

On the third morning of my hibernation the doorbell went. Mum had already gone off to work so I hauled on my boxer shorts and staggered groggily downstairs. Through the glass panes in the front door I could make out his stocky frame. I kissed my teeth and reluctantly opened the door.

'What's up, bredren?'

I didn't answer him. I simply turned and started climbing the stairs. I heard him come in behind me and shut the door. We both climbed the stairs in silence.

We went into my bedroom.

'Find somewhere to sit,' I said. 'I'm going back to bed.'

I crawled back under the quilt. He looked round the room, turning up his nose at the mess of clothes and tapes on the floor, at the overflowing ashtray on my bedside cabinet, at the old superhero comics and footie magazines on the armchair in the corner, at the closed curtain and the haze of smoke hanging like fog in the room, at the musty stench.

Finally he said: 'For fuck's sake, Gabby, man. What's happened to you? You sick, or what?'

'Don't start, Jeff. You sound like the old dear.'

He went over to the window and drew the curtain.

'What the fuck you doing?' I shouted, the summer sunlight blinding me.

'What you think I'm doing? Letting some light in the place. Fucking hell.'

I kissed my teeth and sparked a fag. Silence. Jeff watched me closely. Eventually he said: 'So what you been up to?'

'Nothing much. Sleeping mostly.'

'Sleeping?' He laughed. 'Sleeping!'

'What's wrong with that?'

'I'll tell you what's wrong with it, Gabby. It's loafing, that's what's wrong with it.'

'You calling me a loafer, Jeff?'

Stand off. I got out of bed and went and looked out the window. The flats were quiet at that time of the morning. I saw two dogs shagging by one of the big metal dustbins in the courtyard. The male one came but couldn't pull out of the bitch. They were stuck. Getting more and more desperate, they started pulling each other backwards and forwards. Finally they separated themselves and went off in opposite directions, sniffing the ground for titbits, indifferent to what had just happened, as if they both wanted to forget the whole nasty business as quickly as possible. I turned and faced Jeff. He was standing there with his arms folded, his temples rippling, watching me.

I said: 'Look, Jeff. You say you're my bredren, but bredren don't run each other down, you get me?'

'True. But what d'you expect. I can't stand to see you like this.'

'Like what?'

'Like this.'

He spread his arms, indicating the state of the room, as if it somehow indicated my state of mind, which I suppose it did.

'I'm all right,' I said. 'Just thinking things through at the moment, that's all.'

'Think,' he sniffed dismissively. 'What's there to think about? You think too much, bredren. That's your problem. Life's simple. Make as much money as you can so the white man can't take libs with you. And fuck as many girls as you can so you can have a million yoot to look after you in your old age. That's about all there is to it.'

I shook my head. What a wack philosophy, I thought. I said: 'Boy, Jeff, sometimes you sound like an old man the way you talk.'

'That's 'cause I am. I'm only young in years. You've known me long enough to know that.'

'Only you ain't an old man, are you? You're the same age as me, so how come you think you know all this stuff about life and shit?'

'I don't think I know. I know I know. If you'd studied my old man up close like I have then you'd know as well. I don't mind telling you, bredren, the man's a bum. I ain't turning out like him, you get me? Why d'you think Mum left him? I only wish she'd taken me with her. The only thing that man's good for is to waste his money on horses. He'll die in a bookie shop one day, you mark my words. D'you know he's never given me a thing in his life? Actually that ain't true. He's given me plenty of blows. I was fucking glad when he kicked me out. It's the best thing he's ever done for me. Now I couldn't care less what happens to him. Can't even remember the last time I saw him. If he's waiting for me to come looking for him he can forget it. The man's a bum, I tell you. A good for nothing bum.'

He went silent. I was sure I saw tears welling in his eyes. I didn't know what to say to him. I knew he hated his old man, but until that day I never realised how much.

'Honestly, Gabby. I don't wanna turn out like him,' he said. 'And I don't want you to turn out like him either, without a pot to piss in. But the way you're going . . .' He shook his head at the thought. 'All I'm saying is pull yourself together, bredren. Before it's too late. Get out there and make something of your life. Don't stop in here dreaming about it. I'm out. You know where to find me.'

He left the room. I was tempted to see him out but I couldn't move, my legs were rooted to the spot. I just stood there staring at the poster on the wall of the Spurs cup-winning side of '82. Ray Clemence, Steve Archibald, Garth Crooks, Glenn Hoddle. I'd watched the final in DC. We'd beaten QPR after a replay. No Ossie Ardiles or Ricky Villa that year, both missing because of the Falklands War. Shame, really, because Ricky Villa scored a wicked winning goal in the final against Man City the year before. To my mind that's the best fucking goal scored in any cup final before or since. I heard the front door slam. I finished my fag and crawled back into bed, resurfacing two days later to go to a party Lana invited me to.

* * *

The second I walked into the cramped flat on the Frampton Park estate I knew I was going to have a shit time. I'd found out that Lana was working at a nursery, and while it was good for my status to be going out with someone legit, her working also served to remind me of my own sorry-arse, no-job, no-prospect situation. Her cousin's party was unlikely to cheer me up.

It was one of those typical family dos. As soon as we came through the front door Lana fucked off to find her cousin. Before she went she asked me to get her a drink. I felt like a right plum in a house full of strangers. I stood around in the passage smiling foolishly at people before deciding to go and find some drinks.

I fought my way through the crowd and eventually came to this makeshift counter in the doorway of the kitchen. The bar. There was the usual bunch of people clogging it up. I stood behind them, waiting patiently to order a couple of drinks. Some old biddy in a lopsided wig looked round at me. She obviously knew why I was waiting, but instead of moving aside so I could order a drink she just turned her back on me and carried on gossiping. As far as she was concerned I was a stranger, a nobody, not family, maybe even a gatecrasher, or, worse still (since the birthday girl, like Lana, was Bajan) maybe I was Jamaican. I felt like dragging off her wig. Lana came up behind me and squeezed my arse cheek. I jumped and spun round.

'Only me,' she said. 'Ain't you got the drinks yet?'

'Gimme a chance,' I said.

Another old biddy was serving the drinks.

'Lana, dear,' she said. 'You know this young man?'

Lana smiled and nodded.

'Oh,' said the bartender. ''Cause he standing there like he lost.'

Lana giggled. She stroked my arm, all patronising-like, then said:

'Ah, there, there, poor thing. You lost your mummy?'

'Very funny,' I said, straight-faced.

The people at the bar all looked round at me.

'Can I have a babycham, please, Auntie,' said Lana to the bartender. 'What you having, Gabby?'

'Brandy and lemonade.'

'And a brandy and lemonade.'

'No lemonade, darling,' said the bartender to Lana, as if I wasn't there. 'You friend like coke?'

Lana looked at me.

'Coke's safe,' I said.

'Coke's fine, Auntie.'

I couldn't believe the way they were talking round me. I just wanted to get the drinks and go find some corner to hide in.

We eventually found our way into the front room. A guy my age was spinning some discs. The room wasn't as bright as the rest of the flat, thank God, and I told Lana I wasn't moving again till I was ready to leave. We went and stood in a corner away from the doorway where kids kept running in and out. After a few seconds scanning the faces in the room I turned to Lana and, half-shouting above the music, said: 'So which one's your cousin?'

'She's upstairs. She'll be down soon.'

'Most of this lot your family?'

'Most of them, yeah.'

'Big family.'

'Too big. Dunno half of them.'

Just then a girl and two guys came in. They stood in the centre of the room as if they owned the gaff, as if they were looking for gatecrashers to chuck out. I was sure I recognised the girl.

'That's her,' said Lana.

'Your cousin?'

'Yeah. Those are her brothers.'

'What's her name?'

'Yvette.'

'It's definitely her,' I said. 'Call her over.'

'Why?'

'Go on. I don't fancy her or nothing. Just wanna see if it's really her.'

Lana rolled her eyes then walked to the centre of the room and started chatting with her cousins. I saw them look in my direction. The next minute Lana and Yvette were walking towards me. The two guys left the room.

Yvette stood right in front of me, Lana by my side. Yvette looked me up and down, as if she was thinking of buying me but couldn't be sure I was made of the right stuff. She then looked at Lana and said: 'Nope. Dunno him. Sorry.'

'No. What you mean is you don't remember me,' I said.

Now that she was up close I was even more certain of who she was.

'Where you know me from?' she asked, cheekily.

'I know you, that's all.'

She looked at Lana and said:

'This a wind-up?'

Lana shrugged.

'Remember your little accident in Downs Park?' I asked.

That wobbled her, embarrassed her. Lana, too.

'Look,' said Yvette. 'I gotta mingle. You two enjoy yourselves. Speak to you later, Lana.'

Lana nodded and Yvette left the room. In some hurry.

'Was horrible what happened to her that day,' said Lana.

'I know. She's all right, though, ain't she?'

'Thank God. But it could have been worse. When she told me what happened I couldn't believe it. Wouldn't have happened if it hadn't been for those randy boys from that apology for a school you went to.'

'Whatever. The main thing is she's all right. Fancy a dance?'

At first she didn't want to know, as if she held me personally responsible for what happened to Yvette that day. I had to do the most coaxing to get her to dance with me. In the end she gave in and we danced for three records straight: slow, nasty dancing, with me forcing myself between her legs. At one stage I whispered in her ear: 'Must get some pussy tonight.'

'Don't be so crude,' she said.

'Look who's talking about crude. "I want you to fuck me then use this massive fuck-off dildo on me."'

She laughed and thumped me on my back. I gripped her to me and we danced the remainder of the tune in silence. When the tune stopped I said: 'Let's go outside and build a spliff.'

'Lead the way,' she said, much to my surprise. She wasn't much into weed.

We went and stood outside on the landing, a few feet away from the front door. We were on the fifth floor. I leaned over the landing wall and looked down onto the courtyard. Lana squeezed up next to me and did the same. We stood there looking down onto the cars. We could hear the music coming from the flat, together with muffled bits of conversation and occasional loud laughter. For a time we didn't speak. I gobbed and watched my spit fall slowly to the ground, a big white blob that went splat! as it hit the concrete below. I gobbed three more times. Lana was soon disgusted. She pushed up her face and said: 'You pregnant or what? Cut it out.'

I got my skins out and stuck a quick three sheets together. The cigarette and weed were in it in no time. I rolled them without even looking. The whole thing must have taken all of two minutes. I'd been leaning with my back against the landing wall and when I finished rolling the spliff I turned round and again leaned over the wall and stared down at the courtyard. It was a cool summer's night, with a slight breeze, and I felt very relaxed and clear-headed for the first time since coming home. I sparked the spliff, took two deep drags, held the smoke in for a few seconds, then let it out slowly through my nose, the breeze carrying it away into the night. I closed my eyes, the better to enjoy the buzz. Lana squeezed up next to me. I felt her breast on my arm. Maybe it was the spliff, but my cock rose on me instantly. I grabbed her face, looked deep into her eyes and said: 'Let's get outta here, for fuck's sake. This party's wack.'

We took a minicab back to my gaff. We stayed quiet the whole journey. Partly because of the African cab driver who kept looking at us in his rear-view mirror, like he suspected us of shagging in his car. And partly because of the anticipation of what we were about to do.

When we got to my gaff we sneaked up to my bedroom and locked the door against Mum. We stripped in the dark, jumped into bed and for the first time in our relationship actually made love. That night I didn't go to the toilet on Lana like I'd always done. We didn't just fuck. We made love. After that night I knew the difference between the two.

Lana left early the next morning, before daybreak. She had to get home and get ready for work. I begged her to take the day off and spend it with me but she wouldn't have it. She sneaked out the house half an hour before Mum got up. About an hour later I heard Mum rattle my door knob. I pretended to be asleep. As usual, she cursed me for always locking my door and told me not to sleep my life away and to get my 'lazy arse' down the job centre. Then I heard her stomp down the stairs, muttering curses at me as she went. Seconds later I heard the front door slam. I turned over in bed and tried to get back to sleep but it was useless. There was just too much stuff in my head. It seemed like everyone was getting on with their lives except me. I thought about Jeff and how, in a few hours, even he'd be down the frontline grafting. Yep. Everyone had a life except me. Well, bollocks to that, I thought. I wasn't kidding myself any more. Jeff was right. If I wasn't careful I'd end up like his old man, 'without a pot to piss in'. I needed to face facts. I wanted stuff from life, the good stuff, the kind of stuff I'd become accustomed to since leaving school, nice clothes, jewellery, money, flash cars. There was no shame in wanting that stuff. And I wasn't going to get any of it by doing some poxy nine-to-five. Jeff was right about that as well. Oh yeah, I had a life all right, one that fitted like a suit. All I had to do was take it from the wardrobe, dust it down and put it on. I got out of bed, showered, dressed, then went to see my 'partner'.

FRONTLINE

The frontline was a mad place. Totally fucking mad.

It wasn't much to look at, just a hundred metres or so of two-storey derelict buildings, on both sides of the road, every one boarded up or covered in rusty corrugated iron. In fact they were so badly run down that only one of them actually had a roof. This one became our drug shop.

Come rain, snow or shine it was heaving with bods looking to score dope. They came from everywhere, all over London, even further, the front drawing them in like some big fuck off magnet.

Dope wasn't its only attraction. It quickly developed a rep to give All Saints Road and Railton Road a run for their money. Everyone wanted to be seen hanging out there. And I mean everyone. From the biggest reggae stars to black footballers to notorious Yardies fresh from Jamaica who were biding their time. But the people that really mattered were the dealers themselves, me and Jeff included. We were the heart and soul of the place. We were known as the Sandringham Massive. Our motto: united we stand, divided we fall, fuck with one, fuck with all.

And plenty people tried to fuck with us. The local residents, for a start. Time and again they tried to get the old bill to rid the street of us. They needn't have bothered. The old bill couldn't touch us. They didn't dare. They were seriously impotent against us. Those were the days, you see, of softly-softly community policing, not long after the Brixton riots and Lord Scarman's report on police (mal)practice in the black community. Knowing this, we didn't half take the piss. We sold dope openly. Every now and then, as a token gesture to the locals, Stokey old bill would send their 'community officer', Sergeant Brown (known to us as Dixon) to come and ask us politely to tone things down. In other words, could we keep the dealing indoors. Our answer was always the same. We'd tell Dixon to tell his superiors to go fuck themselves. Dixon would pocket a free bag of weed for him and the 'missus' to smoke later, then return to Stokey station with out blunt message. But not before he'd given us the names and addresses of the complaining locals whose drums we'd stake out then burgle.

There was never a dull day on the front. There was always something going down. Mass footie matches. Car burn-ups. Bike burn-ups. Deadly knife fights. Muck-about knife fights. Drinking sessions. Gambling. Chalice smoking. Nasty sex with groupie Dorises. You name it, we got into it. Yet all that was secondary to the main function of the front: to provide dope to the masses. Jeff hadn't exaggerated. There was serious money to be made and for two years him and me made it hand over fist. Not that the front was a place where bedlam held sway. Far from it. There were rules. And you ignored them at your peril.

For starters, you never tried to poach a rival's punters. When this happened, or even threatened to happen, it usually ended in knives being drawn and no little blood.

That was the first and most important rule, stay away from your rival's punters. But there were plenty of others.

White people were banned from the front. They were all undercover old bill as far as we were concerned. Anyone found trying to court their trade was run off the front for good. (A couple of years later this rule got relaxed when competition for the crack trade got madly intense. Needless to say, quite a few of us ended up behind bars as a result.)

We never sold weed to kids, even if, as a lot of them claimed, their parents had sent them to buy it.

No one was allowed to sell dud weed (usually tea leaves mixed with weed seeds). That kind of behaviour gave all the dealers a bad rep. Anyone caught selling dud weed was banned from the front.

Road-running was a definite no-no. By that I mean sprinting up to punters and shoving your wares under their noses. The punters didn't like it, quite rightly they saw that kind of behaviour as desperate, and if they got treated like that too often, they stopped coming to buy weed from us altogether.

I could go on. The point is, although there was enough of us on the front vying for a piece of the same pie, it wasn't chaos.

Of course, if you're going to have rules there's got to be someone to enforce them. Which brings me neatly to the front's ringleaders, or the Dons, as we rank and file called them.

There were eight of them. Backra was one. That's how come me and Jeff managed to inveigle ourselves onto the front. We'd been his 'boys' since school. We were proud of the fact that we were the only two 'youths' allowed to sell weed on the front. Our peers were mad with jealousy. We didn't half rub their noses in the fact they were still having to go out on the thieve while we were sitting back making easy money.

Backra was a right fucking nutter. He'd split your head open for treading on his snakeskin shoes. Everyone respected him, even the other Dons, since he was the one who'd started the front. He was a big geezer, over six feet tall, with big feet, big hands and a big rep.

Then there were the twins, Pepsi and Coke. They'd got their nicknames because, being identical, you couldn't tell which one was which, just like the drinks. They were both hot-headed as fuck, both skilled in the use of butterfly knives, both always immaculately dressed, and both sickeningly good-looking. I idolised them. Jeff thought they were a couple of 'flash cunts' but could never say so in case he got a fat lip for his troubles.

Ever was completely different to the twins. There was something serious and grim about him. He never smiled. He was ugly beyond description. He took backchat from no fucker. He treated everyone the same. Man or woman. Young or old. If you fucked with him his vengeance was swift and terrible. Whereas all the other Dons respected Backra, they were downright terrified of Ever. He'd got his name because he was once stabbed thirty times in a fight and, according to rumour, walked five miles to Hackney Hospital before finally collapsing in A & E. The sawbones patched him up and must have got the shock of their lives when he discharged himself the next day. From then on he was known as Ever, since it was clear to everyone that he was indestructible and would live for ever. Unlike the guy he'd tangled with. That poor sod died of multiple stab wounds. Ever got off in court on a self-defence plea. To us, this made him even more invincible.

The other four Dons weren't as fearsome but were still quite formidable in their own way.

Mad Neville frothed at the mouth and stammered when he lost it, which didn't happen a lot. Most of the time he was quite easy going. You could have a laugh with him, even take the piss out of him being overweight. But if you got him mad and saw him waddling with grim determination towards his seven-series Bimmer, then you'd have to run for your life. He carried an axe in his boot.

Jo-jo was a joker, a practical one. He was also a muscle-bound black belt in judo who loved going about practising his moves on people, especially me and Jeff. It was his way of trying to toughen us up.

Boxer Ben was a retired professional who longed to be back in the ring. He was forever jogging and shadow-boxing, keeping himself 'in shape' for his big come-back fight. Which never happened. One night at Phoebe's night-club he exploded one of his bombs in the face of one of the bouncers who'd been giving him gyp. The *Hackney Gazette* got wind of the story, then the British Boxing Board of Control. Even though he admitted what he'd done and apologised and begged for leniency, he still had his licence stripped. The papers described him as a 'has-been boxer turned dope-peddler'. Which was true, of course, but nevertheless . . .

And finally there was Drake. He fancied himself as a bit of a historian, always banging on about the origin of stuff: words, places, people. That was on his good days. On his bad ones he could be a moody so-and-so, likely to poke you in the eye or nick you with his cut-throat just to relieve his boredom. To his face he was called Sir Francis, behind his back, Schizo.

These eight geezers ran the front. They had over half the dope trade sewn up between them. They had money coming out their ears and didn't give two fucks who knew about it. In fact, they wanted people to know. That's why the trappings of their wealth were forever on public display.

The money rolled in for me and Jeff as well. And we spent it like it was going out of fashion. Within six months of starting on the front we each had a 323 injection Bimmer. Then there was the tom, grands worth of the stuff dangling from our necks, fastened to our wrists and stuck on every one of our fingers, including thumbs. Don't even mention the garms. Backra was always trying to get us to put a little something away for a rainy day. According to him, the front wouldn't last for ever. The 'gravy train', as he called it, must, he told us, stop one day. We laughed him out of town. To our way of thinking, money was good for one thing and one thing only . . . to be spent. Sure we put a 'little something away' from time to time. We'd always done that, even before the front. But Backra would have had us going to the bank every day. We were too busy living it up for that.

It was around this time that I left home. I was seventeen.

I had to do it. Mum was now on my case night and day, day after day. She'd be damned if she was going to have a drug dealer living under her roof. She just couldn't understand what had happened to me, she didn't know where I had gone wrong, where *she* had gone wrong. Of her three sons she had always been convinced that I would be the one to break with the tradition of underachievement in the family. Hearing her express all her frustrations like that, there was only one thing I could do.

With Backra's help I got a flat round the corner from the front, on Amhurst Road. At first I thought it was an ideal location, since I didn't have to travel very far to work, so to speak. But later on, when the old bill started kicking down my door, I wished with all my soul that I wasn't even living in Hackney, let alone near the front.

It was also around this time that me and Lana finished. I'd sort of hoped things would get serious between us, once I found out she was a working girl. But no. Like Mum, she started lecturing me every day about my lifestyle. In fact she was worse than Mum. She tried to shame me into submission. According to her I was wasting my talents and would end up like so many of my peers: good for nothing, worthless. After a while I just couldn't hack her any more. I realise now that her and Mum were the only two people in my life at the time who really saw where I was headed, the only two people who really cared about where I was headed. Maybe that's why I ripped them out of my life so ruthlessly. Of course, Jeff was made up. To his mind, I'd finally come of age, was facing up to my reality, to my destiny. It was hard to argue with him on that score. The life I was now leading seemed so natural to me. At least most of the time it did. There were, of course, times when I'd shut my door on the world, when I was on my own, when I could drop the act, times when I dreamt of a different life. Slowly the dream faded. It didn't vanish altogether. Just faded.

Now that I was free to do as I pleased, I upped the pace. Even Jeff tried to get me to take a breather. I was deaf to him. It was all right for him to talk about slowing down, now that he was a family man and all that. He had something worth going home for – Gloria and his new-born son, Jordan. I had no such responsibilities. What I had was money and unlimited freedom. So naturally I was going to indulge myself.

I was out every night. If there was a rave on some place I'd find it. Especially if the massive were going to be there. I was never home before five in the morning. And I never came home alone. I always had some Doris with me. They'd get a tired poke before I sent them packing in a minicab.

In those days I was getting by on fuck-all sleep and surviving on takeaways. I was also smoking weed as if there was no tomorrow. It all added up to me being a physical wreck. Still, I could just about cope with being all skin and bones. What I couldn't cope with were the almost daily migraine attacks that left me blinded in one eye and vomiting constantly. My GP confirmed what I already knew, that the headaches were brought on by 'sleep and nutrient deprivation'. I tried to heed his advice but my new healthy lifestyle lasted all of two days. After that I simply stacked up on some wickedly powerful painkillers and resumed my life at its previous pace.

Migraine attacks and weight loss weren't the only side-effects of my unhealthy lifestyle. I lost count of the amount of times I had to go to the VD clinic. And no matter how many times I went there the shame I felt was always the same. Especially since I could never tell the doctors for certain who had given me the latest dose of the clap, or crabs, or NSU, or . . .

By now Mum was lucky if she saw me once a month. And when she did it was for no longer than a few minutes. That's about as long as either of us could hold out before the slanging matches started. As for my brothers, in those days I neither knew where they were nor cared.

Effectively, I was on my Jack Jones. And everything I did, the raving, the dope smoking, the fucking around, all of it was my way of trying to hide from that fact: there was a gaping hole in my life and these activities went some way towards filling it.

But that was the private me. Joe Public saw a different Gabby Power, the one who seemingly had it all and couldn't have been more happy-smiley about it. That's certainly how I tried to appear to Jeff, especially since he now looked like a guy who didn't have a care in the world, what with Gloria and the baby and everything. Actually, it really pissed me off the way he just sort of settled down like that. I mean, I'd always known he was old at heart, but I didn't expect the pipe and slippers routine. That's why I had to stop going round his gaff. To see him and Gloria and the sprog together was more than I could stomach. Besides, although I never told him, I thought his family-man image was completely bogus. And there was evidence to back me up. He was fucking at least two Dorises on the side. He was out with me and the rest of the massive at least two nights a week. And he treated Gloria not as the love of his life but simply as the mother of his son and the person who did round the house. He even confessed to me one day that they hardly fucked any more. Still, I had nothing in my life that came anywhere close to what he had with Gloria and the little one.

Backra was right. The front didn't last. It took just two years for things to go pear-shaped. There were a couple of reasons for this and they were linked. First, a lot of us got greedy and started selling charlie. Second, the old bill got tough with us as a result.

It wasn't clear where the charlie suddenly sprang from, though there were plenty of rumours. Some said Yardies were to blame. Others blamed old East End villains. Others still pointed the finger at bent drug-squad old bill. Whoever was responsible, in next to no time the market was flooded with the stuff.

Suddenly it was the 'in' drug. This put pressure on us dealers to provide it. A handful of die-hard weed sellers refused to touch it, Backra included. But the majority of us caved in under the sheer weight of demand for a drug that only two years before was as scarce as a reggae hit in the national charts.

At first the only way to get it was in powdered form and the only way to take it was up your hooter. Soon, every Arab and his camel was standing about on the front sniffing mounds of the stuff from the back of his hand. The situation was ripe for skullduggery and sure enough there came a time when the punters couldn't be certain what they were buying. Us dealers would cut the charlie with almost anything we could lay our hands on. Flour, bicarbonate of soda, Ajax. Greed, pure and simple. Charlie wasn't expensive in those days, in fact it was dirt cheap, a fiver a gram wholesale, fifteen retail. So as a business, ours was lucrative in the extreme. For about a year, anyway, until the punters got fed up with being ripped off. Things did pick up again, with the arrival of crack from America, but we all knew it was the beginning of the end for the front. Suddenly, if you weren't dealing rocks then you might as well pack up and go home. Backra did just that. He literally started selling weed from his flat on the Kingsmead Estate to the few bods who were still bothering to buy it. Ever got out as well. So did Mad Neville. The other Dons just shrugged and 'moved with the times' as they put it.

The whole culture on the front changed. Everything got hyper. You couldn't trust your own shadow. Backstabbing and bad blood ruled. The crack business was booming and it was dog eat dog. People who before hadn't so much as sold a dummy in a footie match were giving up their day jobs and encamping on the front in the hope of making instant fortunes. An unstoppable momentum built up and the remaining Dons were simply swept aside. The Yardies finally moved in. Their time had come, and with it the front degenerated into a cut-throat free-for-all where the fittest of the fittest survived, where manic junkies with bulging eyes and bloodless lips and rotten breath went to buy the tiny little rocks that would ease their nerves for all of five minutes at a time.

The old bill had to do something. They had to make some dramatic gesture that would send a message to the wider community that they aimed to come down on us like a ton of bricks. They started to raid the front, mob-handed, at least twice a month. I'll never forget the first one I got caught in.

It happened one night in the middle of winter, when the shop was jammed with us dealers trying to shelter from the freezing temperature outside. We were passing the time as we always did, baiting each other, smoking spliffs, dealing. All of a sudden about thirty wooden-tops burst in on us screaming their fucking heads off. Later I found out this was meant to scare us. I don't know about the next bod, but they certainly terrified the shit out of me. Before we knew what was going down, they had us pinned to the walls and were patting us down and rifling through our pockets and getting us to drop our strides.

Every jack one of us got nicked that night, carted off in meat wagon after meat wagon up to Stokey Station. We didn't get released till the following afternoon. About a quarter of us, me and Jeff included, escaped without charge. The rest all got done for possession with intent to supply then let out on police bail to await trial. A month later roughly half of these, the remaining Dons among them, got sent down at the notorious Snaresbrook Crown Court. The other half did runners.

For me the whole thing was a slap in the face, a wake-up call. The way the old bill treated us that night, like motherless scum, plus the fact that people actually got put away, made me realise what I'd become: a hardened drug dealer who could expect no mercy from the old bill and not an ounce of sympathy from society at large. When I left Stokey Station that day I went home very depressed.

Jeff saw the raid as a notch on his gun, and he tried to get me to see it in the same light. He was proud at having slipped through the old bill's dragnet, the idiot, as if it was all down to cunning on his part and nothing at all to do with luck. He'd learned only one lesson from the incident: the old bill would never again catch him with his cock hanging out like that. Next time he'd be prepared for them. I told him, sheepishly, that I wasn't sure there'd be a next time for me, that I was sort of thinking about quitting the game. He called me a pussy, we argued and he stormed off. Two days later I was back on the front. I might have been a lot of things in those days, but a pussy wasn't one of them.

The raids became predictable. With each one fewer and fewer of us were nicked. After a while none of us were. We simply got too wily for the old bill. We made sure they never actually caught us with any rocks in our possession. They'd steam in, throw their weight around, then leave empty-handed, calling us all the racist names under the sun. During this time they never once found the hiding places for our stash. Yet they carried on raiding the shop regardless. We soon got wise to their strategy (courtesy of Dixon). They were hoping we'd get fed up and go away. When this didn't happen they got dark on us.

For a while house raids were the order of the day. Once a week for two months straight the old bill trashed my gaff looking for crack. Not once did they find any. In the end I had to get a solicitor involved. Harassment and all that. Only then did they leave me alone. But from then on I lived in constant fear of them kicking down my door.

Then came the old undercover routine. Since white people were now allowed on the front, the old bill came to us disguised as punters. In this way they were able to find out where in the shop we hid our rocks. It was a successful tactic ... up to a point. Some dealers were nicked, but not many, and those who were nicked got off in court when plummy-sounding barristers in pin-stripe suits argued that their clients had been entrapped.

Next, the police developed informers in our ranks. This ploy backfired as well. The snakes were quickly exposed, knifed and run out of the manor.

So finally, in desperation, they started fitting us up. It was only then that we reluctantly abandoned the front.

OSSIE'S

The police might have won a battle but certainly not the war. They cleaned up the front but all that did was force us to seek out new stamping grounds: illegal gambling dens, shebeens, minicab stations, pubs, amusement arcades, community centres. At each new place we'd cane it for a few weeks then move on. Ideally, what we wanted was a permanent base, and eventually we found one, at least me and Jeff did.

It was kind of ironic that we ended up at Ossie's. It was a stone's throw from the old front, on the busy junction of Sandringham Road and Amhurst Road. We'd been all over Hackney only to end up, more or less, right back where we started.

Ossie's was ideal for us in lots of ways. It was a pool hall for one, pool being a legitimate leisure activity and therefore the perfect cover for our illegitimate activities. It was also full of our peers (that's how come we ended up there) which meant we'd fit right in. But the best thing about the place was the fact that it was run by an amiable old Greek, Ossie, and his wife, Maria, and their two teenage sons, Ossie Jnr and Ulus. No one would suspect a decent, hard-working, law-abiding, old-fashioned, respectable Greek family of harbouring crack dealers at their place of business.

And they'd be right not to suspect anything. Ossie and Maria were as straight as kebab skewers. All right, to give them their dues, they did turn a blind eye to the odd bit of dope smoking. But they were constantly on the lookout for any dealing. They warned us time and again that they wouldn't hesitate to phone the old bill if they so much as thought any of us were indulging in it.

Needless to say it was hard for me and Jeff at first. It took months before we felt we'd perfected a system of dealing that kept Ossie and his eagle-eyed clan in the dark.

Dealing to junkies meant we couldn't afford to have them actually shuffling up to us on the premises. They'd have stuck out something rotten and blown our cover immediately. Instead, we used mobile phones. They were the first ones on the market, great big clunky fucking things with ten-foot aerials. We invested in one apiece. For a while we were the only bods in Ossie's who had them. It was a business tool for us. But the rest of the crew saw them as status symbols and in no time they all had one. Another good thing for me and Jeff. Here was yet another layer on our cover.

So that was our system. The junkies (or cats, as we called them) would ding us on our mobiles and wait round the corner for their rocks. We would take turns to go out and serve them. The pool hall was a busy place so we could slip in and out more or less unnoticed. Or so we thought. Surprise wasn't the word for how we felt the day Ossie took us to one side and whispered in a friendly-uncle-sort-of-way: 'Be careful, you two. Old Ossie is awatching you, no?'

Yet for a while things ticked over nicely. Me and Jeff weren't earning shed-loads any more, those days were gone for good. But we were doing more than just getting by. And because we were scared to draw attention to ourselves, we had to change our lifestyles, which helped even more. We stopped being the two flash plebs we were in the front's heyday. We parked our jewellery at home. We dressed down. We traded in our rides for less sporty ones, though we stuck with Bimmers. Jeff used his money to feather his nest. I banked mine. Backra would have been proud of me. Even when we were out raving, which was happening less and less, things had to be toned down. It was no longer drinks for everyone and showing off. Basically, we were living through some fucked up times. The heat was on everywhere. And the only way to go about your business was quietly. If you had an ounce of common, that is.

Compared to the front Ossie's was chilled. So long as we behaved the old boy and his missus were cool. Of course, to a certain extent, it made good business sense for them to be that way. We spent the most money in their place. And not only on pool. We bought food and drink. We were constantly shoving money in the nudge machines with the tiny jackpots. And the arcade games made noise from the moment Ossie opened at ten in the morning till he or Maria or one of his sons shut up shop again twelve hours later.

I liked Ossie, in the same way I liked Backra, and that old kanga at DC, Mr Davies, and numerous other father-figure types who've featured in my life over the years.

If Ossie spoke to me I was all ears. If he gave me advice I at least considered it. If he offered me anything (a bit of grub Maria had cooked specially for him, a free game of pool, a shot from his ever-present bottle of Jack Daniels) I accepted with a gratefulness that was almost grovelling. Yep, we got on well me and Ossie. I wish I could say the same for him and Jeff. That they didn't like each other was plain for all to see. Ossie was a figure of authority, which Jeff couldn't stand. He had nothing personal against Ossie. It was just that Ossie owned the pool hall and laid down the law as he saw fit. That was his crime in Jeff's eyes. As for Ossie, he could see Jeff had what he called 'attitude problems', something he loathed in 'youngsters'. In the 'old country', as he called Cyprus, kids had to show respect for their elders. This was definitely what he demanded and got from Ossie Jnr and Ulus who were like lambs in his presence.

There's no doubt in my mind that Ossie would have found some excuse to ban Jeff from the pool hall if Jeff hadn't had a certain controlling influence over the troublemakers among us. There was a kind of unspoken deal between them. Jeff kept the rabble in check and in return Ossie pretended to be ignorant of our crack dealing, so long as we kept it outside, that is.

Most of the time it was easy for Jeff to keep order. A lot of the guys knew him from school and knew the level of violence he was capable of. But there were always a few idiots looking to test him, looking to make reps for themselves. With these guys Jeff usually had to open his blade. The sight of it and the look in his eyes was normally enough to frighten the guys off. But if it wasn't, then Jeff would be forced to go the whole hog and cut them up a little. He didn't take pleasure in this, as he was always telling me. He was simply defending his livelihood. Having said that, there were one or two cold fuckers among us that not even he could intimidate. Guys like Brick, Killer and Gunhawk, the ringleaders of the Cromer Posse who Jeff had hooked up with while I was in DC. Brick and Gunhawk were the two I'd met outside Jeff's squat the day I'd gone looking for him.

Brick got his name because he was built like a brick shithouse. In a scrap you couldn't let him get close to you. He'd break every bone in your body. Killer was so-called because he was so vicious when he got going that we all knew it was only a matter of time before he'd kill someone. And sure enough, one day he got done for murder and sentenced to life. Only he wasn't guilty. But more of that later. And then there was Gunhawk, so named because he was the only one among us known to have a gun (a German Luger, in quite good nick) and he wasn't afraid to use it, mostly on the owners of small jewellery shops. If any of these three had decided to make trouble then Jeff would have had his work cut out. And he knew he couldn't rely on me to cover his back. He knew I just didn't have it in me.

Ossie Jnr and Ulus were black in all but skin colour. When their mum and dad weren't around they'd really walk our walk and talk our talk. They couldn't hang out with us enough. They loved all our banter, our bad-boy posturings, our casual dope smoking. Especially Ossie Jnr, or OJ, as we called him. Silly bugger even carried a knife.

At nineteen, he was two years older than his kid brother and his old man's heir apparent. He couldn't wait to take over the business. He was forever telling us what he planned to do when the big day arrived. He was going to do things differently to his old man. For starters, he was going to buy up the empty property next door, knock out the adjoining wall and make the pool hall that much bigger. Next he was going to convert the basement into a casino. And finally, if all went according to plan, he was going to open another pool hall, then another, till he had a chain of them across London.

One day, after he'd told me about his big plan for the zillionth time, I asked him wearily: 'For fuck's sake, OJ, where you gonna get the money to do all that shit? Gonna run round banks with your begging bowl?'

'Bollocks to that,' he said. 'There's easier ways to make money.' He smiled, all cryptic and shit.

'Oh yeah,' I said. 'And what are they then?'

'I could do what you do for a start.'

I raised my eyebrows and said: 'What you on about?'

'Don't gimme that, Gabby. The old man's told me all about it. He knows what you and Jeff are up to.'

I knew that. But it never entered my mind that Ossie talked to OJ, maybe even Ulus, about stuff like that.

'I dunno what you're on about, OJ,' I said.

'Nah,' he said. 'Course you don't.'

He got his chance to take over the pool hall sooner than any of us had imagined. He opened up one day and told us Ossie had gone back to Cyprus for good. Retired. We were all shocked by the news. The place just wouldn't be the same without the old boy. That's what I thought, anyway, and I told OJ as much. I also told him that if he had any sense he'd forget all his crazy expansion talk and carry on running the place exactly as his old man had done. He laughed in my face. I knew right away the pool hall was doomed.

OJ was true to his word. He did things radically different to his old man. He made changes right from the off, like some newly appointed, headstrong football manager determined to stamp his authority on some dodgy team he'd inherited. It didn't take long for us to realise those changes were for the worst.

Like his dad, OJ was an old soak at heart. So he started selling booze, illegally. None of us were heavy drinkers so he'd get through most of the stock himself, him and Ulus. The two of them were like a couple of fishes. They'd drink steadily all day and by early evening would be in no fit state to run the place. Pissed as fucks, they'd chuck us out, lock up, then carry on their quaffing behind closed doors, oblivious to the fact that they were actually losing money by shutting up so early.

As well as booze, OJ loved hash, but he was forever whinging about how far and wide he had to travel to score any. In the end he made it known he wouldn't object to any of us selling it in the pool hall so long as him and his brother were kept in constant free supply. The floodgates opened. Except for me and Jeff and the committed tea-leaves among us, the likes of Brick, Killer and Gunhawk, everyone started selling hash. I couldn't believe the amount of punters who came to buy their little five-pound lumps. I'd had no idea there was such a market for hash. Me and Jeff seriously thought about getting in on it. We didn't because the punters were all kids. And I mean kids. Some were as young as eleven and none looked older than fourteen. It was a sight to behold to see them turning up to buy drugs in their school uniforms.

The whole thing was a ruse by OJ. He made sure the pool hall was packed with hash dealers then turned round and demanded rent from each and every one of them. They grumbled loads but paid up anyway. It was either that or they hit the pavements. And still he wasn't finished with them. He bided his time, sussed out how the hash business worked, then joined the fray. Now he was selling rocky and red-seal and Leb from behind the counter where before his old man had sold crisps and chocolate and fizzy drinks.

Slowly but surely the pool hall went to the dogs. It became a haven for loafers. No one used the pool tables any more except to sit on or roll spliffs or play cards. They were covered in stains, their cushions were wonky, and their baizes were all ripped up and shit. As for the nudge machines and arcade games, all they were good for was taking up space and gathering dust. One day a huge fuck off lorry came and took them away. It turned out that Ossie had only been renting them. Since they weren't paying for themselves any more, OJ got rid of them.

The building was falling apart as well, menaced by subsidence and a leaky roof that flooded us out when it rained. A million calor-gas heaters couldn't have dried out the rising damp on the walls. Try to mask it, and you'd have needed gallons and gallons of paint. Then there were the beams in the ceiling. You could hardly see them. They were black with soot and choking in cobwebs. What was left of the lino on the floor was cracked and turned up at the edges. I lost count of the amount of times I tripped on the damn thing. And if there was ever a place that needed fumigating that pool hall was it. It ponged like nobody's business, a suffocating mixture of BO, dope, fags, booze, damp, dust, food, and Caesar, who I don't think could have had a bath in his entire life. Caesar was Ossie's huge, vicious, long-haired Alsatian who lived in the dank dark cellar barking his head off round the clock, slowly going mad because OJ hardly ever took him out for a walk, and probably going blind through lack of light.

No. Ossie's as we knew it in the days when the old boy and Maria were in charge, was definitely a thing of the past. With OJ now running things, it was nothing but a common dope den. Its rep was sealed and word of it got out. The first old bill raid couldn't be far off.

When it came to raids me and Jeff were old veterans. The ones on the front had given us a kind of sixth sense for when they were likely to happen. The writing was on the wall for the pool hall. Jeff and me knew that as well as we knew our own names. We tried warning OJ. We told him to lock up for a few weeks till the heat was off. He wouldn't have it. He was making more money selling hash than he'd ever dreamed possible and the whole thing went to his head. In the end we gave up on him and left him to his fate.

Caution was the word. We had to use our common. We knew the old bill had to be watching the gaff, so we cut down on the hours we spent there. Our faces were familiar to them. We were known drug dealers. Therefore we had to try and make it look as if we only popped into the pool hall now and then. And while we were there we had to be on our toes the whole time. Under no circumstances could we afford to have our rocks on us. If we were caught with them then it would have been goodnight sweetheart. We're talking serious bird. A-class drugs and all that. Not like those other bods with their hash. All they were likely to get was a slap on the wrist. No. Our rocks had to be hidden. And in a different place every day. Not too hard in a place like the pool hall, with all its nooks and crannies. Still, we had to be vigilant, as there was no honour amongst us whatsoever.

The thing we had to be most careful about was our dealings with the cats. Our whole strategy had to change. We couldn't have them loitering outside any more. Now when they called us on our mobiles we had to give them elaborate instructions where to go and wait for us, usually far away from the pool hall. It was a hazardous strategy to say the least. Remember we're talking about junkies here. Sometimes we'd get to the agreed place and they'd be nowhere in sight. Fuming, we'd get back to the pool hall only for them to call again complaining that it was us who hadn't shown up. That's if they could actually get through to us on our mobiles. They always called us from phone boxes and nine times out of ten their money would run out before they'd even said a word. It was all so frustrating. Business was being badly affected. Nevertheless, as far as we were concerned, it was the price we had to pay to keep our arses out of prison.

The pool hall was now attracting all the wrong types. OJ could do fuck all to keep them out. I remember him appealing to Jeff one day for help. Not pulling his punches, Jeff told him that he had to lie in the bed he'd made for himself. It was kind of sad to see him slowly losing his grip on the place, but he'd been warned not to bite off more than he could chew.

Yep. OJ's open door policy had come back to haunt him. The pool hall quickly filled up with dippers, drummers, muggers, ringers, car-stereo thieves, cheque-book and credit-card merchants, armed blaggers, con artists, all looking to fence their wares. There were some real bargains to be had – even by me and Jeff.

But what we didn't want from all those crooks was all the heat they carried around. Pairs of old bill were constantly walking in on us. They'd bowl up to the counter and ask OJ to help them with their inquiries into this or that crime. And while they chatted to OJ we could see them looking the place over, clocking the layout and shit and making mental notes. *One way in or out, good, good. Extremely thick double door, problem if locked. Lots of pool tables, plenty of hiding places for drugs and other contraband, must search thoroughly. Is that barking? Must bring the dog-handlers. That thing sounds wild. Quite a dark place, must bring torches, halogen lamps even.* And they weren't only interested in the layout. They'd scan our guilty faces as well, trying to suss out who was known to them and why.

Eventually, the cops lulled us into a false sense of security. Months went by and they still hadn't raided us. They'd even stopped coming in twos to question OJ. It was like they'd seen enough to know we weren't up to much, small fry the lot of us. We started to feel safe, and, of course, feeling safe we got careless. We went back to doing full days at the pool hall, once again getting the cats to wait for us outside. Our hands had been forced. Business had slowed to the point where it was hardly worth the name.

One day Jeff turned to me and said: 'I've had enough. Fuck all this pussy-footing around. We gotta start making some bucks again, you get me? Look at them lot. They're selling the hash like their lives depend on it. What the fuck are we doing? I can't be dealing with this shit no more. I got responsibilities. After all, what are we? We're drug dealers, that's what. We gotta *deal* drugs. It's what we do.' He was boosting himself something chronic. And he wasn't finished. 'I mean, set me straight if I'm wrong, Gabby, but life's a battle, right?' I shrugged. 'And if it is, what the fuck are we, losers or winners? Eh, eh? What we gonna do, take prisoners? What are we, cadets or soldiers?' He wasn't really looking for an answer and I didn't give him one. But I was tempted to. I was tempted to say: 'Oh, we're soldiers all right, Jeff, don't you worry about that . . . fucking toy soldiers!'

So, we decided to fuck the police and go for it, but then something happened which made us think twice.

One afternoon, we were all in the pool hall when it started to filter through that there was a riot happening on Broadwater Farm. Now normally, this would have made us rub our hands with glee, not at the thought of sticking it to the old bill, but at the thought of all the looting we could do. Since there was jack worth looting on the Farm, we kissed our teeth, said 'fuck it', and stayed put. Well, everyone except Killer did. There was no holding him back (not that any of us tried). He was out and headed for the Farm quicker than you could say 'Molotov cocktail'.

We didn't see him again till the following evening. He swanned in grinning from ear to ear and started to boast about his part in the old bill's whupping. He'd lobbed X-amount of bricks. Many of them had hit their targets. He was right in the thick of the action. His balls were big, etc, etc. He could see we weren't impressed so he called us all 'pussies' and stormed out, all puffed up like a bull-frog. He only had himself to blame for what happened to him next.

It's as obvious to me now as it was then: there must have been informers in the pool hall the day Killer got back from the Farm. A week later the old bill came for him, and in a way I'd only ever seen in films. One minute it was all quiet quiet, then suddenly BANG!!! . . . Armed cops all over the place, two dozen or so, bullet-proof vests, helmets, riot shields, the works. And these were just the ones who came in. There were at least another thirty outside, all with their sniper rifles trained on the entrance, crouching behind their vans and cars and shit. I was so scared I could barely breathe. Jeff was shaking with fright. I'd never seen him like that before. We were made to lie face down on the floor. We must have been like that a good ten minutes before they started frisking us. Then, one by one, they let us up and told us to line up against the wall. In my terrified state, I thought for a moment they were going to execute us. At this point the copper in charge ordered his men out of there before he himself walked backwards out onto the pavement. We stayed lined up against the wall, even though we'd not been told to. Through the open door we could see frenzied activity going on outside, made even more frenzied by all the flashing blue lights. Then we heard engine after engine rev up, then sirens wailing, then tyres screeching. They were gone. Only then did we realise they'd taken Killer with them.

Along with two others, Killer got done for the murder of a policeman. He spent ten years inside before he had his conviction quashed and was released. Serving all that time inside for a crime he hadn't committed must have been the stuff of nightmares. But Killer had it coming. What did for him in the end was a combination of his rep, his bragging, and being in the wrong place at the wrong time when he didn't have to be there at all.

The whole business affected us badly. For about a week after Killer got snatched the talk at Ossie's was of nothing else. Quite simply, we were awed by the force the police had shown. So much so that whenever we huddled round to relive the incident everyone spoke in hushed tones, whispering like the frightened kids we were, as though the old bill were listening to us outside. Of course, we tried to give the impression we hadn't been affected at all. OJ opened up as usual and the place was heaving, business as usual. Only it wasn't. Something in all of us had changed. I don't know what exactly, but the wind definitely left our sails for a while. We calmed down, became more sombre, reflective, respectful of each other, as if trying to draw strength from each other, the strength to carry on, the strength to face our fucked-up, blighted little lives.

Personally, I needed a break from Ossie's. The place had started to get to me long before all those gun-toting cops showed up. Yet for the life of me I could think of no place to get away to, except to my drum to mope around and get all depressed and shit. My dilemma was solved the day Carlton Cook walked into the pool hall.

I was pleased to see him. No. Scratch that. That's like saying rastas were pleased when Haile Selassie touched down in Jamaica. 'Ecstatic' would be a better way to describe how I felt seeing my old school mate. He hadn't changed much in the four years since I last saw him. I could tell that by the way he walked in with his nose in the air, looking all superior, as if he expected us to curtsey. I went over and greeted him by the door.

'Yo, Carlton, my man, what's up?'

'Gabby! How you doing?'

I offered my fist for him to punch, at the same time he stuck out his hand for me to shake. Then I stuck out my hand, him his fist. We got all confused. To the others we must have looked like we were playing scissor, paper and stone. We forgot the hand greeting and hugged instead.

'What the fuck you doing here?' I asked.

'Looking for you, mate.'

'Looking for me? How you know I was here?'

'Oh, you know, word gets round.'

'Yeah, tell me about it,' I said, sounding all paranoid and shit.

'What d'you mean?' Carlton whispered, sensing some juicy gossip. He was always a gossip.

'Nothing,' I said. 'So. Look at you. Still wearing specs, I see.'

He moved them off then back onto his nose, like Eric Morecambe.

'Well,' I said. 'At least you got rid of them horrible National Health ones.'

He smiled, looked over my shoulder and said: 'Still running with that loser, then?'

I glanced over my shoulder. Jeff was staring at us intensely, more at Carlton than me. 'Ain't that your poofy friend from school?' he'd said when Carlton walked in.

I went over and asked him if he'd mind taking care of business on his own for a while.

'Why, where you going?' he asked, all grumpy-like.

'Out for a couple of hours. Is that all right . . . Dad?'

He looked towards Carlton who was casting his superior glances in every direction and at all and sundry.

'Suit yourself,' said Jeff, and he walked off to chat with Brick and Gunhawk. I rolled my eyes at his back then walked over to Carlton.

'Let's go,' I said, ushering him out the door.

'No. Please. After you,' he said, all posh-like. We blew the gaff. I never set foot in there again. And by the time I clapped eyes on Jeff again a whole year had passed.

NEW WORLD

New World Snooker Club was a huge, sprawling gaff. It had twenty-four professional-size tables. Money had clearly been spent on the place, so apart from what they raked in on the snooker tables themselves (two pounds fifty an hour to rent), the owners obviously had to find ways to recoup their outlay. Which is why there was a licensed bar, and a food counter, and a cabinet jammed with saleable snooker memorabilia, and arcade games, and nudge machines, and, everywhere you looked, posters advertising up-coming raffles, quizzes and in-house snooker competitions.

If you weren't a member then you could forget trying to get in. Entry was via an intercom system linked to CCTV. A small monitor behind the counter let the staff know who you were. If they didn't recognise your face then you had to show your pass. If you couldn't do that, if you'd forgotten it for instance, then you were told to go away and get it. If you then claimed you'd lost it, you had to state your name, address, date of birth, and when the lost pass was issued. If the staff could find your details in the membership book they'd let you in, but snooker was out of the question till you'd paid the one pound fine for losing the original pass, plus the fiver for the replacement one.

For a snooker club it was seriously wack. I mean, we're not talking Fort Knox here, but a poxy snooker club. Under such a regime I wouldn't become a member if you paid me. And if I'd known how I was going to be treated the afternoon I showed up with Carlton I certainly would never have agreed to go along and be his 'guest'. Guest my arse. The word suggests a certain warmth, a friendliness, a little hospitality. I got none of that from the pot-belly bloke behind the counter. He made eye-contact with me maybe three times, smiled not once, and only spoke to me to say I had to pay a two pound guest fee and sign the guest book. Of course, he was excessively chatty with Carlton, the way white guys tend to speak to black guys when they're desperate to show the world they're not racist. Carlton, bless him, sensing my unease, did all he could to make me feel at home. Although I protested, he paid my guest fee, bought a round of soft drinks and insisted that the session (the best of nine frames) was his treat. Like I said, bless him.

Although it was the middle of the afternoon and a weekday, more or less every table was occupied. By young Turks. Literally. It was the catchment area. The snooker club was on Kingsland High Street, or Istanbul, as it was otherwise known. Me and Carlton were the only two black guys in the place. It was weird. I said to Carlton as he was setting up the balls: 'Where's all the brothers, man?'

'Oh, they never show up till gone seven. They keep some strange hours. They get here late evening and leave at dawn. Like vampires.'

I thought he was being a bit harsh so I said: 'You know what us black people are like. We're night owls.'

'Not all of us. Especially those of us who work.'

He'd brought out his soap-box so I didn't pursue it. I changed the subject. The snooker club was open round the clock. Interesting. Maybe membership wasn't such a bad idea after all. I said: 'Twenty-four seven this place then, yeah?'

'Yeah. Right, then. Flip to see who breaks?'

'Go for it.'

He tossed a coin, told me to call it while it was airborne, I said heads, the coin landed tails-up on the snooker table.

'My break,' he said, getting ready to do so. He broke off. It was a good break. The reds had hardly been disturbed and the white, avoiding all the colours, had run on to rest on the balk cushion. Carlton was going to whup me at snooker.

The first frame dragged a bit. Neither of us made any sizeable breaks, we made loads of errors, and eventually I conceded after fouling on the black and leaving myself needing two snookers and a clearance of the table to win. Carlton said: 'Nice one. I like a man who knows when he's beaten.'

'You didn't beat me. I beat myself.'

'Yeah, whatever. Now set 'em up and let's go again.'

I set up the balls then broke off. What a joke break. I hit the reds way too hard, so that they scattered everywhere, and instead of running to balk, the white kissed the blue and ended up mid-table. I shook my head, slumped into my chair, took a quick sip of my drink, then waited for the inevitable. Carlton chalked up and slowly approached the table, barely able to contain his glee at the embarrassment of options I'd left him.

He took his time sizing them up, going round and round the table, working out shots in advance. Finally he decided where to begin and got down to business. I stood up and got ready to pick balls out of the pockets. He made a forty break, ran into trouble, played the safest of safety shots, then leaned against the table looking pleased with himself. Before I took my shot I said: 'Nice break. That's your highest now, right?'

'Yeah. And the way you're playing it's gonna get higher.'

I smiled weakly. I've yet to meet anyone as ungracious in victory as my old mate, Carlton. Maybe he was getting his own back for all those times in school when I'd belittled him for being rubbish at games. If he was I could hardly have blamed him. I took my shot.

Mis-hit white, reds everywhere again, colours all nicely on their spots. For the next ten minutes Carlton had me picking balls out the pockets left, right and centre. He beat his previous break by ten and in the process cleared up all the reds. When I eventually got back to the table I needed a million snookers and a full clearance to win. I did the decent thing and conceded.

After we'd re-set the balls, Carlton chalked his cue and moved away from the table.

'So,' he said, as I was lining up the first red. 'You're a drug dealer now?'

I was immediately pissed off by his judgmental tone. I didn't answer him, not straight off. I focused on the red, as if it was his head, then smashed it into the pocket. The shot was so true it jolted me ... and calmed me, especially since I'd managed to hold the white perfectly for the black. Now I could answer him.

'That's right,' I said. 'Got a problem with that have you?'

I rolled the black in and left myself, at a slight angle, on the only potable red. I cut it in ever so gently and again held the white for the black. I chalked up.

'Yeah, I got a problem with that,' he said. 'I mean, who'd have thought it. You, a drug dealer.'

'Yeah well, takes all sorts, you get me?'

'Sure, I could understand Jeff turning out like that. But you?' He shook his head, all regretful-like.

I slammed the black in and cannoned into the bunch of reds. They opened up beautifully, like an exploded firework in a night sky. My options were now endless. I rubbed my hands mentally. Talking and playing was clearly the key to success for me. It relaxed me, so I said, to keep the conversation going: 'Ain't nothing special about me, Carlton. Never has been.'

'Didn't say you were special.'

'Then how come you're so surprised I ended up dealing?'

''Cause at school you had more brains than all of us. Everyone thought you were going places. Even you thought so at first. I know a few teachers certainly did.'

'Is that so? Pity they gave up on me, then, innit?'

'You gave up on yourself, the moment you started to knock heads with Jeff.'

I sank a red in mid-table and held for the blue. Then I remembered something. I said: 'Hold on a sec. You counting this break or what?'

'Seventeen. That's all. Don't go wetting your knickers just yet.'

'And how come I'm respotting my own colours?'

'Shit. Sorry.'

He waited for me to sink the blue. I sank it and he dutifully respotted it. Well, well, I thought, he wasn't as calm as he was making out, not if he'd forgotten his duties.

I sank four more balls. Two reds and two pinks. That took my break to thirty-six. I ran into trouble on the next red and opted for safety by leaving the white tight on the side cushion. There were loads of reds on but Carlton needed to produce something special to sink any of them. He tried, failed miserably, shouted 'fuck!', and I was back at the table within seconds. I downed a red and held deftly for the black. I chalked up and started to plan a couple of shots in advance. I sank a fairly hard red and left myself not too clever on the pink. The choice was to play safe or try and pot it. I went for broke. The pink trickled in off the jaws of the pocket and the white, which I wasn't even that bothered about, nestled in nicely between two easily sinkable reds. Carlton respotted the pink while I tried to decide which of the two reds to go for. In the meantime I had a question for my conscience.

'So you working at the moment?' I said.

'Me?'

'Nah. Pot-belly over there.'

'I'm a clerk for the DHSS.'

'Oh, right,' I said, unimpressed. I'd never have guessed it – Carlton working down the dole office.

I won that frame comfortably then lost the next three abysmally. The session was over. Despite Carlton trying to provoke me with his gloating, I took my beating on the chin. And even though we'd had our little heated exchange, we left the snooker club that afternoon the same way we'd entered it: as two old mates hooking up for the first time in years, hoping to see a lot more of each other.

Without any firm plan as to what we'd do, we agreed to meet up again in the next couple of days. I dropped him home (I was surprised when I found out he was still living with his parents) then drove like a bat out of hell towards the pool hall, worried about what foul mood Jeff would be in.

The pool hall was closed when I got there, padlocked from the outside. I immediately got vexed and started slagging OJ. Him and his brother had obviously got pissed and had gone home to sleep it off. I stood outside on the pavement for a few minutes not knowing what do. I tried to imagine where Jeff might be. I thought maybe he'd gone home, so I got out my mobile and called his drum. Gloria answered the phone. I could hear the little one crying in the background.

'Gloria, it's me.'

'Gabby. What's up?'

'Jeff there?'

'No. Ain't he with you?'

'No. Don't worry. I'll catch him on the mobile.'

'OK, then, see ya?'

'See ya. Oh. How's little man?'

'He's all right. You can probably hear him.'

'Yeah. Got some lungs on him, I'll say that for him. See you later.'

I hung up and dialled Jeff's mobile. It was switched off. Fuck. Now what? I thought. There was no point standing there looking lost so I decided to walk back to my ride. Where

I was going to drive to I hadn't the foggiest. I'd only taken a few steps when I heard: 'Yow! Gabby! Yow!'

I looked round but couldn't see anyone. I stood still for a bit and waited for whoever it was to shout my name again. He did.

'Yow! Gabby! Over here, man!'

I looked across the road and saw, in one of the many entrances to Pembury flats, a shadowy figure beckoning me over with frantic waves of his hand. I glanced up and down the road. There was no traffic worth fretting about. I sprinted across the road, then across a grassy knoll littered with dog shit, then into the dark entrance leading into the flats. Just inside it, looking for all the world like a day-ghost, was this cat I knew called Alex, a Greek. Once I recognised him I started to rant and rave.

'What the fuck you want? I ain't carrying at the moment. Go away.'

'Nah, nah,' said Alex. 'Listen, listen.'

He tried to grab my arm but I slapped his hand away and said: 'Didn't I just tell you? I ain't carrying. Get the fuck out of it.'

I went to walk off.

'Nah, Gabby, man, you don't understand. Listen. You missed it, man. The raid.'

I didn't wait to hear any more. I legged it back across the road, jumped into my ride, screeched round the corner onto the main road, then hung a sharp left into this narrow little alleyway where street whores took their punters for blow jobs and knee-tremblers. It was where we liked to park our cars, out of sight of the old bill. Sure enough, there it was, Jeff's ride. Why I bothered to check on it I'll never know. Jeff had been nicked, not his ride. Strange the things we do in a crisis. Anyway, the car was safe. At least that was one thing off my mind for the time being. Next I had to give Gloria the bad news. I rang and told her. As I expected she got a little hysterical. She always did whenever Jeff got nicked.

'Calm down,' I told her. 'I'm coming round.'

'So you don't know where he is?' she asked me just after I got there. She was pacing the front room with Jordan cradled in her arms, transmitting all her stress to the poor little thing who just wouldn't shut up crying.

'No I don't. He could be anywhere.'

'We gotta find him, Gabby. They're probably beating him to death right now.'

Tears were welling in her eyes. Jordan wailed on.

'How we gonna find him?' I asked. 'Go round all the nicks and ask for him?'

'Yes. If that's what it takes.'

'Don't be stupid, Gloria. We can't do that.'

'Why not?'

''Cause us showing up like that might make things worse for him. We dunno what he's told them. S'pose he's using a false name? S'pose he's given them a moody address?' I could see I was getting through to her. She was trying to shush Jordan and listen to me at the same time. 'So you see? We just gotta sit tight till he contacts us. There's no other way. But I ain't telling you nothing you don't know. Ain't the first time Jeff's been nicked, is it?'

'No. But at least those other times I knew where he was.'

'We just gotta wait.'

'That could be for ever, though.'

'Trust me. He'll get bail in a few hours. No matter what they've charged him with. *If* they've charged him. Let's just chill, OK? It'll be all right. You'll see.'

She'd calmed down. As a result Jordan's wailing descended to a whimper. We all sat down on the sofa. She started to rock and soothe Jordan (or was it herself?) and eventually the little man, all cried out, fell asleep in her arms. She got up gingerly and went and put him to bed. By the time she got back I'd rolled a spliff.

'All right to spark this?' I asked.

She nodded and sat next to me on the sofa, at a distance, clutching a cushion. I sparked the spliff, sucked on it a couple of times, filled the room with smoke, then offered her some. She didn't want to know. I took another toke on the spliff.

'S'pose you want a drink to go with that?' she asked.

'Wouldn't say no.'

'You know where the kitchen is.'

'Huh? Oh. Yeah. 'Course. You want one?'

She shook her head. I went out to the kitchen. When I came back with my glass of Vimto I could sense she had something to say to me. And sure enough, the moment I sat down . . .

'So where were you?'

'What?'

'When this raid happened?'

I told her about Carlton showing up and about the afternoon spent at the snooker hall.

'Lucky you, eh?'

'Damn lucky,' I said.

She fixed me the coldest stare then said: 'For your sake, Gabby, I hope Jeff sees it like that.'

Maybe it was the spliff, but I just didn't see that coming. It poleaxed me. It took me at least a minute, maybe longer, to fully understand what she was driving at. Once I had, I stood up, straight-backed and rigid, my arms by my side tensed as fuck, my fists clenched ready to ... I looked at her, really looked at her for the first time. I saw a stupid, stretch-marked, flabby-stomached, good-for-nothing bitch who Jeff had picked up in some sweaty shebeen, fucked, got pregnant, and tied down. I saw a silly, going nowhere Doris who'd been given a little status and respect and who was now sitting in front of me accusing me with her damn cheeky self of informing on my best friend. I should have smashed her face to a pulp. Instead I said: 'If you got an itch, bitch, you best just scratch it, you get me?'

'Who you calling a bitch?'

'You. Got something to say to me then say it. Don't beat about the bush.'

'Keep your voice down, if you don't mind. Jordan's asleep.'

'You got some front, ain't you? You know how far back me and Jeff go?' She turned her face away from me. 'Fuck you,' I said. 'I don't have to stand here taking this shit from you. Who the fuck d'you think you are? Stupid bitch.'

I stormed out.

I drove straight home, mad as hell. When I got in I put some sounds on, went out to the kitchen and grabbed two bottles of Babycham from the fridge, went back to the front room and rolled the fattest spliff, then stretched out on the sofa, absolutely determined to get out of my box.

I drank and smoked but the buzz I so desperately wanted was playing hard to get. There was just too much going on in my head. It had been a weird day, one of those days when nothing seems to make sense.

After two spliffs and the Babychams all I had was a headache, one of my sledge-hammering migraines. I swallowed two painkillers and got into bed. It took me four hours of tossing and turning and groaning and vomiting before I finally dropped off. When I woke up my headache had gone but I felt as groggy and as weak as a new-born foal. Food. My first thought was to order a takeaway, but the prospect of yet another Chinese or Indian grease-feast made me retch all over again. What I needed was some good old-fashioned home cooking. Mum. If I went to see her I could kill two birds with one stone. I could reassure her I was still alive and she was bound to have some grub at her place. I had a quick shower, changed, then drove round to see her.

I found her in front of the telly watching *Minder*. She looked sad, old and lonely. As I came into the front room she said: 'Still pushing key in me front door like you live here, eh?'

'You want the keys?' I asked her, holding them out for her to take. She carried on staring at the telly. I put the keys in my pocket and plonked myself down on one of the armchairs. Silence. I looked at the telly. Terry was laying into these two blokes while Arthur, dressed in his trademark sheepskin coat and trilby hat, looked on from a safe distance, wincing like a wimp every time Terry landed a punch. It was a scene I'd seen a million times, and it had stopped being funny after the first time. Mum was enjoying it though. There was a twinkle in her eye. If I hadn't been there she'd have been laughing her head off. Terry saw off the two blokes and Arthur rushed over to him to try and hen-peck him but Terry wasn't having it and stormed off in a huff. Arthur got in his Jag and started cruising slowly behind him, begging him through the wound-down window to quit playing the martyr and get in the car. Eventually Terry got in (as he always did) and the two of them drove off into the sunset. It was time for the ads. I looked at Mum and said: 'So. How you been?'

'Me's alive.'

'How's work?'

'Work is work.'

'Seen your two good-for-nothing sons, lately?'

'Hear you, though. Talk about the pot calling the kettle black.'

'You ain't seen them, then?'

'They does come here all the time. More than you can say, isn't it?'

Minder was back on. We both automatically glued our eyes to the screen. Television. What an invention. Arthur and Terry were now in their local, chatting with the landlord, old gravel-voice. 'You working yet?' Mum said out of the blue, without looking at me.

'What d'you think?'

'Where you living?'

'Just round the corner. On Amhurst Road.'

She shook her head and smiled, all rueful-like.

'Boy,' she said. 'Sometime it hard to imagine you is a son of mine.'

'I'm your son all right.' I was trying to sound jaunty.

'You mean to tell me, Gabriel, that all these months me don't see you, you was only round the corner?'

'Yeah.'

'And you couldn't even stop by and see if your mother want anything? You couldn't even phone?'

She shook her head again, this time even more ruefully, as if, once and for all, based on this my latest fuck-up, she'd realised there really was no hope for me, that maybe it was time she washed her hands of me. I felt as guilty as it was possible to feel. My eyes filled up and I felt a sudden need to hug her, to be hugged by her. I wanted to say how sorry I was, for everything, for all I'd put her through, all the disappointments, the heartache, the stress, the worry, the shame, everything. Yet I couldn't. I just couldn't bring myself to do the one thing I knew would have gone a long way to rebuilding the collapsed bridge that once existed between us. Maybe it would have been easier for me if she'd suddenly broken down and sobbed and pleaded with me to stop killing her. But I knew she wouldn't. I knew Mum. She was as likely to expose her vulnerabilities to me as a lioness would to her cub. So we sat there, in stony silence, pretending to be interested in the banal activities of Messrs Daley and McCann. I had three options. I could sit there in the oppressive silence pretending to watch telly, I could try and talk to Mum, I mean really talk to her, or . . .

'Any food in the kitchen?'

Again without looking at me she said: 'Why you must always ask stupid question?'

I got up and went out to the kitchen. As ever there were pots and pans on the rings of the cooker. I opened them up one by one to see what goodies were to be had. White rice, ackee and saltfish, dumplings, yams and green bananas. I sparked the fire under them then started to lay the kitchen table.

I ate my belly full then went back into the front room. Mum had switched off the telly, put on the main light and was busy doing a word-search, the magazine on her lap, pen in hand, glasses perched on the tip of her nose. I sat next to her on the sofa, close enough to see the magazine.

'You leave some of the food for your brothers?'

'No. Ate the lot.'

She seemed shocked and quickly spluttered: 'But see here, bwoy! You mean to tell me you come here with your hungry belly and eat off all the food?'

'Chill, Mum. I was joking. Remember them, jokes?'

She was not amused.

'Look, here, Gabriel,' she said. 'Don't come here and provoke me, OK?'

She went back to her word-search game. After a minute I said: 'I can see one.'

'See what?'

'A word.'

'Where?'

I pointed. She drew a line threw the word and crossed it off her list. I got carried away.

'I can see another one.'

'And I can see that you need to go from here and leave me to play me game in peace.' The snub cut me to the quick. I almost did get up and leave. But something pinned me to the sofa. She seemed to sense my discomfort and, as though regretting her harshness, continued: 'If you want something to do you can go and clear out that room of yours. There's a whole heap of rubbish in there and me don't know what to throw away from what not to throw away.'

I went to have a butcher's at this so-called rubbish. When I walked into my old bedroom such a feeling of nostalgia came over me that my legs wobbled and I was forced to sit for a moment on the bed. I looked round the room. Far from being a tip, which is what I'd expected, everything looked neat and tidy. There were reminders of my childhood all over the place. The glossy poster of the Spurs cup-winning side of '82 was still stuck to the wall, its shine dulled now. In a corner, stacked on top of each other, were my old Subbuteo teams, twelve in all, which me and Carlton used to play with after school all those years ago. In another corner was the old paraffin heater Mum was always telling me to turn off before getting into bed. I never did. I used to just turn it down. I had a real love-hate relationship with that bloody thing. It saved me from dying of hypothermia, so cold did my draughty room get in winter, but it also gave me chilblains on my fingers and toes because of the amount of times I had to sit hunched over it trying to warm up. Why Mum hadn't thrown it out I'll never know. She certainly didn't need it any more. Just before I left home Hackney Council had put in central heating. Maybe she was keeping the thing as back-up, in case the central heating broke down. Mums think that way. Whatever. There it was in the corner looking redundant, like almost everything else in the room. Including the bed I was sitting on. I bounced on it a few times. It was as rickety and creaky and lumpy as ever. I must have been an idiot to think that Mum, from her room next door, couldn't hear me shafting the Dorises I used to sneak in under her nose. My old single bed. It had seen its best days. And that's even before Mum bought it for me from a second-hand furniture shop on Mare Street.

I carried on looking round the room but still I couldn't spot the 'rubbish'. Then the penny dropped. The old wardrobe . . . or more specifically . . . what was in it. In one movement I leaped off the bed across the floor and turned the key in its door. I stepped back to get a better look. Yep. There it was all right. The 'rubbish', crammed in all higgledy-piggledy-like, as if Mum, maddened by the sight of it all and lacking the heart to throw it out, had decided to stuff it in the wardrobe out the way.

Anything not bagged – clothes, shoes – I decided to leave well alone. They could be dealt with some other day. But the rest of the stuff, the bagged stuff, had to be examined and reminisced over before any chucking could be done. I was in that kind of mood.

There were about ten plastic shopping bags full of comics. All my old favourites were there. *Superman, Spiderman, Batman, Silver Surfer, Daredevil, The Fantastic Four,* comics I'd had since primary school. And these were only the super hero ones. There were dozens of others, all in surprisingly good nick, about an equal amount of funnies and sport. *Beano, Whizzer and Chips, Dandy, Whoopee, Tiger, Roy of the Rovers, Shoot, Scoop.* It was like opening up a treasure-trove. They were all definitely coming home with me. I smoothed them out as best I could, blew the dust off them, then put them back in their bags.

Anything else I found was always going to pale beside those comics. Sure enough, what I found in the other bags was fit only for the bin. Old school reports, old exercise books, cracked cassette tapes, a broken down cassette player, dirty magazines, cheap watches, fake jewellery, Rizlas, football sticker albums, out of circulation coins, out of circulation notes, badges, baseball caps, pens, pencils, toy cars, an old camera, playing cards, and much more besides. Junk. I scooped everything off the floor and stuffed it back in the bags, sneezing now and then because of the amount of dust.

I put my Subbuteo teams into a bag (I was taking them home as well) then put all the bags (comics and junk alike) outside the door ready for when I was leaving. I then went back into my old room, tidied it, took a final look round, thought for a second about taking down and chucking the Spurs poster, decided against it, switched off the light, then went back into the front room. Mum was still doing her word-search.

'Right, then,' I said. 'I'm out.'

'You clear out that rubbish?'

I didn't say anything, just watched while she pretended to be searching for some word. There was a long silence.

'See you, then,' I finally said.

She looked up at me and shook her head.

'Can't wait to leave, can you?' she said.

'Ain't that. Got a few moves to make, that's all.'

'Always in a rush. Well, you mark my words. One day you going to have to slow down, Gabriel. You wait and see.'

'I hear what you're saying, Mum, but I really gotta go.'

'A letter come for you.'

'A letter? Who from?'

'You father.'

Nothing could have prepared me for that.

'You're joking,' I said. She kissed her teeth. 'What's he writing me for?'

'How me must know? Why you don't read the thing and see?'

'Where is it?'

'In me bedroom on the sewing machine.'

I went and got it. I stood there for a minute or so looking at it, turning it over in my hand, the way you do with letters, as if the envelope can tell you something of the letter's actual content. The only thing this one told me (which I already knew) was that Dad was living in America. Washington DC, to be specific. I tucked the envelope into my back pocket and, after picking up the bags in the passage, left Mum's that night feeling no better than I had been all evening, but with a sense of anticipation as to what the man who was my father in name only could possibly have to say to me after so many years.

When I got home I went straight into my bedroom. I switched on the main light, closed the curtains, then lay on the bed and made myself comfortable. I got out the letter. Once again I turned it over in my hand, noticing this time the terrible handwriting. I studied the individual letters of each word, like some airy-fairy handwriting expert trying to decipher the personality of the writer. In a sense that's exactly what I was doing. I knew next to nothing about my old man. Mum hardly ever mentioned him, and whenever she did it was only to suggest I contact him, which I had no intention of doing. The only things I knew about him were his name (Winston), his age (fifty at the time), his occupation before emigrating to the States (bus conductor), and that he and Mum hadn't married. The man was as much a stranger to me as the bloke on the speaking clock. To my mind, I had no father, and when I was growing up, Mum didn't exactly go out of her way to encourage me to think otherwise. It was only after I'd left school that she started to suggest I contact him, no doubt racked with guilt for not having done so earlier.

I won't lie, there were times when he crossed my mind and I found myself asking questions: what did he look like (Mum had no pictures of him), did I resemble him in looks or personality, what sort of life had he made for himself in the States, had he more kids besides me, did he think of me, did he love me? I convinced myself I was indifferent to the answers to these questions when in reality I was anything but. In fact, whenever I thought about my father I usually ended up seeing red. I was angry with him. That was the bottom line. I felt that if ever there came a day when we were face-to-face I'd let him know that in no uncertain terms. And I was angry with Mum too. And secretly ashamed of her. Angry because no matter which way I looked at it she was partly to blame for me not knowing my old man. And ashamed because she'd had three kids by three different men and not one of those men had featured in our lives, me and my brothers, that is. This made me think that at various points in her life she must have put it about a bit, given it up to complete losers who'd only been after one thing, all of them bolting once they'd made her pregnant. No child likes to think of its mother in this way, it's nothing short of blasphemy. Yet I could think of no other explanation for what had gone on. And Mum didn't offer me any. That part of her life was a closed book, she made that clear, and to be honest, I had no desire to open it and peek. I might have had my suspicions about her confirmed. In any case, who was I to question her about her life, who was I to lecture her about morality and shit? Here was a woman who'd given me and my brothers all we could possibly need to equip us for the journey, a woman who'd raised three kids single-handedly at a time when it was unheard of for a woman to raise one child on her own, never mind three. If for nothing else, respect was due to her for that. Obviously my brothers felt the same, since I never once heard either of them question Mum about the absence of their own fathers.

I opened the letter. The first thing that struck me about it was its length. It was more a note than a letter, just one side of a small sheet of writing paper. That got my back up immediately. I was expecting page after page of soul baring and loads of grovelling apologies and pleas for forgiveness. What I actually got was . . .

Dear Gabriel,

I hope you are well. I've been meaning to write to you for some time now but what with one thing or another I just never got round to it. Still, as the saying goes, better late than never.

Anyway, I'm writing now because I was hoping you might like to come and see me here in the States. If you do, then write back and let me know as soon as you can. Don't worry about the plane fare. If you agree to come over then I would be happy to get the ticket for you. I would come and see you myself but I just can't get enough time off work.

I would really like to see you, Gabriel. You must be all grown up now, a big man with plans of making your way in the world. Well, you make sure you listen to your mother. She's a good woman and she knows what she's talking about. And spare a thought for your old man. I certainly think of you a lot and wish you all the happiness in the world.

That's all for now. Write soon. I look forward to hearing from you. Take care of yourself, your father,

Winston

I just couldn't believe it. The man obviously had no shame. He'd been meaning to write to me ... for almost twenty years! It would have been sad if it wasn't so funny. He wanted me to visit him in the States. *Me* go and see *him*. And the way he offered to pay the plane fare, as if that was some major kindness on his part, as if he was saying he might be a heartless cunt but he wasn't tight. He would really like to see me, he said. Well, if that wasn't an understatement I didn't know what was. Listen to Mum, he said, she's a good woman. He had some nerve telling me how good a woman Mum was. She was such a good woman he'd abandoned her with an unborn child. But what really got me was when he asked me to spare him a thought. I'd spare him a thought all right . . . a fucking murderous one.

The letter got me so riled I immediately started to write a reply. I started off by saying I had no intention whatsoever of going to see him. Ever! What's more, I said, if he loved his life he would be wise not to show up on my doorstep. I told him what I thought of his flimsy excuse for not writing in all those years and said that he shouldn't bother wasting paper and ink doing so again. And since in his letter he'd shown no real interest in it, I put him in the picture as to my fucked-up life, just in case he was under any illusions about being reconciled to a son who'd make him proud of all he'd achieved and hoped to achieve. I rattled on and on about all the things I'd done since leaving school. I left nothing out. It was like a confession. By the end of this section of the letter, I realised what I was doing, stopped writing altogether, ripped up what I'd written, put a match to the tiny pieces of paper, then watched them burn slowly in the glass ashtray on my bedside cabinet. The time for writing my life story was some way off yet. When that time came I'd get everything down properly. As for the old man, I never did reply to him, and taking the hint, he never wrote to me again. I kept his letter, though, and read it from time to time, just to remind myself of the fact that, like everybody else, I do actually have a father.

Suddenly I was at a loose end. I had no place to be, no one to see, nothing to do. I lay on my bed staring up at the ceiling, my mind clogged with thoughts. It was getting late but I knew if I got into bed proper I'd have trouble sleeping.

So, as much as I didn't want to, I went into the front room and called Gloria. Her phone rang once before she answered it, as if she was sitting by it, waiting. She sounded frantic.

'Hello.'

'It's me, Gabriel.'

'Oh. What d'you want?'

'What d'you think?'

'He ain't back yet.' There was a short silence. Then she said: 'Sorry about earlier.'

'Me, too,' I replied.

'I'll call you if I hear from him, OK?'

'Do that. No matter what time it is. Didn't wake Jordan, did I?'

'He's dead to the world. See ya.'

'Laters.'

The next morning Gloria called me to say that she'd just spoken to Jeff's solicitor on the blower. Jeff had been charged with possession with intent to supply. He was due to appear before Highbury Corner Magistrates that morning for a summary hearing. I told her I'd be at her gaff in five.

We had to make a detour to Tottenham to drop Jordan off at Gloria's sister's. By the time we got to the court 'Joe Allen' had already been before the magistrate, pleaded not guilty, and had been remanded in custody to await trial at Snaresbrook Crown Court. The old bill were holding him in the cells under the court building and would allow only Gloria down to see him. I went outside to wait for Gloria on the courthouse steps. Eventually I saw her and rushed up to her. When I was up close to her I noticed she'd been crying.

'You all right?' I asked.

She sighed heavily, looked at the ground, then started to shake her head. She didn't know whether she was coming or going, the poor girl. She said: 'I dunno, Gabby. I just don't know no more.'

'What d'you wanna do now? You wanna go home?'

'No.' She looked over my shoulder at a caff across the road. 'Let's go in there. You can buy me a tea.'

Inside the caff, struggling to keep her voice from cracking, she began telling me what Jeff had told her.

After I had left Ossie's with Carlton, Jeff thought about taking the rest of the day off. He felt a vibe that something was going to happen but ignored it, putting it down to simple paranoia. For an hour or so things were quiet. He didn't make a single sale in that time. Even the hash dealers, OJ among them, were sitting around twiddling their thumbs. Then all of a sudden there was a rush on. Jeff had trouble keeping up. He slagged me for not being there to help him. His mobile was ringing every five minutes. It was turning into one of those days when he'd have to go home and get more rocks, so rapid were the cats buying them up. In no time at all he'd finished his stash and was well into finishing mine. He was on automatic pilot now, doing things without even thinking, giddy with exhilaration, careless. After a while he stopped telling the cats to go and wait at some secluded spot. He had them walking right up to the door. And after each sale, rather than hiding it as we always did, he started holding the stash in his hand, just too plain lazy to keep hiding it and fetching it, hiding it and fetching it. When the police burst in he did the worst thing you can do in that situation. He froze. They caught him bang to rights with a fistful of rocks. They had to prise his fingers open to get at them, as if he'd died standing up and rigor had set in.

Everything that happened after that was a blur. He couldn't remember much of it. Too dazed. He knew a lot of the others had been nicked but couldn't say who exactly. He'd been put in a cell by himself, which he thought was strange considering the haul. Later that night, while trying to get some shut-eye on his plastic-covered bunk, he realised why. He was the only one who'd been caught with crack. He was special. He couldn't be allowed to mix with the others. They'd all be getting bail and one of them might cover his tracks for him. Obviously it was the police's intention to spin his drum. Under no circumstances could he have allowed them to do that. Quite apart from wanting to spare Gloria and Jordan the aggravation, he had a fat stash of rocks hidden round his place. If the old bill had found it he'd have been put away for a very long time indeed. That's why he told them he was of 'no fixed abode' and gave them a false name, Joe Allen. Lucky for him he'd been nicked by old bill who didn't know him, the Dalston mob. Still, when the duty solicitor came round to see him in his cell that night, he took a gamble, based on the old boy's kind face. He told the brief his real name and took him into his confidence. The next morning the brief phoned Gloria and, choosing his words carefully so as not to incriminate himself in any conspiracy, told her what Jeff was up against and what he, Jeff, wanted her to do.

I told Gloria to prepare herself for the worst, because even though Jeff had pleaded not guilty, the chances of him walking were slim at best.

'I ain't a fool, Gabby. I know that.'

'In some ways it might have been better if he'd just pleaded guilty and got the whole thing over with quickly.'

'That's what I told him.'

'And he said what?'

She mimicked Jeff's pompous voice.

'"What fart you talking, woman? Ain't my job to make life easy for the old bill."'

I shook my head.

'Sounds like our Jeff,' I said. 'There's just no reasoning with him when he's like that.'

'Tell me about it.'

We sipped our now lukewarm teas. I didn't know what to say except: 'Let's get you home?'

Jeff got five years. Just like that. The trial lasted a week. He didn't really have a defence. He said he'd been fitted up. It was his word against the old bill's. The jury believed the old bill. I didn't go to the trial. I just couldn't face it. Gloria gave me a day-by-day account. Apparently Jeff managed a grim smile when the judge, just before passing sentence, called him a 'carbuncle on society's back'.

No time's a good time to get sent down, but two weeks before Christmas must be the worst time of all. My heart really went out to Jeff. And to Gloria. God only knew what sort of Christmas she and the little one would have.

I genuinely did feel sorry for Jeff, but at the same time I also felt relieved to be shot of him for a while, maybe even for good. It was what I'd wanted for longer than I cared to remember. And despite the sad way it happened, I nevertheless planned to take full advantage of the situation.

I put the crack business on indefinite hold. Like Carlton had said, my heart was never really in it. Besides, now that Ossie's had been closed down, there was no place for me to deal from. Except the streets, which was definitely not an option for me. You had to be a particular type for that cat-and-mouse lifestyle. Your survival instincts had to be razor-sharp. And since I had trouble feeding myself properly, I knew mine were as blunt as a mallet. So, the small stash of rocks I had at home I put, together with what Jeff told Gloria to give me, in my freezer, to be sold at some unspecified future date. The money I would have raised from selling Jeff's stash I drew from my bank account and gave to Gloria. Once I'd done my bit by her, I made a concerted effort not to go round her gaff any more. Not that I didn't want to. Plenty of times I felt the urge to call round and see how she and Jordan were getting on. But to avoid talk of me and her doing the dirty on Jeff, I used the phone to enquire after her and her son's well-being.

My plan now was to see as much of Carlton as possible. The afternoon we'd spent together at the snooker club was the most relaxed I'd felt in years. I wanted more of the same. After all the stress-filled years I'd spent in Jeff's company I felt I deserved some chill-out time.

I became a member of New World Snooker Club. Me and Carlton went there most evenings after he'd finished work. I liked it there. The emphasis there was on relaxation. What Jeff would have called 'loafing'. The place suited me to the max. If anything, it was probably too relaxing. You could quite easily end up staying there round the clock, neglecting other areas of your life in favour of smoking weed, playing snooker and kipping on the comfy sofas in the TV room. This was a trap Carlton never fell into. He always had to get off home and get his beauty in before work the next day. But I had no such commitment, and there came a time when Pot-Belly Dave was forever asking me if I had no home to go.

My snooker game improved. Whenever Carlton left to go home, I'd stay on and practise, either by myself or with anyone who cared to for a few frames. I couldn't get enough of the game, whether playing it or watching it on telly. In no time at all I'd got up to Carlton's level. I liked to think that I even passed his level. It annoyed him no end that I was now whupping him on a regular basis. So it didn't surprise me when one day he announced: 'I gotta take a break from this game.'

'What d'you mean?' I asked, all innocent-like, though I knew full well where he was coming from.

'I'm fed up playing snooker. There's other stuff we can do, you know? That's all we ever do. Play bloody snooker.'

'What other stuff?'

'All sorts.'

'Like what exactly?'

'Well, we could join a sports centre for a start, maybe play some table tennis or badminton, or go for a swim. We could go to some footie matches. You're always on about bloody Spurs. Why don't we go and watch them play? You gonna be an armchair supporter for the rest of your life?'

'I'd love to go and watch Spurs play.'

'Then why don't we?'

'Well,' I said. 'If you're sure you don't mind, then yeah, I think going to watch Spurs play is a fucking inspired idea.'

Spurs had eight games left in the league that season. We went to all of them. It wasn't a vintage season for the Yids by any means. In fact it wasn't a vintage season for English football generally. Heysel and the subsequent ban on English clubs from European competition ensured that. Me and Carlton couldn't have picked a more dismal time to start going to matches. Of the eight games we saw, the highlight has to be our one-nil victory over the old enemy. At the final whistle the Lane erupted and I actually kissed Carlton. He scrubbed his cheek and slagged me off. Not being a true Spurs fan it was hard for him to understand what it meant to me for us to beat Arsenal.

There were one or two other memorable moments that season, though I only saw them on *Match of the Day*. We beat Liverpool at Anfield one-nil. This was no mean feat when you remember how dominant the scousers were in the eighties. And we got as far as the fifth round of the FA Cup, beating Oxford and Notts County (we put five past County), only to lose two-nil to that other bunch of scousers, Everton. Shame. Still, although it was nice to see Spurs win, it wasn't the main reason me and Carlton went to watch them play. We were interested in the event itself, the whole package: getting to the game, buying the programmes, the pre-match excitement, the atmosphere inside the ground, the taunting of the away fans, that feeling of being part of a tribe, applauding the team onto the pitch, the game itself, that feeling of elation or dejection depending on the result, filing out of the ground and analysing the game's key moments, looking forward to the next match. These things, much more so than the matches themselves, are the memories I have of that season.

Watching Spurs play that season had a positive effect on me. This pleased Carlton. He never said, but I knew he took credit for reawakening my passion for the beautiful game. And he wasn't content to stop there. He was on a mission to save me from myself, forever dreaming up things for us to do. He worked bloody hard at that – too hard in my view. The majority of things he suggested were so outlandish and alien to me as concepts I put my foot down and refused outright to even consider them. I just couldn't see myself canoeing, sky-diving and climbing rocks. All that 'outdoor' stuff just wasn't for me. And besides, it would have meant leaving the manor to do them, maybe even the city. I wasn't having it.

The cinema was more my kind of thing. I hadn't been in years, not since primary school (Saturday morning pictures), so when Carlton suggested we start going I instantly agreed.

It became a twice-weekly ritual for us. On Wednesday nights we'd go and take in the latest action-packed Hollywood blockbusters showing at the Odeon Dalston Junction. On Friday nights the Konak Kingsland High Street was where you'd find us watching Kung-Fu triple bills till three or four in the morning.

We went clubbing most Saturday nights. Not to the usual dives I'd always gone to. Carlton would have preferred death by stoning to going to any of those places. No. He was used to up-market clubs with strict dress codes and pricey drinks and bouncers in penguin suits, West End clubs with celebrity DJs from commercial radio stations spinning commercial tracks. These were the type of haunts him and his Buppie work colleagues went to.

The more I went to these clubs with Carlton and his cohorts the more my eyes and mind were forced open. In the end I learned a very important lesson. I realised that people from all walks of life, of different races, nationalities and creeds can, in fact, get on with each other. I learned also that I had loads of prejudices. I'll always be grateful to Carlton for coaxing me into a situation where I was forced to confront them.

For instance, I was gobsmacked, really gobsmacked to see the fittest black girls openly tonguing up pasty-face white boys. I was just as gobsmacked to see black guys doing the same with skinny arse white girls. I felt physically sick at the sight of black guys brazenly mincing about hand-in-hand, squeezing each other's arses and shit. None of this bothered Carlton or his colleagues. They liked to think of themselves as 'liberal minded'. That's the phrase they used to describe themselves time and again. Carlton was especially fond of it. And as if to prove to me how 'liberal minded' he was he said to me one night after I'd been trying to get him to condemn the shenanigans I saw going on around us: 'Judge not, Gabby, lest ye be judged.' And again: 'Let he who is without sin cast the first stone.' I couldn't believe it. He'd actually quoted the bible at me. Still, to give him his dues, at least he'd quoted it appropriately. His advice to me was clear enough: instead of slagging people for doing their thing, I would do well to look at myself and my prejudices. He warned me. He said if I wasn't careful I'd end up, in years to come, a bitter, twisted, bigoted old codger, who spends his time railing against white people, foreigners, gays, a joke figure who no one will take seriously, a black Alf Garnett. He was only having a laugh, but the picture he drew made me shudder nonetheless.

What with his job, plus all the other stuff we were doing together, Carlton eventually stopped going to New World. He just couldn't find the time. At least that's the excuse he used. In reality, he stopped going because he didn't like the way it had changed. Neither did I. But I kept going there anyway. In fact it had become my second home. I'd caught the snooker bug bad. Also, going there got me out of my flat, not to mention off Hackney's mean streets. But most importantly, there were people at New World who could provide me with companionship when Carlton wasn't around. Companionship, mind you, not friendship. The bods who were now cluttering up New World were not, never had been, and never would be my friends.

New World changed in the same way Ossie's changed when the old boy 'retired' and OJ took over. The place was now infested with dealers. The very same mob who did for Ossie's, in fact. Routed by the old bill and with no place else to go, they'd gradually wormed their way into the snooker club, every jack one of them becoming a member. It was always going to happen. I realise now I was a fool to think I'd seen the last of them.

They had no shortage of punters. Being hash merchants, the Turks loved them. They never left the place, except when they were forced to go and restock. Pot-Belly Dave, who worked days, was taken care of with a combination of bribery (hash and money) and intimidation (knives were regularly pulled on him). The night staff, a bunch of casuals who divided the week between themselves, simply turned a blind eye. Security became non-existent. The camera at the front door got vandalised and after a while any old drifter was being buzzed in. On busy days (and nights) the intercom system was actually deemed bad for business and the staff were ordered by the dealers to leave the front door open.

The crew also had new leaders. Now that Jeff was doing his stretch, Brick and Gunhawk were running things. And how! Drunk on power, hardly anyone escaped their tyranny. They extorted money from the dealers. They bullied the punters. They ran up huge bills on the snooker tables. During the day, determined to rid the place of the Turks (despite protests from the hash dealers) they kept up an almost hourly chant of: 'Bubble and squeak, bubble and squeak, look out, look out, it's Nick the Greek!' The tactic worked. After a while the Turks got out. New World Snooker Club was now exclusively black.

At night, Brick and Gunhawk treated the place like their own personal shebeen. They blazed chalices, so that there was a constant cloud of thick white smoke hanging heavy in the air. They got out their ghetto blaster from behind the counter and deafened everyone. They turned the basement into a gambling den where they and their cronies went to shoot dice and play cards. Many a stray Doris got shafted down there as well. And to cap it all, they banned everyone from playing snooker after a certain hour, normally around two in the morning when the place was at its busiest.

And they kept watching me. No matter where I was in the place I could feel their beady eyes on me. The truth is, they just didn't know what the fuck to do with me. I was bad for their rep. Out of respect to Jeff, they couldn't bully and intimidate me the way they did the others. They were obviously hoping I'd just go away, like the Turks. That wasn't going to happen, so the thing to do was to suck me into their entourage, to get me close so they could keep tabs on me. I was a potential threat to their regime, a loose cannon. I had to be kept in check. This must have been the way they were thinking because one day they came to me, or should I say they got word to me through a third party. It was more like a summons, actually. They wanted to see me in their office about something. I laughed when I got the message. Office, indeed. More like the basement. Who the fuck did they think they were? Who were they to summon me? Still, curiosity got the better of me and I duly reported.

I'd not been in the 'office' before. A bare lightbulb dangling from the ceiling. A ripped snooker table used for gambling and fucking. No windows. Dust.

They were perched on the snooker table, side-by-side, their legs swinging beneath them, both clutching spliffs that had gone out.

'Gabby!' Brick shouted in fake excitement as I came down the metal staircase.

'What's up, Brick?' I said. 'Hawk.' Gunhawk nodded.

'Pull up a chair, man,' said Brick.

'What's this about?' I asked, cutting to the chase.

'Hasty, ain't he?' said Gunhawk.

'Go on. Siddown,' said Brick. ''Bout time you and us had a natter.'

''Bout what?' I asked, sitting down, the back of the chair in front of me, a barrier.

'One or two things,' said Brick.

'Like what?'

'We're thinking of going into the crack business.'

'Yeah? And?'

Brick re-lit his spliff. Gunhawk stared me out. Brick took two deep drags on his spliff, let the smoke out slowly through his nose, then said: 'We want you to get the shit for us.'

I smiled. Well, well. So that was the 'something' they wanted to talk about. They were getting into the crack business, but like the novices they were, they didn't know how to get the stuff. How it must have burned their hearts to have to ask me. I had half a mind to tell them to take a running jump. But my business brain and my ego ganged up to rob me of the pleasure. Business-wise, I knew I could make money out of them. Ego-wise, I could have them at my mercy. I said: 'How much shit you want and when?'

And so I went back to 'work'. Not before time, it must be said. My lifestyle of late had all but eaten up my savings. Yet even though I was relieved to get the chance to bump them up again, my heart was still heavy at the thought of going back to dealing.

The stash of rocks I'd put in my freezer had kept well. I

flogged them to Brick and Gunhawk at a tidy profit. I then contacted my supplier, told him I was back in business and that he should stand by for some orders. In days gone by I would have bought bulk from him and sold it, piecemeal, to Brick and Gunhawk. But I decided against this because I knew it was going to take Brick and Gunhawk a while to establish themselves at New World. This would have meant me having large amounts of rocks stashed about my flat for long periods. Risky. Old bill and robbers. Besides, I quite liked the idea of being a delivery man. It struck me as a simple way to make money. Brick and Gunhawk would place their order and I'd pick it up from my supplier and deliver it to them. Clean. Simple. Minimum of fuss or risk.

Brick and Gunhawk took ages to shift that first batch of rocks. A whole month, to be exact. This was much longer than I'd expected. Still, after that, they had me rushed off my feet going backwards and forwards between them and my supplier, who, annoyingly, lived all the way out in fucking Ealing. At one point I was making three, four trips there a week. I didn't half clock some miles on the old Bimmer. But I didn't complain. I was making a killing. All four parties were. We had a good thing going. It couldn't last.

The more time I spent with Brick and Gunhawk (we were hanging out loads now) the less I saw of Carlton. All our plans were going out the window. For instance, the new footie season was almost halfway gone and we'd not been to a single match. Not through any lack of effort on my part. I lost count of the amount of times I went round to Carlton's drum on a Saturday only for his old lady to tell me he was out and that she didn't know when he'd be back. He was clearly trying to avoid me. When I did manage to catch him – weekday evenings on the phone – he fobbed me off with excuses. History was repeating itself, only this time it was Carlton doing the snubbing. In the end I forced a showdown. He didn't pull his punches. To cut it short, I was a low-life and he wanted nothing more to do with me. We had a slanging match, nearly swapped blows, and haven't seen or spoken to each other since.

One night I was in New World when Brick told everyone to clear the office as there was business he had to discuss with me in private. As usual, Gunhawk was sitting next to him on the disused snooker table. Gunhawk spoke first.

'Where you been, man? We been belling you all day.'

'Really?' I got out my mobile. 'Shit. Switched off. Sorry.'

'That ain't good for business, Gabby,' said Brick.

'Yeah, I know.'

Gunhawk looked at his watch. 'Don't even bother, Hawk. Ain't making no run tonight, you get me? I'm whacked.'

I must have sounded convincing because Brick said: 'You're just running low, that's all. You need a boost.'

'A what?'

'A pick-me-up.'

'Fuck you talking about, Brick?' I asked. He looked at Gunhawk and they exchanged knowing smiles.

'You ain't got a clue, have you, Gabby?' said Gunhawk.

'What *are* you two going on about?'

'Listen, Gabby,' said Brick. 'For this life you need energy.

Energy's power. Power's strength. You gotta be strong to survive. There's stuff you can take to give you that strength.' I must have looked bewildered because he added: 'Let me ask you a question, Gabby. You ever smoke a rock?'

I was shocked, offended.

'You crazy? I said. 'I look like a fucking cat?'

'Do I look like one? Hawk look like one?'

'What you getting at, Brick? Empty the bin, for fuck's sake. Spill the rubbish, why don't you?'

'I'll show you what I'm getting at. Do the honours, Hawk.'

Gunhawk jumped off the table and went over to this small walk-in cupboard used for keeping mops and buckets and shit. He opened the door, bent down at the entrance, rummaged around for a second, then stood up again and closed the cupboard door. He'd had his back to me the whole time. When eventually he turned round I saw a strange-looking contraption in his hand. As he walked back to the snooker table I realised it was a small Evian bottle, half-full of dirty water, with what looked like half a biro sticking out of it. A home-made crack pipe. I'd not seen one before but I'd heard enough over the years to know what they looked like. Gunhawk jumped back onto the snooker table. By this time Brick had done something I'd not seen him do before. He'd lit a fag. I thought he was going to smoke it but instead he put it on the edge of the snooker table to burn. He then took the pipe from Gunhawk and wiped the foil-covered head. By now the fag had produced enough ash for him to tip and spread it over the pipe head. Gunhawk took a bag of rocks from his pocket (I couldn't believe it, after what had happened to Jeff), shook a few out, then put the bag back into his pocket. He gave a couple of the rocks to Brick who placed them, gingerly, on the bed of ash he'd prepared. Very carefully he put the stem of the pipe (the biro) into his mouth. Then, using his treasured gold Dunhill lighter, he started burning the rocks while sucking slowly on the stem. When the rocks burned out the pipe was full of smoke. With one, hoover-type suck, Brick cleaned it out. Gunhawk watched him almost enviously. Brick closed his eyes, held his breath, gave the pipe to Gunhawk (he immediately started to prepare it for his go), then, very slowly, let the smoke out through his nose. When he'd let it all out, he opened his eyes and looked at me. He didn't say anything for a while, just stared at me with a buffoonish grin on his face. I focused on his eyes to see how the rocks had affected him. He didn't seem altered in any way. Finally he said, a little breathlessly:

'Twice a day, every day. Do I look like a cat? Don't believe the hype, Gabby. Crack's all right. If you smoke it in moderation.'

Gunhawk had his go on the pipe. Like Brick, he didn't seem affected by it. He cleared the old ash from the pipe head and put on a fresh amount. Then he looked at me and said: 'Your turn.' It was more a dare than an invitation. I didn't say a word. For some reason I'd lost my ability to speak. There was stuff I wanted to say but the fascination of watching those two had struck me dumb. Gunhawk put two tiny rocks on the pipe head then brought it over to me and held it in front of my face. I looked at it, and was suddenly reminded of Adam being tempted in the garden of Eden. What I did next I've regretted ever since, and will go on regretting it for the rest of my days.

I'd heard stories from cats who claimed that the first 'lick' on a crack pipe was the greatest, the one that could never be repeated, no matter how many rocks you smoked for however many years. That's how they became cats, chasing that elusive first lick.

After my first lick I felt like Superman: more powerful than a locomotive, able to leap tall buildings at a single bound, faster than a speeding bullet. My heart was full of love for my two companions. I actually got up off my chair, went over to them and hugged them. 'You two,' I said, gushing. 'I love you two idiots. You're my brothers, you understand? My brothers. We're family. We got the same blood. Don't ever forget it. I love you.' I hugged them again. They pushed me away. It wasn't me talking but the rocks, they said, laughing. I cackled. Like a madman. I carried on expressing my love for them and for human beings generally. Suddenly I was the most tolerant, understanding, forgiving person alive. White people were all right. It was time we stopped blaming them for what their ancestors did to us. Pakis weren't as stuck-up as people made them out to be. Not all Africans hated West Indians. Jews had it in them to be generous. One day the Greeks and the Turks would settle their differences. Gays had rights. So did animals. Then I got all green. As masters of the planet, we had a duty to look after it. Deforestation had to stop. Recycling was the answer. There was far too much waste. Of everything. We had to stop taking the earth for granted.

'Shut the fuck up, Gabby,' said Gunhawk. 'Giving me a headache, na'am saying?'

I waved aside his protest and carried on babbling. I talked and talked for another hour before I realised I was on my own. Brick and Gunhawk were missing. I suddenly clammed up. The silence was deafening. I'd talked so much my mouth and lips were as dry as a stale rock cake. I suddenly felt scared, in mortal danger. I had to get out of that basement. Double fast. I dashed upstairs to the snooker hall hoping to quell my fears. Not a bit of it. As soon as I heard Brick shout from clear the other side of the hall 'Yo, Gabby, you back with us now, are you?' I knew I had to blow the gaff altogether. To avoid making eye-contact with anyone, I kept my head straight and headed briskly for the door. Just before I stepped through it I heard Gunhawk shout: 'Yo, Gabby! Stay sane!' Then I heard him and Brick cracking up. I ran out the door. Once outside, I sprinted to my ride, got in it and drove like a maniac towards my flat.

I woke the next morning feeling on top of the world, better than I'd felt in months. Suddenly the future didn't seem so bleak. I felt rejuvenated, energetic, alive. Brick was right. Smoking those rocks had done me the power of good. Not that I was planning to smoke the stuff on a regular basis. 'Crack's all right. If you smoke it in moderation.' Those words were to be my guide. For a time, anyway.

That morning, a Saturday, I got a letter from Jeff. It arrived almost a year to the day after he got sent down. It didn't say much. In fact it wasn't really a letter at all, more like two questions and a command. Why hadn't I been to see

Gloria? Didn't I take my responsibilities seriously? Come and see him for a 'chinwag'. He'd put a VO in the envelope. I had two weeks to use it. After that it lapsed. Visiting days were Saturdays and Sundays, between one and five. It felt strange holding that VO in my hand. I just kept looking at it and looking at it. And the more I looked at it the more I could see myself at Hollesley Bay. There I am doing circuit training, knackered as hell, but not half as knackered as Punk who's taking a roasting from Farquhart. Now I'm on the parade ground, trying to march in step. I can't. I'm giggling too much. Someone's just shouted 'Birdseye!' There's me in the TV room smoking Old Holborn and watching Trumpton. Fade to Horny Hornby's class. I'm in the front row of pupils, eyeing up her boobs. And finally, I see myself prancing round the unit, winding everyone up. 'Only ten and a breakfast now, boys.' Gate-Happy-Gabby. In the words of the Madness song: oh what fun we had. Somehow I didn't think Jeff was having fun. If I'd got his letter a week earlier, I'd have blown him out. But arriving when it did, feeling as good as I felt that morning, I knew I would drive down to the Ville that same afternoon.

The visiting hall was chocker with people. Parents, wives, girlfriends, kids, mates. The air was dense with smoke, close from the lack of adequate ventilation. Conversations merged into a hum. Kangas stood about the edges of the hall trying in vain to look discreet. Refreshments were being sold from a cubicle by a flustered-looking old biddy who was getting the most grief from the long queue of people waiting to be served. There were kids running amok everywhere. For the second time that day memories of Hollesley Bay came flooding back to me.

Jeff looked completely different to when I last saw him. He'd clearly been at the weights and was in the process of dreading his hair. But these were superficial changes. The most profoundly altered things about him were his eyes. They'd always been cold, full of menace, but now they looked dead, as if his soul had been drained away. Prison had done something to him, as if in the year he'd been locked up, he'd made some kind of pact with the Devil. We touched fists across the table.

'What's up, bro?' I asked.

'What's the coup, Gabby?'

'Oh, you know. Living and shit.'

'You don't sound too with it, blood.'

'I'm all right. I could do with a few more inches. But otherwise . . .' I trailed off.

'You ain't exactly short, you know?'

'I was on about my cock, actually.'

Without so much as a smile, he came straight to the point.

'I want you to keep an eye on Gloria for me,' he said. 'I don't trust her.'

So that's what he'd meant in his letter. He wanted me to spy on Gloria. I wasn't having it.

'I'm sorry, Jeff,' I said, shaking my head. 'But I just ain't gonna do that.'

He stared at me with those lifeless eyes, said 'Fuck you then, pussy,' then got up and stormed out the room. I didn't even get a chance to hand over the bag of weed I'd brought for him.

In the car on the way back to Hackney I felt as deflated as a flat tyre. What a contrast to how I'd woken up feeling. Trust Jeff to be the cause. As I put my foot down and raced towards New World, I realised that what I needed was a pick-me-up. I just didn't care any more. At this point in my life I'd all but given up the lingering hope of becoming anything other than what I was. At twenty-one I felt it was about time I accepted the cards life had dealt me. Especially since there was no one in my life to make me think otherwise. I was now more or less living at the snooker hall. The money kept rolling in. I was in my element as delivery man, on call to Brick and Gunhawk night and day. They'd turned the snooker club into the crack shop to end crack shops. You could hardly move for cats. The hash dealers were sick with jealousy. What they were making a week, Brick and Gunhawk were making in a day. This caused a lot of friction. Not a week went by when there wasn't some kind of flare up, usually Brick and Gunhawk clobbering or stabbing some would-be rival. When this wasn't happening, there were fights between the hash dealers themselves. They were all desperate to cling on to their share of a rapidly dwindling hash market. And there was yet more violence, of the casual type, meted out to the cats by all of us. I say casual because sometimes we slapped them around or kicked them up the arse or burnt them with our spliffs for no reason except the fact they were cats. We saw them as less than human, as filthy animals, and we treated them accordingly.

No matter how much I warned them, Brick and Gunhawk

just kept gobbing in the eye of caution. It wasn't in them to tone things down. Everything they did was loud and up front. It wasn't enough for them to be making shedloads, they wanted the world to know about it. They came to 'work' dripping in tom and decked out in designer fineries, their wallets bulging. No side road was good enough for their flash Bimmers. They parked them right outside the snooker club. Their braggadocio was sickly to behold. The more I observed them in action the more I realised how ridiculous me and Jeff must have looked during our time on the front. But at least in those days we had the excuse of being young and foolish. Brick and Gunhawk were approaching their mid-twenties, for fuck's sake. The way they were carrying on, it could only be a matter of time before they fucked things up for themselves, for me as well. I told them as much. They took not a blind bit of notice of me. Then one night two Yardies walked in.

THE YARDIES

It was like a scene from a Western. A couple of mean-looking coots walk into a noisy saloon-bar. The regulars, busy gambling, drinking and carousing with whores, suddenly go quiet. The piano player loses heart and closes the lid on his out-of-tune instrument. The 'strangers' walk up to the bar and order a bottle of whisky. The bartender, wary as hell, serves them without speaking. It's obvious to everyone that the presence of these two spells danger for the town. A little boy, who's been watching the scene from outside, peeping under the bar's swing doors, runs across town to alert the Sheriff. Minutes later the Sheriff walks in with his deputy. They go up to the bar, stand one either side of the 'strangers', then, after sizing them up for a second or two, start to question them as to their business in town.

Brick and Gunhawk, the Sheriff and deputy of New World, didn't dare approach our two 'strangers' and start questioning them. Instead we all watched as the two Yardies walked up to Pot-Belly Dave at the counter and ordered two shots of brandy. They downed these in one go then got Dave to give them a tray of snooker balls. Then they started scanning the hall, careful not to make eye-contact with any of us. When they had spotted the table they wanted to use, in the most remote corner of the hall, they got Dave to put its light on, then took the tray of balls over to it. For the next couple of hours they pretended to be engrossed in their session. In reality they were taking every opportunity to clock all that was going on around them. Eventually they made contact with us. One of them, a wiry character with scars all over his face, came over to our little corner near the counter. We immediately stopped talking. Addressing all of us, he asked: 'Yo, can get a draw a weed fi buy?'

We all looked at each other to see who'd be brave enough to answer him. Brick did.

'Ain't no weed, you know, bredren. Can get hash if you want, though.'

The Yardie shook his head and said: 'We nuh smoke dat, you see me? Respec still.'

And with that he turned on his heels and walked back down the long aisle to his friend at the table on the other side of the hall. They carried on playing snooker for maybe another hour then left. Believing that would be their one and only visit, we didn't bother discussing them once they'd gone, but my heart sank to my guts the next day when I saw those two Yardies walk in again. And this time they'd brought two more of their compadres with them.

That did it. We got together in the 'office'.

Since I was the only one there who'd had dealings with Yardies, I was asked to interpret the meaning of those four showing up like that, and to say what, if anything, should be done about them. Everyone looked so glum I tried to lighten the mood. I said that maybe our visitors only wanted to play snooker. I didn't get so much as a half-smile from any of them. I could have been Bernard Manning cracking jokes at an ANC rally. I straightened my face and told them the score.

Just like I'd suspected, word had got out about what was going down at New World. The Yardies had moved in looking for a piece of the action. It was as simple as that. As to what should be done, there were three options, each one carrying a certain amount of risk. One, we could allow the Yardies a share of the market. The risk here was that they might see this as weakness on our part and try to muscle us out and take control for themselves. Two, we could get militant. We could unite, open our blades and try to run them out of town. Big risk. If we went down that road, there was no doubt in my mind blood would be shed, a lot of it ours. Three, *we* could get out and try to establish ourselves some place else, leaving the snooker club to the Yardies. The risk here was obvious. Our livelihoods could be badly affected. There was no guarantee of finding another base. And even if we did it would take time – six months, a year – before we had it swinging.

When I'd finished my speech Gunhawk was the first to pipe up. Predictably, he was all for militancy. He wasn't about to share anything with the Yardies. And after all the hard slog he'd put into it, he certainly wasn't getting out and leaving the snooker club to them. He'd rather die first.

Then Brick had his say. He was as steely as Gunhawk in his determination to stay put, but he disagreed with his sidekick about taking on the Yardies. He was for option one, sharing, but he added a string: if and when the Yardies tried to take over then that would be the time to stand up and be counted.

The others were split. Half were ready to fight, half wanted to share. None wanted to get out. Indecisions, indecisions. Everyone looked at me. I felt like a committee chairman with a casting vote. Brick asked me what I would do. I hesitated a second then told him. Options one and two, I said, would lead inevitably to the same thing: violence. The only sane thing to do was to get out while the going was good. Gunhawk rained abuse on me. He called me a pussy, a weak-heart, a faggot. Then he started laying into the Yardies, saying how he had a good mind to go upstairs and show them what he was made of. Like a lot of British-born black guys, he hated Yardies. He was jealous of their fearsome reps.

As usual it was left to Brick to decide our fate. The Yardies would be allowed to deal if they wanted to. 'After all,' said Brick, 'it's a free country.' Gunhawk didn't like the decision one bit. He grumbled loads but in the end fell in line with his co-p. So did the half of the crew who'd backed his call for militancy. I hedged my bets. I'd hang around for the time being, but at the first sign of any trouble I'd be off. Gunhawk said that was typical of my yellowness. We had a quick slanging match before Brick intervened and broke up the gathering. Everyone started filing up the stairs. I stayed put. Brick was the last person through the door. At the top of the stairs he turned, realised I hadn't moved and said: 'What's up with you?'

'Hope you know what you're doing,' I said.

'I do. You coming up or what?'

'Nah. Gonna stay down here for a bit.'

'On your tod?'

'Yeah.'

'What for?'

I didn't answer him. I looked away, all guilty-like. He said: 'Remember, Gabby: moderation.'

Before I could say anything he was out. Seconds later I went over to the walk-in cupboard, opened it and got out the pipe.

We got to know the Yardies as Leffan, Indian, Radics and Scarface. Scarface was the ringleader. He was the one who approached us that first day looking to buy weed. I don't think I've ever known a more vicious-looking hombre. His face was criss-crossed with scars. His eyes were as slitty as Dr Fu Manchu and permanently bloodshot. Rumour had it that during the 1980 Jamaica general election he'd killed over a dozen people in one afternoon. Apparently he'd armed himself with an M16, crossed the 'border' into opposition territory (a shanty-town neighbouring his own), then set about kicking in doors and mowing down anything that moved, including cats and dogs. Even his cohorts seemed to fear him. And they themselves weren't without murderous reps.

They didn't give us any reason to think they would one day try and take over. In fact it was a couple of months before they even started to deal. Befriend the natives, gain their trust, then strike. This, we suspected, would be their tactic. So, try as they might, we never allowed them to get too close. It was a case of them and us. We tried to make that plain to them in our own (non-confrontational) way. They took the hint, and though they clearly had no intentions of going away, mostly kept to themselves. For a time, at least.

Before long they'd colonised a corner of the snooker hall. Yardie corner, we called it. I have to admit I found it fascinating to watch them. And to eavesdrop on them. They had their own particular take on everything. A kind of simple philosophy on life which, at least when they were all together, they stayed true to. For instance, now that they were in affluent Blighty, the only thing to do was make money. Anything else was both a distraction and a waste of time. In that sense they couldn't have arrived in Britain at a better time. Another thing they banged on about night and day was sex. To hear them talk you'd think they invented the bloody thing: how often they fucked, in how many positions, with what girls, how loud the girls screamed, how they begged for mercy, how they rated as ball-lickers, cock-suckers and cum-drinkers. To them, girls were good for one thing and one thing only, and if a girl got uppity with them their solution was simple: blows and babies. When they weren't dreaming of riches or talking about the mother of all orgasms, they spent their time holding kangaroo courts. They'd try, judge and sentence fictitious people who they called 'abominations'. Homosexuals, child molesters, people who practised incest, informers, corrupt politicians. They all deserved to be shot. Listening to them in this kind of mood always made my blood run cold. They seemed to whip each other into a frenzy and would strut about with their blades open and their eyes glaring, as if on the lookout for any 'abominations' who might be lurking nearby.

Shrewdly, they started selling weed, mostly to their Yardie

mates who came and went as if they owned the place, giving us all dirty looks. I say shrewdly because it was obviously an opening ploy to get amongst us. They knew we all smoked weed, and they clearly thought it was only a matter of time before we were buying from them. If that was their thinking, then they were dead right. We did start buying weed from them. From a convenience point of view it made sense. Now there was no need for us to go hunting a draw, we had it right there on the premises. And their stuff was bad. We're talking the living ses, the real McCoy. It was a pride thing with them. Any weed they sold they had to be able to smoke it themselves. And they smoked a lot of weed. Spliff after spliff as though they were smoking fags. And we thought *we* were ganga heads.

Once we started buying weed from them that was it, they were in. Suddenly they got all pally-pally with us, started calling us by our names instead of 'blood' or 'bredren' or 'soldier'. Now they made a point of mixing with us. They deserted Yardie corner and sought us out wherever we happened to be congregating. They wanted in on anything that was going down, from gambling in the 'office' to watching shoot-'em-up flicks on video in the TV room. They were eager to learn from us. As Brits (they actually saw us as British), we could teach them a few tricks on beating the system. They marvelled at our knowledge on how to commit benefit fraud, credit-card fraud, even TV licence fraud. If there was a corner to cut in their quest to make millions they wanted to know about it. They wanted to know about us, too, about our lives, which they saw as criminally privileged compared to their own. They couldn't understand why we were underachieving so badly with all the opportunities we had. How, they wanted to know, could a system that provided free schooling and social security from the cradle to the grave produce so many loafers? It was a good question, one we'd not been asked before, and we were unable to answer it, apart from blaming racism, of course.

By asking us about our life experiences, then comparing them to their own back in Jamaica, Scarface and his crew were able to shed some light for us on what it was like to live in a Kingston slum. All I can say is thank fuck I wasn't born in such a God-forsaken place. Maybe they overstated their case a little, the better to show contrast, but from what they told us, to say they'd known hardship would be like saying Nelson Mandela had spent a few years inside. No. They were brought up on a staple diet of poverty and violence. A lot of violence, illustrated by a story Leffan told us one day.

He was only about thirteen at the time but was already wanted for double murder. He'd shot dead two security guards while holding up a bank. He spent a year on the run before being captured. The police (acting, he claimed, on a tip-off) had cornered him at, of all places, his mum's. Speaking through a megaphone they ordered him to come out with his hands up, warning him it would be suicidal to try and escape since they had the area cordoned. He'd heard it all before and decided he would indeed try and escape. He said he checked the clip in his .44 automatic, brushed aside his mum who was bawling her eyes out and pleading with him to give himself up, opened the door to her wooden shack and started blazing away. Needless to say the police returned fire. When there was a lull in the exchange, Leffan decided to make a run for it, round the back, where there was a maze of alleyways. As soon as he came through the back door a sniper picked him off with a single bullet from an SLR rifle. He got hit in the back and the force of the shot pitched him forward onto his face. (At this point he lifted his silk shirt and showed us the scar from the entry wound.) His mum, hysterical, dashed from the house and flung herself on him to protect him from any more bullets. Seconds later the back yard was swarming with cops and onlookers from the hood. Leffan's mum was hauled away, wailing like a banshee. Leffan was then picked up and thrown into the back of an open-top jeep. A few of the onlookers ordered the police to take him straight to hospital, as he was clearly still alive. The police promised they would and screeched off, cries of 'murderers!' ringing in their ears.

They had no intention of driving Leffan to hospital. Instead, for the next half hour or so, they drove round and round hoping he would bleed to death. They kept checking him to see if he was still breathing. At one stage Leffan heard a couple of them saying to each other: 'This is a stubborn one, bwoy.' 'Can say that again.' 'Wha you say, shoot him again?' 'Could do, I s'pose.' 'You want to do it or . . .' 'Don't mind.' Leffan claimed that at this point he said a little prayer. He asked God to forgive him his sins then got ready to die. He'd barely finished praying when he heard the sudden, deafening noise of someone honking like mad on their car horn. Whoever it was, he knew they were right behind the jeep. Knowing this, he tried to slide to the edge of the jeep so he could signal to the irate driver. He summoned all the strength he had left and managed to move maybe two inches before he felt the weight of a boot on his back, pressing right on his wound. A puff of wind left his body and he passed out.

He came round the next day in hospital. His life had been spared after a bizarre sequence of events. It turned out that his mother and a few of her neighbours had driven straight to the hospital after the police had gone. With a head start on them, surely the police would already be at the hospital by the time they got there. They weren't, so something had obviously gone wrong. The hospital was only ten minutes from where the shooting happened, even allowing for traffic. Leffan's mum and her neighbours decided to take to the road and look for the jeep. They found it crawling down a deserted dust-road.

Leffan recovered fully from his injury. As a juvenile he spent just five years in prison for killing the two security guards. Worried that he might not live to see his nineteenth birthday, his mum scraped together her pennies and bought him a one-way ticket to England. When we met him he'd been in the country two years. He wasn't yet twenty-one.

There were other stories, too. Leffan had got his name because he'd had his left hand chopped off in prison, leaving him with a gnarled stump. Indian was so called because he was once almost scalped after being accused (wrongly, he claimed) of informing. Radics, when he was twelve, had had to stand by and watch his older sister gang-raped at gunpoint. And Scarface's mum was killed before he was out of infant school. She was kidnapped and tortured to death, the victim of mistaken identity. So yes, we heard other stories. But somehow, for me at least, the one Leffan told us about the time he was shot, seemed to sum up the contrast between our upbringing and theirs; comfy on the one hand, hellish on the other. I felt sorry for them, in as much as you can feel sorry for self-confessed killers.

Slowly but surely the tension eased between us and them. I'd even go as far as to say they became part of our crew. It was soon clear to us they had no plans to take over the snooker club. Indeed they spelt out exactly what their plans were.

For the foreseeable future they'd go on selling weed. Yes they knew there was more money in crack but they were doing all right and didn't see the need to tread on anyone's toes. After all they'd been through, with all the hype that surrounded them wherever they went, they wanted the quiet life. Besides, they'd grown to like us. We'd treated them with patience and respect (they were big on being respected). So it was only fair they treated us likewise. As far as they were concerned we all had a good thing going. Everyone was making it and they didn't want to see the boat rocked. And it wouldn't be, not if they had anything to do with it. They guaranteed us they'd allow no outsiders, Yardies or otherwise, to come in and try to take food from our mouths. They assured us we needn't fear anyone while they were around. They'd come to regard us as family, as brothers, and said they'd never stand by and watch any of us being taken advantage of. To put it bluntly, they swore their allegiance to us. In the face of such devotion it was only right that we should swear ours to them. Even Gunhawk allowed himself to be won round, grudgingly.

So we'd misjudged them. Yet we didn't feel guilty about it, more relieved. Not only that, once we knew they were in our corner, we felt invincible, untouchable from anyone, except, of course, those boys in blue.

While all this Yardie stuff was going on my crack smoking had got steadily worse. Now I couldn't go more than a few hours without wanting to blaze some stones. I'd even started free-basing at home, on my own. Not a good sign. At New World I was forever sneaking down to the 'office' for a quick lick of the pipe. When I wasn't doing that I was sucking on crack-and-ses cocktail spliffs. The crew took to warning me. I was fast becoming a cat, they said. I laughed at them. I told them cats didn't dress the way I did, or make the money I did, or drive 3-series BMWs. They countered by saying no, cats didn't, as a rule, drive Bimmers, but, like me, they couldn't keep still or in one place for long, the word 'food' meant fuck-all to them, and paranoia was their constant companion. I couldn't argue with that. Most of the time I was a bundle of nerves, I survived on crisps, and only God himself could have convinced me I wasn't being followed everywhere by the old bill.

Brick and Gunhawk were especially worried about me. They had vested interests in making sure I didn't lose the plot. I was their meal ticket, a situation they were finding harder and harder to deal with. Time and again they tried to get me to introduce them to my man in Ealing. I blew them off every time. I'd lie and say my man wouldn't deal with anyone but me. The truth was I wanted to keep the set-up as it was because it made life easy for me.

The more crack I smoked the more the crew froze me out. They still hung out with me and talked to me and shit, but

I knew I wasn't part of the inner circle any more. Even the Yardies had more status than me. Though I tried not to show it, I was hurting like hell. I couldn't work out what the fuck I'd done to deserve the cold shoulder. OK, so I was smoking a few rocks now and then. Big fucking deal. It wasn't like I was the only one. Brick and Gunhawk were still licking their pipe 'twice a day, every day'. No one said anything to them. Oh no. They saved their scorn for me. God only knows why. I was hardly a junkie. Talk about overreacting.

I was at my wits' end as to what to do. I didn't want to force myself on the crew like some love-starved puppy, yet I felt so isolated and alone that many a night I went home and sobbed, which, funnily enough, made me smoke even more rocks. I was caught in a vicious circle. Something had to give.

Around this time, things started coming to a head at New World. There were a couple of low-key raids. No one got nicked but the old bill frightened off everyone except Brick and Gunhawk. The Yardies were the first to bolt. For them it wasn't only a question of doing bird, they risked deportation as well. Having to go back to Jamaica and dodge bullets was something they'd have done anything to avoid. The hash dealers got out as well. Their market had been slowly dying on them, anyway. It started from the moment Brick and Gunhawk ran the Turks off the premises. No doubt they would have liked to get in on the crack business, but, lacking the balls to take on Brick and Gunhawk, they used the raids as an excuse to move on. Only Brick and Gunhawk stood firm. They were going nowhere. So long as cats kept coming through the door, they'd be there to serve them. Police or no, they aimed to go on dealing for as long as possible. Which meant, of course, that in my role as delivery man I would go on making money for as long as they did. Or so I thought. I was gobsmacked the day they told me they didn't need my services any more, that they'd found their own supplier.

My income dried up overnight. I panicked. I couldn't work out my next move. Back to dealing, maybe. Not a chance. That would have been too much of a head-fuck, a bit like a Vietnam vet donning his fatigues again for more skirmishes in the jungle. I just didn't have the bottle for that kind of lifestyle, my arse had gone. I was too paranoid the whole time.

Actually, my situation wasn't quite as urgent as all that. If I hadn't been so cracked up to my eyeballs I would have realised this. The fact was, by saving my money like a good boy, I'd bought myself some time, time enough to take stock of where I now was and where I wanted to go. The trouble was I didn't know where I wanted to go. I'd never known.

STRUNG OUT

I became a hermit. Apart from weekly stock-up trips to Ealing I didn't leave my flat for months. I cut off my house phone and mobile. I didn't want to see or speak to anyone. There could be no distractions from what I aimed to do, which was to smoke myself into oblivion.

I finally emerged from my flat a fully-fledged junkie. And skint, to boot. And ripe for some serious asset-stripping. First to go was the tom. Then everything in the flat, including the shag-pile carpet. Then finally the ride. The only things I had left to call my own were the smelly clothes on my back.

I saw my man in Ealing less and less. He dealt only in bulk. I could now afford just a few stones at a time. I saw him when I had no choice, when there were droughts in the hood. And I didn't like going to see him even at those times. I didn't like him to see how far I'd fallen. Plus I always had to beg him to serve me, even though I'd been putting good business his way for years. Mostly I was forced to score closer to home, from dealers who abused me verbally and physically even as they were taking my money. I wasn't bothered. If their shit was good they could slap me around and call me names to their hearts' content.

They weren't easy to find, these dealers. The police had really turned the heat up on them, driven them underground. Crack dealing – dealing of any class-A drug – was no longer for the faint-hearted. The courts were now dishing out stiff sentences, as much as ten years in some cases, first offence or no. Serious bird. I knew dealers who quit the game for fear of spending that length of time inside. And the ones who didn't had to keep their wits about them at all times. Even so, I was like a bloodhound when it came to sniffing them out. No matter where they happened to be holed up I'd find them. So long as I kept my ear tuned to the junkie grapevine I had no problem scoring.

What I did have problems with was coming up with the money to score. It got to the stage where I was devoting more time and energy to that than actually licking my pipe. I resorted to petty crime. I went full circle back to the adolescent capers me and Jeff got into after leaving school: strolling into offices and lifting wallets and purses, grabbing money from shop tills, snatching handbags, pick-pocketing. As a teenager I'd had a devil-may-care attitude towards that kind of stuff. I'd been totally blind to the consequences of being caught. Eight weeks' DC had knocked that giddiness out of me for good. So that now, when I was forced to hit the bricks daily in order to get my hands on some quick cash, my arse would twitch at the thought of getting nicked. No matter. Driven by a force too powerful to deny, my cowardice always went out the window at the decisive moment.

In any case, there were other things for me to worry about besides getting nicked, what you might call the occupational hazards of your average petty crook. I got cornered in offices and had to kick, punch, scratch and bite my way out. I had shop tills slammed shut against my fingers. Fleeing with handbags, I had vigilantes chase me down till I got so knackered I had to stop running, turn, open the dull little blade I always carried with me, and frighten them off. Picking pockets, I ended up with fat eyes, fat lips and broken teeth. It was all in a day's work.

For me, one of the most depressing things about being a junkie was the company I was forced to keep: other junkies. It never ceased to amaze me how much they'd deteriorate from one day to the next. It was like watching one of those speeded-up nature films. I didn't like to think that the same thing was happening to me.

But everybody needs somebody. I certainly needed the companionship of my fellow cats. There was a bond between us, strong and deep, the kind that exists between any reviled group of people in any society anywhere in the world. We had things in common that linked us together almost umbilically. We shared the same fucked-up experiences, harboured the same unrealistic dreams, whinged about the same mistakes we'd made. When we got together around a crack pipe the atmosphere could get almost spiritual, so intent were we on baring our souls to each other. That's why if you give crack heads the choice of smoking on their own or in groups, they choose groups every time.

I soon learned that there were certain cats you just didn't

smoke with. These were cats who had the ability to fuck up a vibe by the way they behaved when they got the lick. Unhinged is the word that springs to mind. For instance, there's your 'hummers'. Between licks they'll sit cross-legged on the floor, eyes closed, hands clasped in the praying position, humming to themselves like Zen Buddhists. There's your paro cats. Now every cat's paranoid to a certain extent. It's part of what defines them. But there's paranoia and there's paranoia. Most cats, like I did, suffer from it mildly. Others, like some I made the mistake of smoking with a few times, have really got it bad. When smoking indoors they have to have their backs against the wall at all times in case they get bludgeoned from behind by one of their countless enemies, real and imagined. If they're smoking outside, to put themselves out of harm's way, they'll think nothing of climbing trees. They really have to be seen to be believed. And finally there's your pervs. Crack makes these lot so randy they won't think twice about whipping out their tools and tugging them off all over the shop. Yep, I realised that cats like these had to be avoided at all costs.

The bunch I ended up running with were cut from a different cloth altogether. Sure, they had no illusions about what they were, they accepted they were junkies, were only too aware of their status in the manor (scum), but that didn't mean they lacked dignity, self-respect, pride, feelings. The fact that they acted like animals didn't mean they actually *were* animals. They did look rough, they smelt, they couldn't, by and large, be trusted, but how much of that was their true character and how much down to the crack? To them, if not to others, the answer was obvious. It didn't strictly follow that they planned to stay in the gutter for ever. In fact the opposite was true. Most of the cats I ran with would have sacrificed a testicle if it meant they could come off crack. They'd tried all sorts in an effort to kick their habits. I wanted some of that stubborn hope to rub off on me. I wasn't planning on being a junkie the rest of my life.

My flat became a crack den. My cat mates came and went as they pleased. We used it as our base, took to calling it HQ. Some of them even took up permanent residence there. I didn't mind, companionship was important to me. Not that it was the only reason I let them use the place. No. They had to weigh me off with crack for the privilege of kipping on my floorboards. As rap stars are always reminding us, 'you gots to get paid'. Too right.

My neighbours in the building soon worked out what was happening. They got on to Hackney Council who sent me the most threatening letters. I'd be evicted if I didn't stop being a nuisance to the other tenants; if I didn't 'refrain from illegal activities on council property'; if I failed to 'clear the considerable rent arrears which has steadily built up in the last year'. I say they sent these letters to me, in actual fact they were addressed to a Mr A. Benjamin, an identity I'd been assuming for some time. After a while I wrote back to the council. I told them that whoever A. Benjamin was he'd long gone, that I, G. Power, was now living at the address, having found the property empty. I told them I was squatting and that I knew my rights as a squatter. I never heard from them again. As for my neighbours, let down by the jokers at Hackney Town Hall, they had no choice but to put up with it.

As known junkies, we were easy targets for any old John, Jim and Jeffrey to pick on. We were persecuted. Shop keepers wouldn't let us on their premises, as if we didn't need milk and bread like everyone else. Bus drivers never stopped for us, nor cab drivers. Mums frowned if their babes-in-arms so much as looked at us. People crossed roads to avoid us. The old bill stopped us simply for something to do. Tearaway kids stoned us then set their dads on us for boxing their ears. All this on top of what we had to go through to raise cash to feed our habits. No wonder it was such a wrench for us to leave HQ when the crack ran out. The streets held real terror for us. And for me personally there was the added terror of bumping into my brothers.

Devon and Malcolm had taken it on themselves to clean me up. They weren't, they assured me, going to stand by and watch me slowly kill myself. Two, three times a week they'd barge into HQ, physically remove my weakling cat mates, smash to smithereens our crack smoking equipment, then start knocking me about in order to knock some sense into me. They'd leave me battered and bruised and plotting how I would murder them when the time was right.

That was indoors. If I ran into them on the street they'd grab me by the scruff of the neck, frisk me down in full view of Joe Public, confiscate my rocks (if I had any on me), slap me around a little, then send me packing, warning me to 'get with the programme' before it was too late. They really thought they were helping me, but all they were doing was terrorising me. My own brothers. Then, obviously realising they'd never get through to me with violence, they went from one extreme to the other. They stopped coming round to HQ. And if they saw me in the street they ignored me. They effectively disowned me.

In times of drought some crack heads make do with whatever substitutes they can lay their hands on. They'll take speed, acid, amyl nitrate, heroin, whatever they can find to tide them over till the crack market picks up again. Others travel far and wide in search of their fool's gold. I was one of those. My hunt would take me all over London, starting with areas notorious for crack, like Finsbury Park and Tottenham. If these sources were dry, I'd end up in areas as far afield as Kilburn and Harlesden. Once or twice I even crossed the water to Brixton. If I didn't manage to score in any of these places then I'd swallow my pride and get on the tube to Ealing.

Since I wasn't known in most of these manors, I was able to get away – literally get away – with stuff I couldn't have got away with in Hackney. I robbed people left, right and centre, knowing it would be months before they saw my face again, by which time they would have forgotten what I looked like. As well as civilians, I also robbed dealers, grabbing their stash and fleeing for my life. A risky business, but I always targeted street-corner dealers, lone figures, relatively new to the game, desperate for trade, young bods with a lot to learn, basically.

During this whole period, the one place I refused to go and score was New World. The police were apparently still raiding the place regular as clockwork. They always came away empty-handed: no drugs found, no arrests made. Obviously fed up with the fact that Brick and Gunhawk kept slipping through their fingers, they put pressure on the owners to put their house in order or face closure, maybe even prosecution for 'harbouring'. The owners had to get tough. They installed security cameras. They put up signs outlawing both the use and selling of illegal substances. The staff were told to report anyone found breaking either rule. Admittance was tightened, as it was in the days when me and Carlton first started going there. Tighter, in fact. Now guests were banned. Even the opening time changed, from twenty-four hours to twelve. By midnight everyone had to vacate the premises. Brick and Gunhawk finally bowed out. Soon afterwards New World Snooker Club ceased to exist. It was burned to the ground in an arson attack.

There'd been a drought on for weeks. I'd traipsed all over London trying to sniff out some crack. There was nothing doing anywhere. I had no choice but to go and see Levi, my man in Ealing. I was desperate. I went to his house and begged him to serve me but he refused and sent me away. I had to endure a miserable tube ride back to Hackney. To break up the journey I started reading the names of all the stations on the Central Line. Buckhurst Hill, Loughton, Debden. Right backwaters. I got depressed just thinking about them. After a while I got bored trying to imagine life in Fairlop or Hainault, and instead started looking round the carriage at the few people in it with me. I knew they'd all been staring at me. Now, caught out, they looked away. Fuck 'em all, I thought. I decided to stare at the window opposite me, at my reflection. I was shocked when I saw it. A skeleton in a baseball cap was staring back at me. I lowered my eyes, overcome with shame. That's when I noticed it. On the seat next to mine. I reached over, picked it up, scanned the first page, then scrunched it into a ball and dropped it on the floor. I just couldn't believe it. What were the odds? I thought. What were the odds of me, feeling as I did at that exact moment, finding some pamphlet entitled: 'Kick That Habit: How To Give Up Narcotics'? What were the odds of that? A zillion to one? I felt like Elvis, all shook up. I looked round the carriage again. My fellow travellers, caught out again, all looked away. I wanted to be on that tube about as much as a budgie in a cage. Finally it pulled into Bethnal Green station. I was standing in front of the doors well before they were due to open. When they did, without thinking, I turned round, swooped on the ball of paper, stuffed it hastily into my pocket, then jumped off the tube just as the doors were about to close.

A few days later I went to see Brick and Gunhawk. I hadn't seen them since I'd got out of New World. Rumour had it they were now outing their rocks from Aces, a run-down nightclub in the manor. Norris – the owner, a skinflint Bajan – was always on the lookout for easy money, and was apparently letting them deal from his place in exchange for regular backhanders. When I first heard this rumour I couldn't help but think Brick and Gunhawk had landed on their feet, since they were, in effect, not only paying Norris to look the other way, but through him they were also paying the old bill to look the other way.

Benjy, the doorman, opened the flap in the door and put his face in it.

'Three pounds,' he said.

'Benje, man. It's me.'

He cocked his head to one side and gave me a funny look.

'Me know you?' he asked.

'Course you do, you big oaf. It's me, innit? Gabby.'

He pulled back a little, the better to examine my face.

'Youngster? Is you that?' I nodded eagerly. 'Well bless my soul. What the raas happen to you, bwoy?' I lowered my eyes. 'Oh, don't tell me. Let me guess. You smoking that blasted crack business, right?' I kept my eyes fixed on my battered, stinking trainers. 'Well,' said Benjy. 'All me can say is you really, really let me down, Youngster. Me never think for a minute that you . . .' he pulled up. Even with my eyes lowered I could tell he was shaking his head. Eventually he added: 'So you going to stand there looking at the pavement all night?' By the time I lifted my head he was already holding the door open for me. I smiled guiltily at him. He gave me a look bursting with pity and regret.

It was empty inside. For a second I thought about jumping over the bar and robbing the till, but then thought better of it. I headed for the toilets. I saw Sharon, the barmaid, coming out of the ladies. She cut her eye at me and walked by without saying a word. Like Benjy she hadn't recognised me. I ogled her as she walked by. She looked as fit as ever. Tits and arse packed tightly into her black boob-tube, thighs and calves rippling as she tottered off in her black stilettos. The girl was sex on legs. I shook the image of her naked body from my mind and pushed open the door to the men's loo.

I stood in the doorway holding the door open with my foot. Our eyes met. They then looked at each other and smiled.

Unlike Benjy and Sharon, they definitely did recognise me. There was maybe a ten-second silence before Brick said: 'Well, well, look who it aint.'

'Heard you were dead,' said Gunhawk. 'OD'd.'

'He might as well be, by the looks of him,' said Brick.

They punched fists and laughed. God, they were funny. I stood in the doorway watching them, trying to keep as serious a face on me as possible, hoping to freak them out with my madman's eyes, my 'here-to-kill-you' zombie stare. The ploy worked, because Gunhawk was clearly spooked. I relaxed my face and smiled, which seemed to unsettle them even more. They tensed up, ready for I didn't know what. I was sure I even saw Brick feeling his back pocket for his blade.

'Relax you two,' I said eventually. 'I'm here on business.'

We took Gunhawk's spoiler-covered six-series Bimmer. The two of them sat up front in stony silence. I sat in the back trying to steady my shaky nerves. Gunhawk kept staring at me through the rear-view mirror. He must have noticed the state I was in because at one point he said: 'You sure you're up to this, Gabby?'

'Just drive the car,' I replied, then turned and stared out the window.

Half an hour later we pulled up outside Levi's drum. Gunhawk killed his lights and his engine. 'Right, then,' he said. 'Let's make this shit happen.' He opened the glove compartment and, to my horror, took out a gun: his infamous German Luger.

'What the fuck you doing?' I shrieked.

'Get a grip, Gabby,' said Brick. 'We haven't come all this way to play.'

'But . . .' I sputtered.

'But what? asked Gunhawk. 'What did you expect? Knuckle dusters?'

'Look, Gabby,' said Brick. 'Don't go pussying out on us now. Just do your bit and leave the rest to us. Let's go.'

We got out of the car and strode purposefully across the quiet road and up the stairs to Levi's front door. Brick and Gunhawk positioned themselves to one side of it, away from the peep-hole. They nodded at me to say they were ready. My heart was racing like mad. Suddenly I had a bad feeling about the whole thing. My bottle was going. I looked at Brick and Gunhawk. With their eyes they told me to get on with it. I took a deep breath and rang the doorbell. There was no going back now. Levi took ten years to answer the door. I heard him dragging his feet along the corridor, after which there was a brief silence while he spied on me through the peep-hole. Then . . .

'Gabby?! What the . . . Right! That's it. I fucking warned you not to come back here.'

He started to unlock the door. It took him a while due to all the security locks. Eventually the door swung open. I didn't see the fury in his eyes, only that he had nothing on but his boxer shorts. He lunged at me with his fist. I stepped back out the way. His momentum carried him out onto the steps. Brick and Gunhawk stepped forward. Levi clocked them. We all froze for a second. Brick was the first to thaw. He calmly put the muzzle of the gun to Levi's forehead and ordered him back inside. Levi did as he was told without a squeak.

Knowing the layout of the gaff, I rushed ahead into the front room. Pearl was in there. Levi's bit of stuff. Fit. Black as the ace of spades. Bald. Wearing a white bra and white knickers. She'd been snorting charlie, white lines round the edges of her nostrils. I'd forgotten all about her. As soon as we came into the room she started screaming down the place. Brick pointed the gun at her and said: 'Shut the fuck up, bitch.' She swallowed her screams instantly. Brick then ordered her and Levi to kneel with their hands behind their heads facing the wall. He was conducting the whole business with the flair of a character from the *Godfather*, his favourite film. Speaking calmly, he said:

'Right. Let's not waste time. We want the money and the rocks. The sooner we get it the sooner we'll be out of your hair.' He looked at Pearl, chuckled, then added: 'Or bald head, as the case may be.' He chuckled at his own joke. 'So. Start talking.'

'You might as well shoot me,' said Levi, ''cause I ain't telling you fuck all.'

Brick looked at Gunhawk and smiled and said: 'Have it your way, hombre.'

He went over and pointed the gun at Levi's head.

'What the fuck you doing?' I shouted, terrified.

'Button it,' said Gunhawk.

'Fuck you,' I said. 'Didn't come here to kill no one.'

'If you don't shut the fuck up,' said Gunhawk, 'you might get it.'

Pearl started to whimper, like a dog expecting rain. Brick took careful aim then . . . BANG!!! . . . shot Levi in the back of the leg. My heart almost gave out. Gunhawk looked awe-struck. Levi groaned and rolled over on his side, clutching his leg, blood slowly trickling through his fingers. Pearl screamed. Brick walked over to her, trained the gun on her and said: 'Shut up. Shut up, I tell you. I swear, bitch, I'll fly your brains.'

Pearl did her best to calm down, her screams now a kind of breathless panting, almost like hiccups.

'Now, then,' said Brick. 'I'm trying not to lose it here, but I mean it, unless one of you starts talking soon . . .' He shook his head at the thought of what he would do.

'I know where it is,' said Pearl, wimpering.

'What was that?' asked Brick.

'Shut your fucking mouth, Pearl,' groaned Levi, clutching his leg.

'No, Levi!' screamed Pearl. 'They'll kill us both.'

'Smart Doris,' said Gunhawk.

'Talk, bitch,' said Brick.

Mustering all his strength, Levi shouted: 'PEARL!!!'

'You got five seconds,' said Brick to Pearl. 'One. Two. Three. Four. Fi . . .'

'Inaspeakerboxupstairsinthebedroom,' Pearl blurted out in the nick of time.

'Foolish, bitch,' said Levi, his voice a hoarse whisper now. He groaned and clutched his leg. Brick nodded at Gunhawk who quickly left the room. 'Foolish fucking bitch,' Levi repeated.

'No she ain't,' said Brick. 'She's smart.' He ran the muzzle of the gun over her left breast. 'And fit.'

'You better finish me off, pussy,' said Levi, grimacing, ''cause if I ever see you again, you're dead. You hear me, dead!' He groaned and gritted his teeth and clutched his leg. Gunhawk came back smiling and holding up a plastic shopping bag, as if he'd just won a trophy and was posing for the cameras.

Brick walked over to Gunhawk, took the bag, looked inside it, smiled, gave the bag back to Gunhawk, then turned to Levi and Pearl and said: 'Peace and love, kids. We're out.'

He tucked the gun into his trouser waist, took one last look at our brutalised victims, then we blew the gaff.

An hour later we pulled up outside my drum. It was time to divvy up the spoils. Brick chucked two coin bags full of rocks at me and said: 'Kill yourself.'

'Yeah,' I said. 'And the rest.'

'Don't push your luck, Gabby,' said Brick. 'Now get the fuck out the car before we change our minds and you end up with jack shit.'

'But . . .'

'You still here?' asked Gunhawk, cutting me off.

They turned their backs on me. I sat there watching them, seriously tempted to throw my arms round their necks. But then I remembered how weak I was. I couldn't have strangled a chicken let alone two strapping guys like them. And they were armed. I didn't want to end up like Levi. Without another word to them, I calmly got out of the car. Within seconds they'd screeched away, beeping me tauntingly.

I found a few of my cat mates indoors. They didn't hear me come in. They were sitting on the dusty floorboards, in a circle, round a lit candle, as if they were practising witchcraft, every jack one of them gouching. In the circle I noticed the remains of a heroin binge: stained silver foil, burnt matches, needles. The crack drought had driven them to extremes. My heart bled for them. I thought, if their mothers could see them now. I threw a bag of rocks into the circle. The sound of it hitting the floorboards woke them with a start. They fell on it like a pack of starved wolves. I said I was going into my bedroom and that I didn't want to be disturbed. I might as well have been talking to myself. I shook my head and went next door.

Twelve hours later I came to in Hackney Hospital. A nurse was sitting beside my bed. She said: 'Hello there.' I was struggling to keep my eyes open. 'You're OK,' said the nurse. 'You're in Hackney Hospital.' I tried to speak. I had questions. 'Don't,' said the nurse. 'Just lie there. Take it easy.' Within seconds of her saying that I was out again. When I woke up again some four hours later, a doctor was standing beside my bed: white coat, stethoscope, professional smile. She said: 'Back with us, are we? How do you feel?' What a question, I thought. 'You gave us all a bit of scare, young man. You ought to try giving up, you know. That stuff's no good for you.' I smiled weakly. She could have been talking about caffeine. 'You're extremely lucky, you know that? If it hadn't been for your friends, if you'd been alone . . .' I didn't hear the rest. Not till much later, when my 'friends' came in to see me. By now I was feeling slightly better.

This is what I remember of it. I'd gone into the bedroom with the intention of getting out of my tree. I got my pipe ready and put two fat stones on it. Just as I was about to spark them, I suddenly felt cold. Scratch that. I was suddenly freezing. I couldn't work it out. It wasn't a particularly cold night. Yet there I was shivering. Anyway, I put it from my mind, deciding that the temperature must have suddenly dropped. I sparked my stones. Nothing. Maybe I hadn't burned them right, or they weren't big enough, or I'd inhaled too quickly, or too slowly. I put on four the next time, all fatter than the first two. I sparked these extra-carefully, taking my time to fill the pipe with smoke before taking the lot into my lungs. I sat back and waited. Still nothing. I was getting angry and frustrated. I reloaded the pipe, this time putting on six stones. I remember thinking how ridiculous the pipe-head looked with all those stones crammed onto it. I sparked them. It took me ages to burn them out. By the time it came to clearing the smoke I had fuck all air left in my lungs. I went for it anyway. That's it. I don't remember any more.

According to my cat mates, this is what happened next.

They were in the front room debating whether to knock on my door and ask me for more stones. Suddenly they heard some 'fucked up' noises coming from my bedroom. They went and investigated and were shocked to find me on the floor, on my back, convulsing and frothing at the mouth. They did what they could for me on the spot – freed my tongue and turned me over so I didn't choke on my own vomit – then called an ambulance.

With tears streaming down my cheeks, I told them I owed

them my life. They waved me away all modest-like, promised to visit me again the next day, then left. The nurse fussed over me for a while – she plumped my pillows, straightened my covers, lowered my bed – before she too left. In no time at all I'd drifted off again.

I slept right through the night and woke up around midday the next day, starving. Every other bed on the ward was empty. Unlike the day before when they were all occupied by wheezy old men and blue-rinsed old women. I rang for a nurse. One showed up two years later. I complained that she'd taken her time. She said I wasn't the only patient on the ward. I didn't care for her tone. I wanted the other nurse, I said. The one who'd tended me the day before. She was off duty. I asked if there was any chance of something to eat. The bossy nurse told me I'd missed breakfast and that lunch wasn't for another hour. I groaned. Bossy asked me if I'd like something to drink, a cuppa maybe. I shook my head and asked her what had happened to all the old fogies and, more to the point, why had I been put into the geriatric ward with them. She answered the second part of my question first. I was on that ward due to a shortage of beds elsewhere in the hospital. As to the first part of my question, the other patients were all watching TV in the TV room and would be back on the ward in time for lunch. I made up my mind there and then. I wasn't going to be around when the oldsters got back. Despite protests from Bossy, I quickly hauled on my garms and discharged myself.

It was a warm spring afternoon. With no real idea where I was going, I somehow ended up in Downs Park. The walk from Hackney Hospital left me feeling knackered and ready to collapse. I slumped onto the first park bench I came across, even though it was next to a stinking rubbish bin and was covered in mildew and pigeon shit. From where I sat I could see my old school, closed now for the Easter break. The memory of my time there came flooding back. No matter how hard I tried not to, I couldn't help but think those had been wasted years. And there'd been no improvement in the subsequent ones. A summary of my life to that point made sorry reading. Shameful past, blighted present, bleak future. The future. 'You ought to try giving up.' I smiled at the thought. Easier said than done, Doc.

I looked round the park. Brilliant sunshine, majestic trees swaying in the wind, green grass, birdsong, parents playing with their kids, lovers canoodling. A strange feeling came over me. How can I describe it? The best way, I think, is to go for contrast. Where I was freezing the night of my overdose, now I was burning up. From inside. I felt like I'd eaten a dozen chilli peppers raw. A few days earlier I would have panicked and fled the park. That afternoon I was anything but panicky. Maybe it had something to do with coming so close to death. Once you've stared the grim reaper in the eye, maybe nothing can ever panic you again.

Eventually the heat died, leaving in its place a tremendous feeling of well-being. I felt calm. Truly calm. I started to cry. The tears streamed down my cheeks in bucket loads. They were tears of joy. I knew without a shadow of doubt that what I was experiencing wasn't of this world. And whatever it was I didn't want it to end. I was, as religious types say, in rapture. 'You ought to try giving up.' Once again I smiled at the thought, only this time, instead of dismissing it, I took from my pocket the crushed pamphlet I'd found on the tube.

EPILOGUE

Gabriel felt the time had come for him to move on. He had got all he could from the house. The staff disagreed. They thought he was ill-prepared to go back out into the world. They tried talking to him but he was resolved. As a result, they decided to do all they could to help him make the transition.

They put him in touch with the Portobello Small Jobs Project, an agency devoted to finding cash-in-hand work for the long-term unemployed. He signed up as a general handy-man and managed to get work almost immediately. And on a daily basis for the rest of that summer. Gardener. Window cleaner. Messenger. Dog-walker. Cat-sitter. Leaflet-distributor. The agency had so much work on he was able, at various times, to pick and choose his jobs. Compared to the sums he used to handle, the money was not great. He was not bothered. Doing an honest day's work was reward enough. In any case, his measly earnings were considerably augmented by all the things he got given for jobs well done. One old woman, noticing how he eyed up her bookshelves whenever he came round to vacuum her house, said he could have her entire collection of John le Carré paperbacks. Another woman, a widow (he did a lot of jobs for rich old widows), who lived in Holland Park and for whom he did a bit of gardening, gave him an electronic typewriter she no longer used. He could hardly believe his luck. It was in perfect working order and just the thing, he decided, for typing up his manuscript.

Two weeks after telling them he was leaving, he found himself being taken by the staff to view property. He was surprised at how quickly they had got things moving, and wondered, in spite of evidence to the contrary, whether they were in a hurry to see the back of him.

The first two flats he rejected out of hand, but the third, a conversion job on the fourth floor of a five-storey mansion block on Cambridge Gardens, was perfect. It was just a stone's throw from Marcus's place and exactly the kind of thing he had hoped for, in exactly the right location. The gods had smiled on him.

The build-up to the carnival had everyone in the house feeling excited. Especially Gabriel, who had not been to one before. Marcus was shocked by this admission: 'You really is a strange one, Gabby, boy. You don't smoke weed and you never been to a carnival. What kind of black man you call yourself?'

With a week to go the preparations gathered momentum. Bunting. Posters. The sound of steel bands practising. The whole area was abuzz with anticipation. The talk on the streets, in bars and cafés, was of nothing but the upcoming festivities. There was a consensus of opinion. That year's carnival would be the biggest and best to date.

When it finally arrived, the first day was a complete washout. It rained steadily and heavily from daybreak till dawn. People stayed away in their droves. There seemed to be more police out than revellers. Those who did brave the elements got soaked through. The procession snaked its route devoid of its usual mass, whistle-blowing following. By seven o' clock the streets were dead. No one in the house ventured out that day.

The following day the weather improved dramatically and Gabriel spent the first half of it with Marcus under the Westway on Portobello Green. Neither of them were able to move much due to the crush. They suffered a succession of minor reggae singers doing battle with a dodgy PA system. By lunch-time they had had enough. Marcus went off to check out some ragga sounds. Gabriel went and met up with Marcia in Talbot Square, having agreed to do so earlier that morning.

Out of curiosity, they decided to go and seek out one of the many acid-house sound systems playing at the carnival that year, acid-house being the musical phenomenon of the year. But no sooner had they started walking than Gabriel said: 'Shit! Let's go back.'

'Let's do what?'

'Too late. He's clocked me.'

'Yo, yo, yo,' said Jeff. 'Thought it was you. What's up, Gabby, man?'

They stood sizing up each other. Marcia was at a loss.

'You looking good, Gabby,' said Jeff. 'Heard you were on crack. Just goes to show, you mustn't follow rumours. So, where you been hiding yourself, blood? Ain't seen you since I hit street.'

'I been around.'

'Around where? Went round your drum one day, bunch of Pakis living there. Who's this, then?' He looked scornfully at Marcia. Gabriel did the belated honours. Jeff and Marcia nodded at each other.

'Anyway, Jeff,' said Gabriel, 'gotta splurt. Catch you later.'

'Hold your mules, bredren,' said Jeff. 'What's the rush?'

'Gotta meet someone down the road. Can't stop, honestly.'

'Don't gimme that,' said Jeff. 'Look. Brick and Gunhawk are hereabouts somewhere. Why don't we link them and . . .'

'No. Seriously Jeff. In a hurry right now. Ready, Marce?'

Marcia nodded. She and Gabriel started to walk off. Speaking to their backs, Jeff said: 'Well at least let me know where you gonna be. We can hook up later.'

Gabriel didn't answer him. He gripped Marcia's arm and strode away without looking back. Before long they'd disappeared from Jeff's view, swallowed up by the throng of revellers.

A few minutes later . . .

'Mate of yours I take it,' said Marcia.

'Was a mate.'

'Think he knows that?'

'Let it go, Marce.'

'Charming, wasn't he?'

'Look at that,' said Gabriel, suddenly. 'Just have a butcher's at that?' He held out his hand. It was trembling like a mirage.

'Not surprised,' said Marcia. 'That's what happens when your past slaps you in the face like that. You OK?'

'I'll live.'

They fought their way through the crowd, going nowhere fast. Gabriel said: 'Actually, Marce. I'm gonna head back to the house. You mind?'

'Not at all.'

'It's just that I don't wanna . . . you know?'

'I understand, honestly. Want me to walk back with you?'

'Nah. You stop out here and enjoy yourself.'

'You sure?'

'Yeah. Go on. I'll catch you later.'

'All right, then. Wish me luck.'

Gabriel waved her away before he and she parted company.

He was fighting his way through the crowd when he suddenly felt a hand on his shoulder. His heart sank. He did not need to look round to know who it was.

'Where's your white woman?' said Jeff, smiling. Brick and Gunhawk, who were standing beside him, chuckled and punched fists. Gabriel was poker-faced. 'What's up, bredren?' Jeff added. 'Cat get your tongue?' Gabriel did not rise to it. 'Look,' said Jeff. 'You wanna hang out with us or not? We're gonna go check out Coxsone. Coming?' Gabriel shook his head and said: 'Can't, Jeff.'

'Why not?' asked Jeff.

'Oh leave him,' said Gunhawk. 'Can't you see he don't want nothing to do with us?'

'Yeah, Jeff,' said Brick. 'Let's splurt. My man Gabby's on a different tip these days.'

'Look,' said Jeff to Gabriel. 'Here's my digits.' He got out a pen and his little black book, scribbled his number on one of the pages, then ripped it out and handed it to Gabriel. 'Ding me if you want. If not, have a good life. Laters.'

They walked off. Gabriel watched them disappear into the crowd. He looked at the scrap of paper in his hand. It briefly entered his mind to pocket it, but instead he threw it away.

Pride prevented him from saying so, but Gabriel was disappointed at his send-off. What an anticlimax, he thought. What a way to go out after more than four months at the house. Kevin and Jo had said their goodbyes to him the week before and were now both abroad on holiday. The Support Group were all out on prior engagements, having promised to visit him in his new flat at their earliest convenience. Jack and Lou-Anne had wished him all the best before going off to their rooms. John had presented him with a card signed by everyone, had told him not to be a stranger, before going out to meet his girlfriend for a drink. Marcia accompanied him to his new flat. Outside it, they stopped to say their farewells.

'Well,' said Gabriel. 'This is it now. The great unknown and shit.'

'Nervous?' asked Marcia.

'Like hell.'

'You'll be fine. You know where we are.' She paused then said: 'Well.'

'Well.'

'See you, then.'

'Yeah. Take care walking back.'

'I will.'

She kissed him on the cheek then turned to go.

'Marce?'

'Yes?'

He stared into her eyes. Even under the dim street-lamp he could see how incredibly blue they were.

Finally he said: 'Come up for a bit?'

With thanks to:

Antony Bryan, Shenagh Cameron, Tim Clark, Nick Cohn, Walter Donohue, George and Terry Forbes, Yasmin Hassan, Kenneth and Violet Israel, Jaimini Jani, Karen Jeffrey, Lizzie Kershaw, Carole King-Burrowes, Hanif Kureishi, Vicki Lowe, Courttia Newland, Helen Solomon, Laura Susijn, Neil Taylor, Sidney Williams, Uriah Williams, and with special thanks to Lucille Thompson.

NICHOLAS BLINCOE
THE DOPE PRIEST

'Blincoe skilfully manages to address a deadly serious theme – Israeli-Palestinian real-estate trafficking – while at the same time offering the reader a fast-paced, funny, page-turner of a book . . . Underlying Blincoe's humour and his characters' likeably nonchalant behaviour is a slingshot-accurate perception of exactly what is going on and why. Ironically it is David's dope-obscured gaze that enables us to bring the surreal, cheek by jowl reality of Jerusalem into focus . . . assured and spirited' *Lisa Darnell*, GUARDIAN

'It has become customary to compare every young novelist who writes thrillers set in exotic climes to Graham Greene, but Blincoe is perhaps most deserving of that tag . . . Blincoe's brave decision to set his thriller in one of the most charged political climates takes his sharp storytelling to new heights' *Matt Thorne*, LITERARY REVIEW

'Deceptively light-hearted with an artfully hidden persuasive agenda' *Ra Page*, EXPRESS

'Combines intelligence, pace and simple prose to produce an intriguing yarn of drug-smuggling in Jerusalem'
James Hopkin, THE TIMES' Books of the Year

'Scary. Very funny, very black' COSMOPOLITAN

SCEPTRE

JAKE ARNOTT
THE LONG FIRM

Meet Harry Starks: club owner, racketeer, porn king, sociology graduate and keen Judy Garland fan. There is a business like showbusiness – it's what Harry does. Fronting violence with rough charm and cheap glamour; performing menace while trying to jump the counter into legitimacy.

'This gangster novel set (mainly) in sixties London is one of the smartest, funniest and original novels you will read all year. It is a gloriously accomplished re-creation of the city in the era of the Kray Twins when aristocratic politicians mixed freely with gangsters, rent boys and actresses of dubious repute in a decadent demi-monde. Arnott is quite brilliant at excavating the cultural minutiae of the time to bring the period vividly to life'

INDEPENDENT ON SUNDAY

'*The Long Firm* manages to hook you from the first. It is compulsive reading, powerful writing with an evocative feel for the bleaker side of the Swinging Sixties' THE TIMES

'Gripping . . . slumming it doesn't get much better than this'

TIME OUT

SCEPTRE

Sceptre Paperbacks

The Dope Priest	Nicholas Blincoe	0 340 75045 6	£6.99	☐
The Long Firm	Jake Arnott	0 340 74878 8	£6.99	☐
Ghostwritten	David Mitchell	0 340 73975 4	£6.99	☐
Eating Cake	Stella Duffy	0 340 71563 4	£6.99	☐
A Sort of Homecoming	Robert Cremins	0 340 71723 8	£6.99	☐

All Sceptre books are available from your local bookshop or newsagent, or can be ordered direct from the publisher. Just tick the titles you want and fill in the form below. Prices and availability subject to change without notice.

Hodder & Stoughton Books, Cash Sales Department, Bookpoint, 39 Milton Park, Abingdon, OXON, OX14 4TD, UK. E-mail address: order@bookpoint.co.uk. If you have a credit card you may order by telephone – (01235) 400414.

Please enclose a cheque or postal order made payable to Bookpoint Ltd to the value of the cover price and allow the following for postage and packing:
UK & BFPO – £1.00 for the first book, 50p for the second book, and 30p for each additional book ordered up to a maximum charge of £3.00.
OVERSEAS & EIRE – £2.00 for the first book, £1.00 for the second book, and 50p for each additional book.

Name ____

Address ____

____

____

If you would prefer to pay by credit card, please complete:
Please debit my Visa/Access/Diner's Card/American Express (delete as applicable) card no:

Signature ____

Expiry Date ____

If you would NOT like to receive further information on our products please tick the box. ☐